Additional Praise for
SALT to SE

"Harrowing, tender, surprising, tragic, and hopeful . . . *Salt to the Sea* is a timely reminder that behind every tragedy are names and faces. Behind every statistic, there are stories."
—*Chicago Tribune*

"A haunting story . . . Sepetys's novel serves as a reminder that despite unthinkable tragedies that fall upon the innocent, there is always something or someone to fight for." —*InStyle.com*

"This swift-footed, kind-hearted historical is intensely satisfying in just about all the ways a novel can be satisfying."
—*Parade.com*

"Another stunning historical novel . . . Ruta Sepetys is known for creating vivid, historical fiction that takes a very human look at war." —*Hypable.com*

"Beautifully told . . . readers will feel as if they are there, in the freezing cold Prussian winter, struggling to survive."
—*Examiner.com*

"A lush love story." —*Teen Vogue*

"Ruta Sepetys is a master of historical fiction. In *Salt to the Sea* the hard truths of her herculean research are tempered with effortless, intimate storytelling, as her warm and human characters breathe new life into one of the world's most terrible and neglected tragedies."
—Elizabeth Wein, *New York Times* bestselling author of Printz Honor Book *Code Name Verity*

"Brutal. Beautiful. Honest."
—Sabaa Tahir, #1 *New York Times* bestselling author
of *An Ember in the Ashes*

"A haunting, heartbreaking, hopeful and altogether gorgeous new novel . . . one of the best young-adult novels to appear in a very long time."
—*The Salt Lake Tribune*

"Sepetys's meticulous research and clear writing bring this story to life in a way that is captivating and inspires readers to learn more."
—*The Deseret News*

"[Sepetys] provides insight into an aspect of this truly hideous time in history . . . Each of the four narrators is interesting in his or her own way."
—RT Book Reviews

"Sepetys combines research with well-crafted fiction to bring to life another little-known story . . . Heartbreaking, historical, and a little bit hopeful."
—*Kirkus Reviews*

"This novel will break readers' hearts and then put them back together a little more whole."
—*VOYA*

"A haunting tale that questions whether small acts of kindness are enough to hold back the tide of human cruelty."
—*BCCB*

Awards and Accolades for

SALT *to the* SEA

A #1 *New York Times* Bestseller

An International Bestseller

Winner of the Carnegie Medal

Winner of the Golden Kite Award

A *New York Times* Editors' Choice

A *New York Times* Notable Book

A *Wall Street Journal* Best Book

A *Publishers Weekly* Best Book

A *School Library Journal* Best Book

A *BookPage* Best Book

A *Shelf Awareness* Best Book

A New York Public Library Best Book for Teens

A Chicago Public Library Best Book

A Barnes & Noble Best Young Adult Book

A *Seventeen* Best YA Book

A *Paste* Best YA Book

An Amazon Best Book

Winner of the Goodreads Choice Award
for Best Young Adult Fiction

#1 on the Indie Bestseller List

Winner of the Indies Choice Award
for Best Young Adult Book of the Year

SALT *to the* SEA

RUTA SEPETYS

PENGUIN BOOKS

PENGUIN BOOKS
An imprint of Penguin Random House LLC, New York

First published in the United States of America by Philomel Books,
an imprint of Penguin Random House LLC, 2016
Published by Penguin Books, an imprint of Penguin Random House LLC, 2017

Text copyright © 2016 by Ruta Sepetys
Map illustrations copyright © 2016 by Katrina Damkoehler
Page 419 sketch copyright © 1973 by Michal Rybicki
Page 435 photo © *Ashes in the Snow* / Sorrento Productions
The Fountains of Silence teaser text copyright © 2019 by Ruta Sepetys

Cover photos: Arcangel, Getty Images

The author would like to give special thanks to Leigh Bishop, Cathryn J. Prince,
Edward Petruskevich, Mara Lipacis, and Michal Rybicki for their contributions to this edition.

Penguin supports copyright. Copyright fuels creativity, encourages diverse voices, promotes free speech, and creates a vibrant culture. Thank you for buying an authorized edition of this book and for complying with copyright laws by not reproducing, scanning, or distributing any part of it in any form without permission. You are supporting writers and allowing Penguin to continue to publish books for every reader.

Penguin Books & colophon are registered trademarks of Penguin Books Limited.

Visit us online at penguinrandomhouse.com

THE LIBRARY OF CONGRESS HAS CATALOGED THE PHILOMEL BOOKS EDITION AS FOLLOWS:
Sepetys, Ruta. Salt to the sea : a novel / Ruta Sepetys. pages cm
Summary: "As World War II draws to a close, refugees try to escape the war's final dangers, only to find themselves aboard a ship with a target on its hull"—Provided by publisher.
1. World War, 1939–1945—Juvenile fiction. [1. World War, 1939–1945—Fiction.
2. Refugees—Fiction.] I. Title. PZ7.S47957Sal 2016   [Fic]—dc23   2015009057
ISBN 978-0-399-16030-1 (hc)

Penguin Books ISBN 9780142423622

Printed in the United States of America

Edited by Liza Kaplan. Design by Semadar Megged.
Text set in 11.5-point Adobe Garamond Pro.

This is a work of fiction. Names, characters, places, and incidents either are the product of the author's imagination or are used fictitiously, and any resemblance to actual persons, living or dead, businesses, companies, events, or locales is entirely coincidental.

25th Printing

For my father.
My hero.

DENMARK

SWEDEN

1936 PRE-WAR OVERVIEW

Steuben

BORNHOLM
(DENMARK)

Kiel

Sassnitz

Berlin

GERMANY

Heidelberg

Baltic Sea

LATVIA

LITHUANIA

Biržai

Wilhelm
Gustloff

Goya

Pillau

Tilsit

Kaunas

Vilnius

Insterburg

Königsberg

Nemmersdorf

Gotenhafen

EAST
PRUSSIA

Frauenburg

Warsaw

POLAND

Lwów

CZECHOSLOVAKIA

We the survivors are not the true witnesses. The true witnesses, those in possession of the unspeakable truth, are the drowned, the dead, the disappeared.

—Primo Levi

SALT *to* *the* SEA

joana

Guilt is a hunter.

My conscience mocked me, picking fights like a petulant child.

It's all your fault, the voice whispered.

I quickened my pace and caught up with our small group. The Germans would march us off the field road if they found us. Roads were reserved for the military. Evacuation orders hadn't been issued and anyone fleeing East Prussia was branded a deserter. But what did that matter? I became a deserter four years ago, when I fled from Lithuania.

Lithuania.

I had left in 1941. What was happening at home? Were the dreadful things whispered in the streets true?

We approached a mound on the side of the road. The small boy in front of me whimpered and pointed. He had joined us two days prior, just wandered out of the forest alone and quietly began following us.

"Hello, little one. How old are you?" I had asked.

"Six," he replied.

"Who are you traveling with?"

He paused and dropped his head. "My Omi."

I turned toward the woods to see if his grandmother had emerged. "Where is your Omi now?" I asked.

The wandering boy looked up at me, his pale eyes wide. "She didn't wake up."

So the little boy traveled with us, often drifting just slightly ahead or behind. And now he stood, pointing to a flap of dark wool beneath a meringue of snow.

I waved the group onward and when everyone advanced I ran to the snow-covered heap. The wind lifted a layer of icy flakes revealing the dead blue face of a woman, probably in her twenties. Her mouth and eyes were hinged open, fixed in fear. I dug through her iced pockets, but they had already been picked. In the lining of her jacket I found her identification papers. I stuffed them in my coat to pass on to the Red Cross and dragged her body off the road and into the field. She was dead, frozen solid, but the thought of tanks rolling over her was more than I could bear.

I ran back to the road and our group. The wandering boy stood in the center of the path, snow falling all around him.

"She didn't wake up either?" he asked quietly.

I shook my head and took his mittened hand in mine.

And then we both heard it in the distance.

Bang.

florian

Fate is a hunter.

Engines buzzed in a swarm above. *Der Schwarze Tod*, "the Black Death," they called them. I hid beneath the trees. The planes weren't visible, but I felt them. Close. Trapped by darkness both ahead and behind, I weighed my options. An explosion detonated and death crept closer, curling around me in fingers of smoke.

I ran.

My legs churned, sluggish, disconnected from my racing mind. I willed them to move, but my conscience noosed around my ankles and pulled down hard.

"You are a talented young man, Florian." That's what Mother had said.

"You are Prussian. Make your own decisions, son," said my father.

Would he have approved of my decisions, of the secrets I now carried across my back? Amidst this war between Hitler and Stalin, would Mother still consider me talented, or criminal?

The Soviets would kill me. But how would they torture me first? The Nazis would kill me, but only if they uncovered the plan. How long would it remain a secret? The questions propelled me forward, whipping through the cold forest, dodging branches. I clutched my side with one hand, my pistol with the other. The pain surged with each breath and step, releasing warm blood out of the angry wound.

The sound of the engines faded. I had been on the run for days and my mind felt as weak as my legs. The hunter preyed on the fatigued and weary. I had to rest. The pain slowed me to a jog and finally a walk. Through the dense trees in the forest I spied branches hiding an old potato cellar. I jumped in.

Bang.

emilia

Shame is a hunter.

I would rest a moment. I had a moment, didn't I? I slid across the cold, hard earth toward the back of the cave. The ground quivered. Soldiers were close. I had to move but felt so tired. It was a good idea to put branches over the mouth of the forest cellar. Wasn't it? No one would trek this far off the road. Would they?

I pulled the pink woolen cap down over my ears and tugged my coat closed near my throat. Despite my bundled layers, January's teeth bit sharp. My fingers had lost all feeling. Pieces of my hair, frozen crisp to my collar, tore as I turned my head. So I thought of August.

My eyes dropped closed.

And then they opened.

A Russian soldier was there.

He leaned over me with a light, poking my shoulder with his pistol.

I jumped, frantically pushing myself back.

"Fräulein." He grinned, pleased that I was alive. "*Komme*, Fräulein. How old are you?"

"Fifteen," I whispered. "Please, I'm not German. *Nicht Deutsche.*"

He didn't listen, didn't understand, or didn't care. He pointed his gun at me and yanked at my ankle. "Shh, Fräulein." He lodged the gun under the bone of my chin.

I pleaded. I put my hands across my stomach and begged.

He moved forward.

No. This would not happen. I turned my head. "Shoot me, soldier. Please."

Bang.

alfred

Fear is a hunter.

But brave warriors, we brush away fear with a flick of the wrist. We laugh in the face of fear, kick it like a stone across the street. Yes, Hannelore, I compose these letters in my mind first, as I cannot abandon my men as often as I think of you.

You would be proud of your watchful companion, sailor Alfred Frick. Today I saved a young woman from falling into the sea. It was nothing really, but she was so grateful she clung to me, not wanting to let go.

"Thank you, sailor." Her warm whisper lingered in my ear. She was quite pretty and smelled like fresh eggs, but there have been many grateful and pretty girls. Oh, do not be concerned. You and your red sweater are foremost in my thoughts. How fondly, how incessantly, I think of my Hannelore and red-sweater days.

I'm relieved you are not here to see this. Your sugared heart could not bear the treacherous circumstances here in the port of Gotenhafen. At this very moment, I am guarding dangerous explosives. I am serving Germany well. Only seventeen, yet carrying more valor than those twice my years. There is talk of an honor ceremony but I'm too busy fighting for the Führer to accept honors. Honors are for the dead, I've told them. We must fight while we are alive!

Yes, Hannelore, I shall prove to all of Germany. There is indeed a hero inside of me.

Bang.

I abandoned my mental letter and crouched in the supply closet, hoping no one would find me. I did not want to go outside.

florian

I stood in the forest cellar, my gun fixed on the dead Russian. The back of his head had departed from his skull. I rolled him off the woman.

She wasn't a woman. She was a girl in a pink woolen cap. And she had fainted.

I scavenged through the Russian's frozen pockets and took cigarettes, a flask, a large sausage wrapped in paper, his gun, and ammunition. He wore two watches on each wrist, trophies collected from his victims. I didn't touch them.

Crouching near the corner of the cellar, I scanned the cold chamber for signs of food but saw none. I put the ammunition in my pack, careful not to disturb the small box wrapped in a cloth. The box. How could something so small hold such power? Wars had been waged over less. Was I really willing to die for it? I gnawed at the dried sausage, savoring the saliva it produced.

The ground vibrated slightly.

This Russian wasn't alone. There would be more. I had to move.

I turned the top on the soldier's flask and raised it to my nose. Vodka. I opened my coat, then my shirt, and poured the alcohol down my side. The intensity of the pain produced a flash in front of my eyes. My ruptured flesh fought back, twisting and pulsing. I took a breath, bit back a yell, and tortured the gash with the remainder of the alcohol.

The girl stirred in the dirt. Her head snapped away from the dead Russian. Her eyes scanned the gun at my feet and the flask in my hand. She sat up, blinking. Her pink hat slid from her head and fell silently into the dirt. The side of her coat was streaked with blood. She reached into her pocket.

I threw down the flask and grabbed the gun.

She opened her mouth and spoke.

Polish.

emilia

The Russian soldier stared at me, mouth open, eyes empty.

Dead.

What had happened?

Crouching in the corner was a young man dressed in civilian clothes. His coat and shirt were unfastened, his skin bloodied and bruised to a deep purple. He held a gun. Was he going to shoot me? No, he had killed the Russian. He had saved me.

"Are you okay?" I asked, barely recognizing my own voice. His face twisted at the sound of my words.

He was German.

I was Polish.

He would want nothing to do with me. Adolf Hitler had declared that Polish people were subhuman. We were to be destroyed so the Germans could have the land they needed for their empire. Hitler said Germans were superior and would not live among Poles. We were not Germanizable. But our soil was.

I pulled a potato from my pocket and held it out to him. "Thank you."

The dirt pulsed slightly. How much time had passed? "We have to go," I told him.

I tried to use my best German. In my head the sentences were

SALT TO THE SEA   *11*

intact, but I wasn't sure they came out that way. Sometimes when I spoke German people laughed at me and then I knew my words were wrong. I lowered my arm and saw my sleeve, splattered with Russian blood. Would this ever end? Tears stirred inside of me. I did not want to cry.

The German stared at me, a combination of fatigue and frustration. But I understood.

His eyes on the potato said, *Emilia, I'm hungry.*

The dried blood on his shirt said, *Emilia, I'm injured.*

But the way he clutched his pack told me the most.

Emilia, don't touch this.

joana

We trudged farther down the narrow road. Fifteen refugees. The sun had finally surrendered and the temperature followed. A blind girl ahead of me, Ingrid, held a rope tethered to a horse-drawn cart. I had my sight, but we shared a handicap: we both walked into a dark corridor of combat, with no view of what lay ahead. Perhaps her lost vision was a gift. The blind girl could hear and smell things that the rest of us couldn't.

Did she hear the last gasp of the old man as he slipped under the wheels of a cart several kilometers back? Did she taste coins in her mouth when she walked over the fresh blood in the snow?

"Heartbreaking. They killed her," said a voice behind me. It was the old shoemaker. I stopped and allowed him to catch up. "The frozen woman back there," he continued. "Her shoes killed her. I keep telling them, but they don't listen. Poorly made shoes will torture your feet, inhibit your progress. Then you will stop." He squeezed my arm. His soft red face peered out from beneath his hat. "And then you will die," he whispered.

The old man spoke of nothing but shoes. He spoke of them with such love and emotion that a woman in our group had

SALT TO THE SEA   *13*

crowned him "the shoe poet." The woman disappeared a day later but the nickname survived.

"The shoes always tell the story," said the shoe poet.

"Not always," I countered.

"Yes, always. Your boots, they are expensive, well made. That tells me that you come from a wealthy family. But the style is one made for an older woman. That tells me they probably belonged to your mother. A mother sacrificed her boots for her daughter. That tells me you are loved, my dear. And your mother is not here, so that tells me that you are sad, my dear. The shoes tell the story."

I paused in the center of the frozen road and watched the stubby old cobbler shuffle ahead of me. The shoe poet was right. Mother had sacrificed for me. When we fled from Lithuania she rushed me to Insterburg and, through a friend, arranged for me to work in the hospital. That was four years ago. Where was Mother now?

I thought of the countless refugees trekking toward freedom. How many millions of people had lost their home and family during the war? I had agreed with Mother to look to the future, but secretly I dreamed of returning to the past. Had anyone heard from my father or brother?

The blind girl put her face to the sky and raised her arm in signal.

And then I heard them.

Planes.

florian

We had barely crawled out of the potato cellar when the Polish girl began to cry. She knew I was going to leave her.

I had no choice. She would slow me down.

Hitler aimed to destroy all Poles. They were Slavic, branded inferior. My father said the Nazis had killed millions of Poles. Polish intellectuals were savagely executed in public. Hitler set up extermination camps in German-occupied Poland, filtering the blood of innocent Jews into the Polish soil.

Hitler was a coward. That had been one thing Father and I agreed upon.

"*Proszę . . . bitte,*" she begged, alternating between Polish and broken German.

I couldn't stand to look at her, at the streaks of dead Russian splattered down her sleeve. I started to walk away, her sobs flapping behind me.

"Wait. Please," she called out.

The sound of her crying was painfully familiar. It had the exact tone of my younger sister, Anni, and the sobs I heard through the hallway the day Mother took her last breath.

Anni. Where was she? Was she too in some dark forest hole with a gun to her head?

A pain ripped through my side, forcing me to stop. The girl's feet quickly approached. I resumed walking.

"Thank you," she chirped from behind.

The sun disappeared and the cold tightened its fist. My calculations told me that I needed to walk another two kilometers west before stopping for the night. There was a better chance of finding shelter along a field road, but also a better chance of running into troops. It was wiser to continue along the edge of the forest.

The girl heard them before I did. She grabbed my arm. The buzzing of aircraft engines surged fast and close from behind. The Russians were targeting German ground troops nearby. Were they in front of us or beside us?

The bombs began falling. With each explosion, every bone in my body vibrated and hammered, clanging violently against the bell tower that was my flesh. The sound of anti-aircraft fire rang through the sky, answering the initial blasts.

The girl tried to pull me onward.

I shoved her away. "Run!"

She shook her head, pointed forward, and awkwardly tried to pull me through the snow. I wanted to run, forget about her, leave her in the forest. But then I saw the droplets of blood in the snow coming from beneath her bulky coat.

And I could not.

emilia

He wanted to leave me. His race was his own.

Who was this German boy, old enough to be in the Wehrmacht, yet dressed in civilian clothes? For me he was a conqueror, a sleeping knight, like in the stories Mama used to tell. Polish legend told of a king and his brave knights who lay asleep within mountain caverns. If Poland was in distress, the knights would awaken and come to the rescue.

I told myself that the handsome young man was a sleeping knight. He moved forward, his pistol at the ready. He was leaving.

Why did everyone leave me?

The swarm of planes strafed overhead. The buzzing in my ears made me dizzy. A bomb fell. And then another. The earth trembled, threatening to open its jaws and eat us.

I tried to catch up to him, ignoring the pain and indignity beneath my coat. I had neither the time nor courage to describe why I couldn't run. Instead I told myself to walk as fast as I could through the snow. The knight ran ahead of me, darting in and out of the trees, clutching his side, wrenched with pain.

Strength drained from my legs. I thought of the Russians approaching, the pistol on my neck in the earthen cellar, and

I willed my feet to move. I waddled like a duck through the deep snow. Then suddenly, the sweet sound of Mama's nursery rhyme began to sing in my head.

All the little duckies with their heads in the water
Heads in the water
All the little duckies with their heads in the water
Oh, such sweet little duckies.

Where were all the duckies now?

alfred

"Frick, what are you doing?"

"Restocking ammunition, sir." I pretended to fumble with something on the shelf.

"That's not your assignment," said the officer. "You're needed at the port, not in a supply closet. The order will be issued. We have to be ready. We'll be assigning every available vessel. If we get stuck here, some murderer from Moscow will make you his girlfriend. Do you want that?"

Certainly not. I did not want a glimpse of the Soviet forces. Their path of destruction lay large and wide. Panicked villagers spilled stories in the street of Russian soldiers wearing necklaces made from the teeth of children. And now Russia's army was headed right for us with their allies, America and England, blowing wind into Stalin's sail. I had to get on a ship. Remaining in Gotenhafen meant certain death.

"I said, do you want to become Moscow's girlfriend?" barked the officer.

"No, sir!"

"Then take your things and get to the port. You'll receive further instruction once you get there."

I paused, wondering if I should pilfer anything from the supply closet.

"What are you waiting for, Frick? Get out of here, you pathetic slug."

Why, yes, Hannelore, the uniform, it suits me quite well. If time allowed I would have a photograph made for your bedside table. But alas, leisure time proves scarce here for valiant men. On the topic of heroism, it seems I will soon be promoted.

Oh, certainly, darling, you can tell everyone in the neighborhood.

joana

The wandering boy found a deserted barn a ways off the road. We decided to settle there for the night. We had been walking for days and both strength and morale waned. The bombs had set nerves on edge. I moved from body to body, treating blisters, wounds, frostbite. But I had no treatment for what plagued people the most.

Fear.

Germany had invaded Russia in 1941. For the past four years, the two countries had committed unspeakable atrocities, not only against each other, but against innocent civilians in their path. Stories had been whispered by those we passed on the road. Hitler was exterminating millions of Jews and had an expanding list of undesirables who were being killed or imprisoned. Stalin was destroying the people of Poland, Ukraine, and the Baltics.

The brutality was shocking. Disgraceful acts of inhumanity. No one wanted to fall into the hands of the enemy. But it was growing harder to distinguish who the enemy was. An old German man had pulled me aside a few days earlier.

"Do you have any poison? People are asking for it," he said.

"I will not administer poison," I replied.

"I understand. But you're a pretty girl. If Russia's army overtakes us, you'll want some for yourself."

I wasn't sure how much was exaggeration and how much was true. But I had seen things. A girl, dead in a ditch, her skirt knotted high. An old woman sobbing that they had burned her cottage. Terror was out there. And it chased us. So we ran west toward parts of Germany not yet occupied.

And now we all sat in an abandoned barn, trying to create a fire for warmth. I removed my gloves and kneaded my chapped hands. For four years I had worked with the surgeon at the hospital in Insterburg. As the war raged and the staff dwindled, I moved from stocking supplies to assisting him in surgery.

"You have steady hands, Joana, and a strong stomach. You'll do well in medicine," he had told me.

Medicine. That had been my dream. I was studious, dedicated, perhaps overly so. My last boyfriend said I preferred my studies to him. Before I could prove it wasn't true, he had found another girl.

I tried to massage warmth into my stiff fingers. My hands didn't concern me, but the supplies did. There wasn't much left. I had hoped the dead woman on the side of the road might have something—thread, tea, even a clean handkerchief. But nothing was clean. Everything was filthy.

Especially my conscience.

We all looked up when they entered the barn, a young man carrying a pistol, followed by a short blond girl in braids and a pink hat. They were both haggard. The blond girl's face was red with exertion. The young man's face was also flushed.

He had a fever.

florian

Others had beaten us there. A teetering collection of weathered horse carts was tucked beyond the brush, a sober portrait of the trek toward freedom. I would have preferred an abandoned site, but knew I couldn't continue. The Polish girl pulled at my sleeve.

She stopped in the snow, staring at the possessions outside the barn, evaluating the contents and whom they might belong to. There was no evidence of military.

"I think okay," she said. We walked inside.

A group of fifteen or twenty people sat huddled around a small fire. Their faces turned as I slipped in and stood near the door. Mothers, children, and elderly. All exhausted and broken. The Polish girl went straight to a vacant corner and sat down, wrapping her arms tightly around her chest. A young woman walked over to me.

"Are you injured? I have medical training."

Her German was fluent, but not native. I didn't answer. I didn't need to speak to anyone.

"Do you have any food to share?" she asked.

What I had was no one's business.

"Does she have any food?" she asked, pointing to the Polish girl rocking in the corner. "Her eyes look a bit wild."

I spoke without looking at her. "She was in the forest. A Russian cornered her. She followed me here. She has a couple potatoes. Now, leave me alone," I said.

The young woman winced at the mention of the Russian. She left my side and headed quickly toward the girl.

I found a solitary spot away from the group and sat down. I lodged my pack against the barn wall and carefully reclined on it. It would be warmer if I sat near the fire with the others but I couldn't risk it. No conversations.

I ate a small piece of the sausage from the dead Russian and watched the young woman as she tried to speak with the girl from the forest. Others called out to her for help. She must have been a nurse. She looked a few years older than me. Pretty. Naturally pretty, the type that's still attractive, even more so, when she's filthy. Everyone in the barn was filthy. The stench of exertion, failed bladders, and most of all, fear, stunk worse than any livestock. The nurse girl would have turned my head back in Königsberg.

I closed my eyes. I didn't want to look at the pretty girl. I needed to be able to kill her, kill them all, if I had to. My body begged for sleep but my mind warned me not to trust these people. I felt a nudge at my feet and opened my eyes.

"You didn't mention she was Polish," said the nurse. "And the Russian?" she asked.

"He's taken care of," I told her. "I need to sleep."

She knelt down beside me. I could barely hear her.

"What you need is to show me that wound you're trying to hide."

emilia

I thought of the carts outside the barn. They towered with the belongings of refugees. Trunks, suitcases, and furniture. There was even a sewing machine like Mama's.

"Why aren't you making any dresses?" I remembered asking Mama from my sunny perch in our kitchen.

Mama turned to me from her sewing machine. "Can you keep a secret?"

I nodded eagerly and moved toward her.

She put her hands on her wide belly and smiled. "I think it's a boy. I just know it's a boy." She hugged me close, her warm lips against my forehead. "And you know what? You're going to be the best big sister, Emilia."

And now I sat in a freezing barn, alone, so far from home. These people had time to pack. I wasn't able to pack, had left my entire life chewed to pieces. Who was using Mama's sewing machine now?

The knight hadn't wanted to come inside. What was his name? Who was he running from? I had examined the carts and belongings, evaluating the items and their potential owners to determine if it was safe to enter. But we had no choice. Sleeping outside meant certain death.

I sat in a corner and stuffed straw into my coat for warmth.

Once I stopped moving, the pain subsided. I buried my face in my hands.

A hand touched my shoulder. "Are you all right?"

I looked up to see a young woman above me. She spoke in German, but with an accent. Her brown hair was pulled behind her ears. Her face was kind.

"Are you injured?" she asked.

I tried to control it.

I fought it.

And then a single tear rolled down my cheek.

She moved in close. "Where does it hurt?" she whispered. "I have medical training."

I pulled my coat tight around me and shook my head. "No. *Danke.*"

The girl cocked her head slightly. My accent had given me away.

"*Deutsche?*" she whispered.

I said nothing. The others stared at me. If I gave them my food perhaps they'd leave me alone? I pulled a potato from my coat pocket and handed it to her.

A potato for silence.

joana

The arrival of the German and the young girl made me uneasy. Neither spoke openly. The girl's eyes darted with trauma and her shoulders trembled. I walked over to Eva. Eva was in her fifties and giant, like a Viking. Her feet and hands were larger than any man's. Some in our group called her Sorry Eva because she often said appalling things, but inserted the word *sorry* before or after, as if to soften the sting.

"Eva, you speak a bit of Polish, don't you?" I whispered.

"Not that you know of," she replied.

"I'm not going to tell anyone. That poor girl is suffering. I think she's Polish. Will you try to speak to her? Convince her to let me help."

"Who's the German she came in with and why isn't he in uniform? We don't have permission to evacuate. If Hitler's henchmen find us with a deserter we'll all be shot in the head. Sorry," said Eva.

"We don't know that he's a deserter. I don't know who he is, but he's injured. He found the girl in the forest." I lowered my voice. "Cornered by a Russian."

Eva's face blanched. "How far from here?" she asked.

"I don't know. Please try to talk to her. Get some information."

Eva's husband was too old to serve in the military but had

been recruited into the Volkssturm, the people's army. Hitler was now desperate and had called up all remaining men and boys. But somehow, the young man on the other side of the room had not been part of the recruitment. Why?

Eva's husband insisted that she trek to the west. He was certain Hitler was going to lose and that Russia would occupy East Prussia—and destroy everything in the process.

In school we were told that East Prussia was one of the most beautiful regions, but it had proven treacherous for those of us fleeing. Bordered to the north by Lithuania and to the south by Poland, it was a land of deep lakes and dark forests. Eva's plan was the same as the rest of ours—trek to unoccupied Germany and reunite with family after the war ended.

For now, I tended to people in the barn as best I could. Many had fallen asleep as soon as they sat down.

"Their feet," the shoe poet gently reminded as I passed him. "Make sure to treat their feet or all is lost."

"And what about your feet?" I asked. Poet's short frame was concave, like he had caught a large ball and never put it down.

"I could walk a thousand miles, my dear." He grinned. "Excellent shoes."

Eva pulled me aside.

"You're right—Polish. Her name is Emilia. She's fifteen, from Lwów. But she has no papers."

"Where's Lwów?" I asked.

"In southeastern Poland. The Galicia region."

That made sense. Some Galicians had blond hair and blue

eyes like the girl. Her Aryan look might protect her from the Nazis.

"Her father is some sort of math professor and sent her to East Prussia where she might be safer. She ended up working on a farm." Eva lowered her voice. "Near Nemmersdorf."

"No," I whispered.

Eva nodded. "She wouldn't talk about it. Just said she fled through Nemmersdorf and has been on the run."

Nemmersdorf.

Everyone knew the rumors. A few months ago the Russians stormed the village and reportedly committed vicious acts of brutality. Women were nailed to barn doors, children mutilated. News of the massacre had spread quickly and sent people into a panic. Many packed up instantly and began to move west, terrified that their village would be next to fall into the hands of Stalin's armies. And this young girl had been there.

"Poor thing," I whispered to Eva. "And the German told me a Russian had found her in the forest."

"Where's the Russian now?" said Eva, full of concern.

"I think he killed him." My heart ached for the girl. What had she seen? And deep down I knew the truth. Hitler was pushing out Polish girls like Emilia to make room for "Baltic Germans," people with German heritage. Like me. My father was Lithuanian but my mother's family had German roots. That's why we were able to flee from Stalin into the barbed arms of Hitler.

"You know, I think it could be worse," said Eva.

"What do you mean?"

"My husband told me that Hitler suspected the Polish intellectuals of anti-Nazi activity. The senior professors in Lwów, they were all executed. So the girl's father, sorry, but he was probably strangled with piano wire and—"

"Stop, Eva."

"We can't bring this girl with us. Her coat is splattered with blood. She's clearly in trouble. And she's Polish."

"And I'm Lithuanian. Are you going to toss me out too?" I was sick of it. Sick of hearing the phrase *German Only*. Could we really turn our backs on innocent homeless children? They were victims, not soldiers. But I knew others felt differently.

I looked over at the girl in the corner, tears streaking her filthy face. She was fifteen and alone. The tears reminded me of someone. The memory opened a small door in my mind and the dark voice slipped through it.

It's all your fault.

florian

I watched as the nurse girl moved from person to person, treating each one with items she carried in a brown leather case. I had a fever and knew I had to get rid of it to continue. The wound extended too far beyond my side for me to see or reach. I didn't need to trust her. I would never see her again. She looked my way and I nodded.

"Reconsidered?" she asked.

"When everyone's asleep," I whispered.

It didn't take long. The cold barn was soon full of twitching muscles and nasal whinnies. The nurse girl cooked a potato over the fire and ate it. She ate slowly, neatly, placing small bites in her mouth, patient despite her hunger. She was highborn.

She then brought her bag over to me.

"Bullet wound?" she whispered.

I shook my head. I slowly pulled off the sleeve of my coat, biting back the wince. I lay on my side, my head turned away from her. She peeled my sticky shirt from the mass of congealed blood.

She didn't gasp or cry like other girls did when they saw something gruesome. She didn't make a sound. Maybe nurses were used to it. I looked over my shoulder to see if she was still there. Her face was an inch from the wound. She examined it intently and then leaned forward and whispered in my right ear.

"Shrapnel. About two days ago. You stopped the bleeding by applying pressure but that pushed the fragments deeper, causing more pain. It's infected. You poured liquid on it at some point."

"Vodka."

Her voice resumed in my ear. "There are a couple of pieces. I want to take them out. I don't have any anesthetic."

"Do you have anything to drink?" I asked.

"Yes, but I'll need the alcohol to clean the wound before I dress it." I felt her hand on my shoulder. "I should do this now, before the infection becomes too advanced."

Small boots appeared in front of my face. The Polish girl knelt in front of me with snow wrapped in a handkerchief. She swept my hair aside and pressed the cold compress to my forehead.

"Go away," I told her.

"Wait." The nurse looked to the Polish girl. "Could you please go outside and find a large stick?" The girl nodded and left. The nurse then sat down in front of me. I watched her mouth as she whispered.

"Her name is Emilia. She's from southern Poland. Her father sent her away for safety . . . near Nemmersdorf."

"Holy hell," I breathed.

She nodded and opened her bag. "I'm Joana. I worked as a physician's assistant for a few years. I'm not German. I'm Lithuanian. Is that a problem?"

"I don't care what you are. Have you done this before?"

SALT TO THE SEA   33

"I've done similar procedures. What's your name?" she asked.

I paused. What should I tell her? "What's the stick for?"

She ignored my question and returned to hers. "What's your name?"

The fever burned, making me weak and dizzy. My name. I was named for a sixteenth-century painter my mother adored. No. I would not tell her. No conversations.

The nurse sighed. "You'll need the stick to bite down on. This is going to hurt."

I closed my eyes.

Florian, I wanted to say. *I'm Florian.*

And I'll be dead soon.

emilia

The giant woman, Eva, told me that the nurse girl was Lithuanian. Her name was Joana. She seemed kind, but how could I be sure? If she was going to treat the knight I felt I should stand watch. I owed him a debt now, didn't I?

He told me to go away. His voice was another in the chorus of those who wanted the Poles to disappear. Forever. After fleeing through Nemmersdorf, I met an old woman from Lwów on the road, her eyes stormed with death. She told me the Nazis had killed thousands of Polish Jews in Lwów.

"The Weigels?" I asked.

"Gone."

My voice fell to a whisper. "The Lempels?"

"Why do you keep asking? I told you, they're all dead. Probably hundreds of thousands."

Why was I asking? Because Rachel and Helen were my friends. When Father sent me away to East Prussia, they sneaked over the night before and brought me sweets and gifts.

Dead. How could she say it with such finality? I didn't want to believe it.

The pretty Lithuanian girl, Joana, had told me to find a large stick. I walked outside the barn. Wind and snow lashed my face. Every movement felt awkward in my layers and bulky coat.

Should I confide in Joana? Maybe she could help me. But I knew what would happen. She would be disgusted.

I heard a noise and looked up. That's when I saw it. Perched on top of the barn was the largest nest I had ever seen.

alfred

Hello, dear Hannelore!

How writing or just thinking your name alters my mood. Sometimes I lie on my cot and whisper it oh so slowly into the darkness. Han-ne-lore. Little Lore.

It is late evening. I imagine you at home, finger twirling in your hair while reading one of your beloved books. Perhaps the snow falls there as it does here?

Home in Heidelberg feels so very far away. Buffered by distance, I feel compelled to share a secret. Perhaps it is naughty of me to mention, but did you ever realize that your kitchen window stands opposite our lavatory window on the main floor? I could often smell your mother's duck in the oven from our bathroom. Yes, I frequently watched you eating your breakfast before school. Oh, do not be embarrassed, Lore. Neighbors share close quarters. We of course shared more. Those memories, they are the coals that shield my heart from frost.

But time for reflection is scant. Relaxation is nonexistent for a brave man of the Kriegsmarine. As you know, I am quite an accomplished watchman. Attention to detail has always been one of my great strengths, hence I am making note of everything to report to you. There is word of a massive naval evacuation and

SALT TO THE SEA   37

we are preparing at the port. I will finally be at sea, traversing the waterways into the oceans, like the adventurers you so love to read about in your precious novels.

And it will be an adventure, Lore. People are already arriving at the port to stand in line for one of the big ships. Some have carried all of their earthly belongings with them, piled high upon horse-drawn carts and sleds. Expensive rugs, clocks, china, chairs, they have brought it all. Certainly there won't be space enough and some items will be denied. I saw a lovely crystal butterfly on a cart today. It brought you instantly to mind—how your dark, silken hair floats like wings of gossamer. If the butterfly is not permitted on board, I have decided I will keep it. Redistribution to those who are worthy makes the most sense.

Your kind heart would break if you saw the people at the port. They are weary and filthy from their long treks. Some have escaped from countries as far away as Estonia. Can you imagine? Stalin has stolen more than land, Hannelore, he has stolen human dignity. I see it in their forlorn eyes and broken posture. It's all the fault of the Communists. They are animals.

And now Stalin's army is closing in and people are panicking. No, no, fear not. I am quite confident and assured of my abilities. After all, a human being cannot be trained for these situations, he must be born for them. And thanks be to God that I was.

I rolled over and slid my duffel out from beneath the cot. I reached inside for my well-worn copy of Hitler's book, *Mein Kampf*, and spotted the writing paper Mutter had given to me. Perhaps tomorrow I would actually put pen to paper.

joana

I lit a match to sterilize the scalpel and began talking. The doctor in Insterburg taught me that talking to patients often calmed them. "When Stalin occupied Lithuania, my family fled," I said. "My mother had German heritage, so Hitler allowed us to repatriate and come to Germany. I only got as far as Insterburg."

"Insterburg is East Prussia," he said. "So Hitler, he's your savior?"

He didn't say more, but his sarcastic snort spoke for him. He was either critical of the Nazi Party, critical of me for repatriating, or both. I didn't need his criticism. I carried enough guilt on my own. I had done everything wrong. I had the highest marks in school but couldn't master common sense.

"I know it's cold, but let's remove your coat entirely and have you lie on your stomach," I told him.

As I pulled off the sleeve, his pale green identity card peeked out from his interior jacket pocket. Perfect. If he wouldn't tell me his name, I'd take a look for myself.

"I'm going to press the surrounding area of the wound to see how far the infection has spread." He didn't respond. "Tell me when it hurts." I gently pressed around the perimeter of his wound with one hand, making note of tender areas. With my other hand, I tried to wriggle the papers from his coat pocket.

"Stop." The ferocity of his command made me jump. "Hand me my papers."

"What?"

"You heard me. Now."

He reached back and I placed the identity card in his hand.

"And the folded paper. It's also in the pocket," he said.

I pulled out the cream sheet of paper, trying to get a look at it. I couldn't see through the fold. He snatched it and slid both under his chest.

Emilia returned, carrying a stick, white flakes glistening atop her pink hat.

"It's snowing again?" I asked. She nodded. That would inhibit our progress tomorrow.

"Let's get this over with," said the patient.

His tolerance for pain exceeded anything I had seen. He bit the stick, not out of necessity, but in defiance.

Emilia was an attentive assistant, anticipating both my needs and his. But she appeared fatigued so I sent her back to her corner to rest. She didn't sleep. She watched my every move.

The final piece of shrapnel was lodged deep. My knuckles disappeared as I reached inside the wound for it. I was concerned about gangrene but didn't mention it. The pain was enough for him to contend with. I leaned down and whispered, "I think I got it all. It was deep and the wound is wide. I'm going to wake the shoemaker and have him sew it up. He's probably got a tighter stitch."

He spit out the stick. "No, you do it." He paused. "Please."

I looked at the open wound. Poet sewed a lot of leather and would seam it cleaner than I could, but if blood and flesh bothered the old man, it would only make things worse.

I sewed and dressed the wound. "So I didn't see your papers, but I did spy cigarettes in your pocket," I told him, wiping my hands.

"You didn't tell me there was a fee."

He looked up at me, eyes flickering like gas lamps. His face spoke of pain—physical pain like I had seen in the hospital but also emotional pain, like I had seen in my parents. He stared at me, his eyes slowly traveling over my face.

"There are matches in the same pocket," he finally said.

I pulled out a cigarette and ran it through my fingers, trying to straighten it. I lit the end and sucked a grateful drag. The hot smoke warmed my cold chest. I leaned toward him and gently put the cigarette to his lips, allowing him to inhale. The glow of the tip illuminated his face. There were hints of handsome beneath the bruises and dirt.

"How old are you?" I asked.

"Save the rest. They're hard to come by," he said, exhaling.

I stubbed the cigarette out against my shoe and returned it to his pocket. "Do you want to see the shrapnel I removed? This big piece is nearly the size of a bottle cap." I reached over to show it to him. He grabbed my wrist.

"Don't ever try to steal from me," he whispered.

"What are you talking about?" I said, trying to pull away.

His grip tightened. "You saw my papers."

SALT TO THE SEA *41*

"No, I didn't. Stop, you're hurting me."

"You know something about me, this wound." His voice was weak but carried concern. Or was it delirium? He mumbled for a while and then said, "Tell me something about you." He released his grip slightly.

"You want to know something about me?" I asked.

I stared at his tired face. He waited, eyelids beginning to droop. They fluttered closed and his fingers softly released my wrist. I watched him breathe for a while, his identity papers still tucked under his torso. He wanted to know something about me. I leaned over and put my mouth to his ear. It was barely a whisper.

"I'm a murderer."

florian

Thoughts of the nurse girl followed me through sleep and lingered after I awoke. Did I dream that I spoke with her? It made me angry. With each day that passed the threat mounted. Had they made the discovery in Königsberg yet? I couldn't let a pretty girl sidetrack me.

The barn was still dark, hollow with the emptiness of the displaced people it housed. My wristwatch said it was approaching 4:00 a.m. I pulled myself to a sitting position, gritting my teeth to fight the pain. My pack was untouched, my papers still beneath me. I returned the documents to my jacket and got to my feet.

I took a couple of steps toward the barn door and the blind girl sat up, her milky eyes blinking. The nurse slept next to her, her suitcase open, pretty brown hair scalloped around her face. What did she say her name was? No, it didn't matter. She was ugly. That's what I told myself.

I knelt and rummaged through the nurse's suitcase. The blind girl's nose rose toward the roof. She rotated her head and stared straight at me. What could she see? Were her eyes frosted over like an icy window, allowing light and dark to filter through? Or was her world curtained black? My hands silently sifted through the nurse's belongings. What was I doing? This girl had possibly saved me, saved me for a single drag of a cigarette. I told myself it wasn't stealing. It was protection.

I sorted through clothes, a medical book, the fork she had eaten the potato with, and then I pulled out something unexpected. I looked at the nurse's loose brown curls for a moment, slipped the item into my jacket pocket, and left.

There were Russians in the woods. I knew that already. Most likely scouts or drifters who had been separated from their unit. I could handle one soldier. But how long before full troops swarmed the area? Originally, I'd had two weeks to get to the port. That was the plan. I'd get on a ship, sail to the West, and the mission would be accomplished. Once outside the barn, I reorganized my pack. I saw the letter with my identity card and couldn't brush it from my mind.

Dr. Lange.

Dr. Lange was the director of the museum in Königsberg. He had hired me as a restoration apprentice, trained me, even sent me to the best school. I looked up to him and wrote detailed letters from the institute, sharing all of my thoughts on art and philosophy. Dr. Lange claimed I was brilliant. He said that my talents would provide Germany with a great service, one that would bring the Führer's dream of a national art museum in his hometown of Linz to fruition. Then Dr. Lange introduced me to Gauleiter Erich Koch. Koch was the leader of the regional branch of the Nazi Party.

He was also a monster.

When the belted crates of art started arriving at the museum, Dr. Lange's enthusiasm was infectious. Some pieces made him weep. At times, I had to steady him as a new addition was unveiled. He would put me to work immediately when each crate arrived. Sometimes I'd work through the night on a restoration so Dr. Lange could report to Koch the very next day. I went without sleep, without eating, even missed my father's birthday to complete the tasks and please Dr. Lange. "We make a great team, don't we, Florian?" he would say, grinning.

One morning Dr. Lange sent me searching for a roll of misplaced twine. While looking, I found all of my letters to him from the institute, carelessly thrown in a bottom drawer with ink and supplies. My letters were unopened. He hadn't even cared enough to read them.

A voice rose behind me in the dark, pulling me from my thoughts. I grasped my pistol and reeled around.

"Wait. Please!"

The Polish girl, pink and out of breath, ran toward me in the snow.

emilia

I could not trust the people in the barn. The giant woman recoiled when she learned I was Polish, so I willed my legs to move faster, telling myself that once I told the knight my story, he would understand. He would know what I had done for his country. He would protect me.

My stomach complained. Would the hunger ever fade, retreat in a kind and gentle way and stop its constant knocking? I couldn't remember not being fearful and hungry, when my stomach didn't feel pulled with yearning. My mental pictures of Lwów seemed to be fading, like a photograph left outside in the sun.

Lwów, the city that always smiled, a place of education and culture in Poland. How much of Lwów would survive?

The knight's silhouette came into view and inspired me to move faster. I called out and he turned, gun aimed.

"Wait. Please," I said. "I'm coming with you."

He turned away from me, then continued on his path.

I followed his fresh tracks in the snow and felt stronger, the January morning air sharp and crisp in my nostrils. I kept walking, following. After several meters he stopped and turned, furious. "Go away!"

"No," I protested.

"It's safer for you to stay with the others," he said.

Safer? He didn't realize.

I was already dead.

joana

Mornings held the promise of progress, dangling hope with thoughts of the next stop. We all fantasized of more than a barn. The shoe poet talked of grand manors owned by Junkers, wealthy East Prussian aristocrats. The countryside was dotted with their estates and we were bound to come upon one. Poet said he had visited one such manor house prior to the war and thought it was close by. We dreamed the wealthy family would take us in, ladle thick soup into porcelain bowls, and let us warm our frozen toes by the fire.

Poet walked around the barn, tapping the bottoms of people's feet with his walking stick. The wandering boy followed. "Time to rise. Feet are strongest in the morning," said the shoemaker. He arrived in front of me. "Still in fine shape, those boots. Any blisters?"

"No, Poet."

I stood up and brushed myself off. "Is everyone ready to go?"

"The German deserter and the runaway Pole are gone," he announced.

They all thought he was a deserter. My mind flashed to him snapping the identity card and letter from my hand. "I'm surprised he felt well enough to move on so early."

"His boots were military issue, but modified," said the shoe poet. He sighed, shaking his round head of white hair. "This war . . . do you realize that young people are fighting on tiny islands in the Pacific Ocean and marching through the deserts of North Africa? We are freezing and they are dying of heat. So many unfortunate children. The young Polish girl was exhausted. Her feet were swollen, rising like yeast buns in those boots. But sadly, it's probably for the best. We don't want them caught among our group. If my mind still serves as well as my feet, we'll come upon the estate before nightfall. No one will let us in with a deserter and a Pole."

"Of course it's for the best," said Eva. "A deserter and a Pole? I'm sorry, but they'll be dead on the road in a day."

"Oh my, you're a blister, Eva. A sour little blister." The shoe poet laughed and shook his walking stick at her.

SALT TO THE SEA   49

alfred

The morning sky draped cold shadows over the dock. Was my beloved Deutschland losing her footing? Was such a thing possible? Lübeck, Köln, Hamburg. Reports said they were all rubble.

The U.S. Army Eighth Air Force had bombed the harbor a few months prior. More than a hundred American planes dropped steel suppositories exploding into Gotenhafen. The ship *Stuttgart* was hit and sunk.

They had bombed before. They would do it again. Three air-raid alerts had been established in a tier of severity. I memorized them:

Rain.

Hail.

Snow.

In the event of attack, I imagined I'd fire back into the air, wildly shaking a fist of ammunition at them. In my mind, I scaled such mountains of combat often.

But in the meantime, I employed my keen powers of observation rather than beastly force. The Führer insisted on meticulous record keeping. I had every intention of proving myself worthy of promotion to documentarian. After all, I was a watchman. Noting and repeating my observations only sharpened my mental catalog. My recitations seemed to bother my fellow sailors, but could I really blame them for being jealous of my archival facilities?

I had a secret device. To keep track of the Reich's racial, social, and political enemies, I had put the Führer's list to melody. It was easier to remember when I sang it, similar to a child reciting a lesson in song. It was a rather catchy tune:

> *Communists, Czechoslovaks, Greeks, Gypsies,*
> *Handicapped, Homosexuals*
> —insert breath here—
> *Jews, Mentally ill, Negroes, Poles, Prostitutes, Russians,*
> *Serbs, Socialists*
> —insert breath here—
> *Spanish Republicans, Trade Unionists, Ukrainians and*
> —insert breath for big ending here—
> *Yu-go-slavs!*

The Yu-go-slav finale was my favorite. Three syllabic punches of power. I mentally sang my melody while performing my other duties.

A formal operation was in progress at the port, but specific details had not yet been revealed. Conversations were fraught with nerves and fear. I listened carefully.

"Don't just stand there eavesdropping, Frick, move! You want to be blown up by a Russian plane?"

"Certainly not." I balanced the stack of blue life jackets and peeked out from the side. "Where am I taking these?" I asked.

The officer pointed to an enormous slate-gray ship that matched the menacing sky.

"That one," he said. "The *Wilhelm Gustloff.*"

florian

"Leave! Go away!" I was annoyed. Angry. Why wouldn't she leave? Walking clearly exhausted her.

"I follow far behind. You don't see me," she said in her broken German.

"I can't protect you."

"Maybe I protect you," she said, her face earnest.

"I don't need protection."

"Then why you're not taking the road?" She kicked at the snow that had turned to ice overnight. "Road is much faster. More chance of food. Countryside prettier, but takes longer. You don't want to be seen?" She pulled her pink hat farther down over her ears.

What I didn't want was to waste time. I turned from her and resumed walking. I heard her speaking Polish, talking to herself. Eventually she would get tired and have to stop. Her weary body wouldn't carry her far. Thoughts of my younger sister pecked at me, and finally, I turned. As soon as I stopped, she stopped, lingering to rest against a tree. I reached into my pack and retrieved the Russian soldier's gun. I walked back to her.

"Take this. If you need to use it, hold it with two hands when you pull the trigger. Do you understand? Now go away."

She nodded but I was certain she didn't understand. The gun looked huge in her knitted glove.

I walked away. Was I crazy? Three steps back was a Pole with a Soviet gun, following me—a Prussian carrying enough secrets to blow up the kingdom. My wound cried out and so did my judgment. If I didn't report to a checkpoint soon, it would all be over.

joana

We trudged along the road, the sky gray and heavy. I looked up at the clouds.

"It's going to snow," said Ingrid, sensing my evaluation.

"You can feel it?" I asked.

"Sometimes." She nodded, adjusting her grip on the rope tied to the back of the cart. "Tell me about them," said Ingrid. "The boy and the Polish girl. I have an idea. I want to know if I'm right."

It was fascinating that Ingrid could feel what people looked like. She told me that she could sense a person's build, demeanor, sometimes even hair color. But it was the internal qualities that came to her first.

"The girl was fearful," said Ingrid. "Her motions were taut and full of panic. Her breathing was pinched, almost panting. The boy was the opposite. His movement was smooth and lithe, like he was accustomed to moving silently."

For days he had been moving with shrapnel the size of a bottle cap inside of him. I thought about his wound and wondered if he still had a fever.

"What was her name? The frightened girl," asked Ingrid.

"Emilia."

"Yes, that matches," said Ingrid.

SALT TO THE SEA   55

She tripped over a rock in her path and nearly fell. She clung to the rope and scrambled to regain her balance.

I set my hand on her shoulder. This trek was difficult enough for someone with sight. Two weeks ago, amidst mad chaos at a train station, Ingrid became separated from her aunt. The train departed. Ingrid was not on it. She stood alone on the platform for two straight days, shivering, waiting for her aunt to return. The aunt never came back. On the third day Ingrid asked people for help. They ignored her. Her luggage was stolen. A young girl finally noticed Ingrid and brought her to my attention.

"Don't feel sorry for me," said Ingrid. "I am able to see things. Just not the same things you see. So, the girl, she's blond?"

"Yes, Emilia's fair-haired with braids, blue eyes, and a round face. The young man is fairly tall, has broad shoulders and brown hair that falls in waves. His hair is a bit long. I don't know his name or what city he's from."

"And his eyes?" asked Ingrid. "What color are they?"

"I don't remember. Maybe brown?"

"I don't think so. I think they're gray," said Ingrid.

"Gray? No, people don't really have gray eyes."

"The thief does," said Ingrid.

I turned to her. "You think he's a thief?"

Ingrid said nothing.

The temperature dropped and the exposed parts of my face began to sting. We had been walking for over six hours. Eva complained incessantly. She hated the trek, she hated the cold, she hated the Russians, she hated the war. The shoe poet had promised that today we would find the manor house he had known. I doubted him and warned that he shouldn't get people's hopes up, especially the little one. The wandering boy's spirits were already so low.

"Ah, but if I am right," said Poet, "you will massage my feet by the fire."

I wasn't sure I wanted to accept that wager.

emilia

I busied myself on the walk. I looked at the trees and thought of the big stork's nest I had seen on top of the barn. It made me think of Mama. I thought of the warm sunny days when she would take me to pick mushrooms in the forest. In the forest near Lwów was a beautiful old oak tree with a hollow large enough to sit in. We'd take our baskets to the tree and I'd scramble into the cavity. Mama would sit with her back against the trunk, legs crossed at the ankles beneath her skirt.

"You love stories, Emilia. Well, the trees hold hundreds of years of stories," she'd tell me, touching the bark. "Think of it, everything these trees have seen and felt. All of the secrets are inside of them."

"Do you think the trees remember each and every stork?" I'd ask from inside the cool hollow.

"Of course the trees remember. Like I said, they remember everything."

Just as trees were Mama's favorite, storks were mine. I had them six months of the year. At the end of each summer the storks would leave and fly to Africa, where they'd live in warmth along the Nile for the winter. In March they would return to Poland to the nests they had left. To invite a stork to nest, families would nail a wagon wheel to the top of a tall pole. We had one in our yard. Every March we would celebrate when our stork returned to the nest. As August faded, the departure of the storks symbolized summer's end.

Six years ago, the day our stork left, Mama left too. She died giving birth to what would have been my younger brother.

My throat tightened. I swallowed, reminding myself she wasn't really gone. I felt Mama among the trees. I could feel her touch and hear her laughter in the leaves. So I talked to the trees as I walked, hoping their branches would carry messages up to Mama and let her know what I had done, and most of all, that I would try to be brave.

joana

"Why should we believe a cobbler?" lamented Eva. "He's a shoe-maker, not a prophet."

I didn't admit it, but I had begun to lose hope as well. "He said he knew the area," I told her. "He said when he was young he traveled by the estate with his family."

"We've been walking too long. If we push much farther the horse will be broken and won't be able to continue tomorrow."

Eva was right. We had spotted a small barn a few kilometers back. Some left the group to spend the night. We had decided to press on, following the shoe poet and his ambitious walking stick. Only one horse remained. A few days prior we had two carts and three horses but some German soldiers we encountered had taken one of the wagons and two horses, claiming they were needed for the war effort. Since they did not ask for our evacuation orders, we didn't argue.

The German army had taken everything—cars, petrol, radios, animals, food. It was clear that they were sinking under the weight of the Allied forces, but Hitler's regional leader, Gauleiter Koch, refused to allow civilians to evacuate. Rather than fall into the brutal hands of Russian marauders, some people defied the Reich and left without orders, like us.

If Poet's estate did exist, it was sure to be a shell of its former self, stripped and plundered by the German army. Or worse, German soldiers could be staying in the house themselves. They might question us for not having formal evacuation orders.

"The snow will fall soon," said Ingrid quietly.

The shoe poet stopped and thumped his stick against the icy road. "Aha! This is it!"

"It" was nothing. We were stopped near the same pine forest we had been trekking alongside for hours.

Poet called to the wandering boy and whispered in his ear, pointing into the woods. The boy took off running. We waited, shivering.

"My dear Eva, if I am right and there is in fact an estate, will you apologize to me?" asked the shoe poet.

"If there's an estate I'll dance with you, old man," snapped Eva.

"A close dance." The shoe poet nodded. "A waltz, please."

The wandering boy suddenly appeared on the road in front of us. His tiny body bounced up and down with excitement and he waved us forward. He stood amidst a small gap in the trees revealing a narrow, overgrown drive.

"Very smart! The noble Junkers have concealed their drive," said Poet. "Move those large branches away, my boy. We must steer the horse and cart behind the trees."

The boy did as instructed. We pushed through the small opening and the path widened into a larger mouth. Once we were all inside the brush, the shoe poet and the boy replaced the branches.

SALT TO THE SEA *61*

"Should we cover our tracks leading into the trees?" I asked.

"Forget about that," Eva called out. "The snow will cover our tracks. Hurry."

We plodded down the narrow band, the trees soldiering up around us, dark and tall. We arrived at a clearing. In the distance, perched on a low rise, was an elegant, stately home with long windows and multiple chimneys.

"Well, I'll be damned," whispered Eva.

florian

I paused, eating snow for a drink of water. I pulled out my small notebook and looked at the map I had sketched earlier, trying to orient myself. I had to be closer to the coast, didn't I? Once we reached the lagoon, I would cross the ice to the boats on the other side. Should I have stayed with the group from the barn? By walking through the woods, had I accidentally moved farther from my destination? If so, I might be walking directly toward the Russians.

The back of my neck ached. The fever had returned. I pulled the remainder of the sausage from my pocket and prepared to shove it all in my mouth. The Polish girl plopped down in the snow and ate handfuls. I wished she'd leave me alone. But then I thought of my sister.

I took out my knife and cut the sausage in half. I whistled to the girl and tossed a piece of sausage to her. She caught it and smiled. Cupping it in her small gloves, she raised it to her nose before popping it in her mouth.

"Your home is here? East Prussia?" she asked. "You speak like East Prussian."

The pink in her cheeks matched her hat. I knew where her home was and I knew what had happened there. Did she know? "Yes, East Prussia. Königsberg," I said. I probably could have told her the truth. I was actually from Tilsit, just northeast of Königsberg. I wondered if the Russians had taken Tilsit yet. And what would become of East Prussia? It was a former German kingdom, perched south of Lithuania and north of Poland on the Baltic Sea. Stalin had already taken Lithuania. He would take East Prussia too.

The girl chewed, her gaze at me unbroken. "Heil Hitler?" she asked quietly.

I said nothing.

The girl looked up at the sky. She pointed and started talking about the trees and the stars.

I would abandon her tonight.

alfred

Anxiety swelled in the harbor with each minute that passed.

Rumors circulated that the German front had fallen two weeks ago. Temporary, I assured my fellow sailors. We were told the Russian forces had restored their medieval military order of "rape and pillage." And now the vile Russians were closing in. Refugees, weary souls displaced from their homes, would throng toward the port, desperate to flee the Communists. There would be hundreds of thousands, perhaps millions, of them.

The German High Command had quickly organized a massive water evacuation. They called it Operation Hannibal, after one of the greatest military strategists in history. An enormous convoy of ships would be dispatched to the West. Ambulance trains loaded with wounded German soldiers barreled toward the ports. *Goya, Ubena, Robert Ley, Urundi, General von Steuben, Hansa, Pretoria, Cap Arcona, Deutschland*, and *Wilhelm Gustloff*—ships all designated for evacuation from various ports.

This would be my first-ever journey at sea. My maiden voyage had already presented its challenges. I noticed an unbecoming rash had appeared on my hands and in my armpits. I blamed the Communists.

SALT TO THE SEA

The sailors continued to speak of evacuation plans. I sensed my input was needed.

"There is not enough time," I remarked to one of my superiors. "To register and board hundreds of thousands within a matter of days, I don't think it's possible, sir."

"You will make it possible" was the order.

I looked across the dock, imagining the scene. The entire population would be driven to the coast. The ports would be mayhem. German soldiers would have priority, of course. Desperate refugees would be selected, registered, and processed to board the ships. Thousands had already arrived in ox-driven carts piled high with their belongings. They were haggard, falling asleep in the snow. I saw a man so hungry he was eating a candle.

"Please, sailor. Help me," they would plead as I walked by.

I would do something this time.

Maybe.

For some.

I sang my melodious list of enemies. *Yu-go-slav!*

I imagined myself home in Heidelberg when the war was over. Crowds of women and children would flock around me while I doled out oranges from burlap sacks.

Yes, Hannelore, it is dangerous. I have been selected for a very important mission to disinfect this land. But we heroes eat danger atop our porridge for breakfast. It is nothing, dear one.

Nothing. If the evacuation failed and the ports were bombed, more than half a million people would die.

A thundering *boom* echoed near the water. Someone screamed. Desperate. Panicked. Strangled with fear.

My fingers twitched. A tingle ran up my spine.

emilia

The Prussian knight walked ahead. He had secrets.

I had secrets too.

My legs ached, tired of walking. I missed school. I loved my desk, my teachers, the smell of freshly sharpened pencils waiting patiently in their box.

I had arrived at school that day, anxious for the math exam. Mama used to tease that I was all nature and numbers, like my father. As I approached the school yard I saw it. Our desks and chairs were stacked in the back of an open truck, our textbooks smoldering in a heap. One of my teachers ran toward me crying.

"Hurry, Emilia, go home. They've shut down the school."

"But why?" I asked her, moving closer to the truck. "Wait, I have things in my desk."

"No, run home, Emilia!" she sobbed, tears streaming down her face.

The Nazis claimed I didn't need an education. Polish schools were closed. Our desks and equipment were taken to Germany. Would a German girl open my desk and find my treasures inside?

The Nazis said the people of Poland would become serfs to the Germans. They thought we only needed to count and write our name. My father was part of the Lwów School of Mathematics. He would never agree with children not being taught reading, writing, and arithmetic. They had burned our books in the Polish language. But I had learned to read very young. They could never take that away from me.

I continued walking, thinking of food, rest, a soft bed, and a warm blanket. I would settle for hay and a potato. Snow was falling, making everything appear fresh. The white snow covered the dark truth. Pressed white linen over a scarred table, a crisp clean sheet over a stained mattress.

Nature.

That was something the war couldn't take from me either. The Nazis couldn't stop the wind and the snow. The Russians couldn't take the sun or the stars.

I dropped back slightly and stepped into the trees, thinking I would feel better if I relieved myself. The knight continued walking. I was crouched on my heels when I saw it. A uniformed soldier slipped out of the trees behind the knight.

He had a gun.

He was pointing it.

I jumped up and screamed.

Bang.

florian

Bang.

I saw the girl first, legs apart, gun drawn. Then I saw the soldier between us, writhing on the ground, a bullet torn through the shoulder of his coat. His pistol lifted, but I shot first.

The gunshots bounced hollow in my head. I scanned the woods. Were there more? I kicked the pistol away from the soldier and quickly fleeced him of his ammunition, food, papers, and canteen. This was bad. Very bad.

"What's wrong with you?" I whispered to the Polish girl. "He was German, not Russian." I looked around quickly. "Hurry. Someone heard those shots." I piled up the supplies. "We have to run. Put these in your pockets." I held out the items to the girl.

But the girl didn't respond. She stood, cemented in shock, pink gloves on the gun, her body trembling.

The Russian pistol fell from her hand and dropped into the snow.

joana

We marched up the hill toward the estate. Tonight we would have thick walls, a warm fire, and a solid roof to shield us from the snow.

"Just as I remember it," said the shoe poet. "Extraordinary! We shall walk around back. I expect that's where the kitchen entrance will be."

I painted a visual for Ingrid. "It's beige sandstone. Large tall windows across the front and upstairs. The entry door sits in a diamond-shaped alcove."

Ingrid clutched my arm. "I don't like it," she whispered.

"What's not to like? It's shelter."

Ingrid's nostrils pulled at the surrounding air, but she did not reply.

We made our way around the back of the manor house and entered through a snow-covered garden hedge. Poet's feet stopped short. Tall glass doors with shattered panes stood open into the garden, torn damask curtains flapping like a loose tongue in the wind. The courtyard was littered with clothing, broken crockery, shoes, books, and various personal items. A baby carriage lay mangled on its side, dusted with snow.

The wandering boy stepped in close. I put my arm around him.

"Sorry, but what did we expect?" Eva laughed. "Servants waiting outside in a receiving line?" She shrugged and walked inside.

Eva was right. Nothing was intact anymore. The entire region was broken, bombed, and looted. How could we have expected anything different? The cold wind blew, banging the crippled doors as we went inside.

The main floor of the house was divided into five large rooms with high ceilings, all connected by tall double doors. Standing in what had been the garden library, we could look through the door and see across to the opposite end of the house. Floor-to-ceiling shelves lined the library walls. The books, raped and rummaged of their dignity, lay in heaps on the floor. We stepped over the books and through the doorway.

"Let's choose a room to sleep in, close off the doors, and start a fire to warm up the space," commanded Eva. She stopped midway through the house. "This'll do."

"Where is the kitchen?" I asked. "Maybe there is food or drink."

"Yes," Eva sighed. "A drink."

Eva instructed the shoe poet to collect any wood or paper he could find for the fireplace.

"Not the books. Please, Poet," I whispered.

He nodded and patted my arm. "We won't disturb their things."

I set down my bag and walked through the house, admiring the ravaged ghostly splendor of each room in its panicked disarray. I reached the end of the main floor, the dining room,

72   *Ruta Sepetys*

and saw a small silhouette. The wandering boy stood next to the long dining room table, his head bowed by an overturned chair. I approached quietly and looked over his shoulder.

A basket of mossy bread in the center of the table was crawling with brown mice. Flowered china bowls skinned with half-eaten soup sat on a dusty tablecloth, the spoons still in them.

They hadn't even been able to finish their dinner.

florian

I dragged the dead German into a wooded thicket and covered him with snow. But what if someone found him? I gripped my pistol and searched through the trees for light. Using the scent of fire as a guide, I walked quickly through the forest. I should have known. It had been too quiet today. The Polish girl saw the gun and thought he was going to shoot. She thought she was defending me.

The girl followed. When I looked to the right I heard her breathing stop, trying to swallow the tears. My sister, Anni, did the same thing the day Father sent her away up north. She did not want to cry. She held her breath in one hand and her suitcase in the other.

The memory brought pain to my stitched wound. I still smelled smoke and hoped it signaled a resting spot. If I couldn't rest, I wouldn't get far tomorrow.

We emerged from the woods. The Polish girl pointed. In the distance, a large manor house sat on a loaf of frozen earth. The house was dark, but smoke coughed from one of the center chimneys, grayer than the gray sky.

Was it a trap? The frozen meadow leading to the warm house could be a minefield.

The girl moved close. I shared her concern. What if the

house was nested with Germans or Russians? Either would be a problem. The Russians would kill me or take me hostage. The Germans would demand to know why I wasn't in uniform.

I didn't want to imagine what they would do to the girl.

"We'll follow the tree line until we're closer," I whispered. "We'll see who's there."

One thing I knew for sure—we would not find a kindly old couple enjoying an evening pipe and needlepoint in the drawing room.

emilia

We walked toward the large house. With each step, I felt increasingly ill.

I shot him.

I shot a man.

The knight saved me and now I had saved the knight. Why didn't that make me feel better?

The sound of gunfire had ripped a seam in my mind. Discarded memories were now leaking, dripping through.

Boots. Screaming. Glass shattering. Guns firing. Skull against wood.

I tried to push them away.

Please go away.

I couldn't make them stop. The memories rolled at me, faster. Faster.

All the little duckies with their heads in the water
Heads in the water
All the little duckies with their heads in the water
Oh, such sweet little duckies.

A searing pain tore through my body and I collapsed in the snow.

joana

The shoe poet sat by the glowing fireplace, polishing his boots with lampblack he had scraped from the hearth. The wandering boy watched intently at his side, mimicking the strokes on his own small ankle boots.

The fire cracked and popped, rolling waves of heat in front of my face. Glorious. I wrapped the scarf around my head and buttoned my coat.

"If I can find an oak tree, I can boil the bark to treat some of the blisters," I told Poet.

"I'll come with you," he said.

"Rest. You'll need your strength for the days ahead."

"I'm fit as a lad, my dear girl." He pulled up the leg of his wool trousers to reveal his bony knee. It was covered in white. "Shoemaker's secret," he whispered to the wandering boy. "There's mercury in white shoe polish. Fights off the arthritis. Fit as a lad, I am." The wandering boy pulled up his pant leg to inspect his own tiny knee.

Poet smiled and patted the boy's head. The old man was still full of energy. He refused to buckle under the burden of grief and loss. "Be careful out there, Joana," he told me.

I walked through the darkened shell, back to the library with its smashed glass doors. A book lay open, its pages flipping

SALT TO THE SEA   77

in the icy wind. I bent to pick it up and the name on the cover daggered me with guilt.

Charles Dickens.

Grandma had given *The Pickwick Papers* to both Lina and me for Christmas.

Lina.

What had I done?

I set the book on a table and walked out into the cold, making my way toward the trees. Two dark figures sat in the snow halfway between the forest and the estate. I looked closely and saw blond braids blowing beneath a pink hat. It was the Polish girl and the young man with the shrapnel. I made my way toward them.

"Were you following us?" I called out.

"Hurry," he shouted. "Something's happened to her."

I ran. Emilia sat in the snow, her chin dropped to her chest.

"What's wrong?" I asked her. She didn't respond.

"I think she's in shock. She shot a soldier in the woods. She won't move," he said.

I knelt beside her. She quickly wrapped her arms around her body, trying to inch away from me. "It's okay, Emilia, tell me what's wrong. Let me help you," I said. "Let's go inside."

She wouldn't move. Instead, she lay down in the snow and started to unbutton her coat.

I helped her with the buttons, then sifted through her many layers of clothing.

I gasped when I saw it.

"Oh, dear God."

florian

We brought her into the house. My stomach pushed up into my throat. The Polish girl was my sister's age. What had human beings become? Did war make us evil or just activate an evil already lurking within us?

The day was a loss. I had left ahead of the group, yet they had arrived before me. Pathetic.

My senses were so misaligned that I was nearly killed in the woods.

And now the fifteen-year-old kid who saved my life was probably going to die.

The pretty nurse tended to the girl, whispering. I watched her. After several minutes, the nurse appeared at my side. Her fingers grazed my shoulder. "Come away from the fire," she said.

"I'm cold."

"You're cold because you have a fever. Come away from the fire."

She led me past the man they all called the shoe poet. He and a small boy were in their stocking feet. Their boots, arranged in a row against the wall, shone to mirrored perfection.

The little boy waved at me. "Hallo, I'm Klaus!" he announced. I gave him a discreet wink. He smiled.

"Sit down here," said the nurse.

I felt uncomfortable with her, yet somehow relieved she was there.

"What did you say your name was?" I asked her.

"Joana. What did you say yours was?"

I opened my mouth but caught myself. A hint of a smile pulled at her lips. Was she laughing at me? Would she still be laughing when she realized that I had taken something from her suitcase?

"I want to see the stitches. Take off your shirt," she said.

Inappropriate jokes ran through my mind. But she wasn't looking at me. Her eyes were fixed on the Polish girl and the fold between her brow deepened.

"Will she make it?" I said, unbuttoning my shirt. I wished I hadn't asked. I couldn't afford to care about the girl. She was just another tragedy of war.

The nurse turned to me. "Since her survival depends on you, let's see how you're doing." She carefully peeled back my bandage. "Hmm, not as bad as I expected."

"I can't take care of her. I'm already behind schedule."

She knelt in front of me. I could barely hear her. "The Russians have this region surrounded," she said. "There are only two escape routes, through the port at Gotenhafen or the port at Pillau. We're all headed the same way. It will be safer if we travel together."

Her cold fingers whispered across my chest as she buttoned my shirt.

She had no idea. It wasn't "safer" for anyone to be with me.

joana

"He's cute," said Eva, stretching her mammoth feet by the fire.

"He's young."

"Too young for me, yes, but not too young for you. What is he, nineteen, maybe twenty? Look, he's staring at you."

I glanced over at him. He looked away. Eva's estimation of his age seemed correct. And Ingrid had been right. His eyes were gray. My record with boys was not exactly successful. I seemed to have a talent for picking the wrong ones.

"But something's not right with him," said Eva. "Maybe he's a spy."

Ingrid's words echoed back to me. *He's a thief.*

Eva leaned back in a broken chair. "But even a spy can keep a girl warm, you know." She surveyed the room. "The Nazis destroyed this place. It must have been beautiful."

I nodded.

She let out a laugh. "They certainly don't trust the old Prussian nobles now, do they?"

Eva was right. Prussian Junkers didn't quite blend with other Germans. "Junker" meant "young gentleman." The Prussian aristocracy was serving in the German army, fighting for their land and titles. But some of their ideologies didn't align with Hitler's. Back in July, Prussians were involved in

SALT TO THE SEA   *81*

an assassination attempt on Hitler. The plot failed and the Junkers were executed.

"So what's wrong with the girl?" asked Eva. "Exhaustion? Or has she realized that her father won't be doing any more math? Sorry."

I shook my head. "I want you to speak to her privately. I need details to try to help her. Can you do that, Eva?"

"Why me?"

"Because you understand more Polish than the rest of us."

"She seems terrified," said Eva.

"She probably is," I told her. "She's eight months pregnant."

emilia

I liked the Lithuanian girl, but the towering woman called Eva spoke bad Polish and always seemed impatient. I had never seen such a tall lady.

"That." Eva pointed to my belly. "From Nemmersdorf?"

"No. From the farm last spring," I told her.

"The farm?"

I nodded. Should I tell her? Should I explain that my father had sent me from Poland to work on a farm in East Prussia? Should I mention that the farm was owned by Father's friends, the Kleists? Father had said it would be safer for me there. The Kleists had a son named August. Heat brushed my cheeks as I thought of him.

"Emilia," Mr. Kleist had said, pointing to a tanned boy dragging a sledge of wood. "That is our oldest, August."

I smiled, remembering his gorgeous face. I put my hands on my belly. "I am on my way to meet August," I told her. "It is the plan." Eva nodded and walked away.

I lay back and thought of August, our wedding, and how we'd make a big nest for the storks above our cottage, just like the nest I had seen on top of the barn. The images were so peaceful, so perfect, that I soon fell asleep.

alfred

Greetings, sweet Hannelore!

The cold continues and I am braving temperatures of minus fifteen. My eyelashes freeze and stick when I step outside. This climate is unsuitable for tender-skinned women of course, so I prefer to think of you at home, soaking your stockings or drawing a bath.

Today I have news to share. I am confirmed to sail on the MV Wilhelm Gustloff, the most impressive ship in the harbor! She is enormous, two hundred and eight meters long, fifty-six meters high, and only eight years old. A true beauty. She was originally built for vacation cruising and has amenities I think you would enjoy, such as a pool, a formal dining room, a ballroom, and a library. But ho, let me tickle your thoughts with this—the ship even has a movie theater, a music room, a beauty salon, and a promenade deck completely enclosed in glass. Can you imagine? All of the cabins are the same, except the private luxury suite on B deck for the Führer himself. Perhaps I'll be invited to lodge in the private cabin at some point, but I must decline. Sacrifices, Lore. I am making these types of sacrifices every day, allowing others to eat from my spoon.

I imagine the Gustloff was once quite pretty for leisure cruising, but the ship is now painted a chalky gray for the war effort.

It once served as a hospital ship but was most recently used as barracks for a submarine training school. No matter, she is my boat now.

Yes, how fortunate I am to be a sailor of priority, taking voyage on a grand ship instead of digging tank trenches like most of the lads my age. My services are quite in demand, so I must close. I will leave you, however, with the most impressive fact of all—the capacity of the ship is 1,463 but I am told we may have as many as 2,000 on board.

Imagine, my darling, your Alfred is saving two thousand lives.

"Have you cleaned the toilets yet, Frick?"

"Not yet," I replied.

florian

I sat in the corner, watching. They didn't have much food, but what they had, they shared. The small boy discovered an old gramophone and dragged it across the floor. He found a single disc, a Swedish starlet named Zarah Leander singing "Davon geht die Welt nicht unter." They played the record over and over. The squatty shoemaker made the giant woman dance with him. For his age, he was a good dancer, much better than she was.

I remembered dancing.

Dr. Lange had asked me to accompany his daughter to two balls. Unfortunately, I was a better dancer than she was and it made her angry. She was a selfish girl with a nose like a woodpecker.

The nurse walked over to me. "It's only bean soup, but it's warm." She held out the cup.

"Give it to the girl," I told her.

"She's already had some. Take it, you'll feel weaker tomorrow if you don't eat something."

I took the cup from her.

She sat down next to me, uninvited. "I've heard this song before. I know she's singing in German, but I don't completely understand the lyrics," she said.

I spooned the warm soup into my mouth. "She's saying it's not the end of the world."

The nurse folded her legs up under her skirt and rested her chin on her knees. "Well, that's good to know. It's nice to hear music. At the hospital, we sometimes played music for the patients. The soldiers loved the song 'Lili Marleen.'" She looked at me. "Do you know it?"

"No," I lied.

"It's beautiful. It's about a boy who longs to see his sweetheart."

I wasn't going to correct her, but the song was based on a poem written by a German soldier during the first war. The song was about him meeting his girl under a lamppost. Then he leaves for war. By lantern under a barricade he thinks of his *Lili of the lamplight*.

"So you like to dance," she said. It was more of a comment than a question.

"Me? No."

The shoemaker glided over to us. "Come, my dear Lithuanian, let us have a dance." He extended his knobby hand to the nurse. "Do you understand what she is singing?"

"Of course." She smiled. "She's saying it's not the end of the world."

"Very good! Let us dance and celebrate. Tonight we sleep as aristocrats," said the shoe poet.

"I doubt the aristocrats slept on the cold floor," the nurse whispered to me before accepting Poet's hand. I wanted to laugh, to keep talking with her, but instead I said nothing.

The shoemaker danced her around the room, holding her appropriately and closing his eyes. He had probably danced with a lot of pretty girls in his day. He seemed like a wise man, a kind man. I imagined he worked by oil lamp, cutting and sewing leather well into the night. He probably employed an apprentice and taught him an honest trade, unlike Dr. Lange, who had lured me with lies.

Lange must have considered me an easy target. I was so eager, captivated by all the old paintings, staring at them for days until they confessed their secrets to me. Dr. Lange taught me to carefully dissolve and remove discolored varnish. I studied pigments and tinting to match antique patinas. We spent months experimenting with the methods the old masters used to create real gesso. I learned quickly. I came to recognize all the crack patterns and each type of canvas and stretcher used by every school of art. Dr. Lange was impressed with how quickly I could detect a repainting, fake, or touch-up. My restoration work always passed, completely undetected.

"Stunning, Florian," he would whisper over my shoulder. "You, my boy, are the Reich's best-kept secret."

My boy. My stomach turned with disgust. What an idiot I was. If I could detect a flawed painting so quickly, why had it taken me so long to see the truth about Dr. Lange?

The song ended and the nurse returned and sat down. I got up and carefully lifted my pack onto my shoulder. "I don't suppose there's a working commode?"

"You can leave your pack." She looked at me, her brown eyes earnest. "No one will take it."

I would not leave my pack. Ever. It had my supplies, my notebook, my future, my revenge. I walked across the stone floor, away from her. As I neared the tall doorway, the shoe poet raised his hand to stop me.

"What do you want?" I asked.

He stared at me and then looked down at my boots. "The shoes tell the story," he whispered.

My heel. He had heard the hollow in my step as I walked across the room.

He knew.

joana

Ingrid sat silently braiding her hair. "When will we reach the ice?" she asked.

The ice. The goal we trekked toward. If we crossed the frozen Vistula lagoon, we could then make our way down the narrow strip of land to either Pillau or Gotenhafen. Ships would be leaving from both ports.

"Poet says we're only a day from Frauenburg," I told her.

"That's where we'll cross the ice?" asked Ingrid.

"Yes."

Ingrid's fingers stopped moving. "You're nervous about it."

I *was* nervous about it. The closer we moved to an actual village, the more military and wounded we'd encounter.

"If there are soldiers," whispered Ingrid, "can you convince them?"

"The bandages will fool them," I told her.

Ingrid had reason to worry. Hitler considered those born blind or disabled, inferior. They were called garbage children, life unworthy of life. Their names were added to an official registry. A doctor in Insterburg confided that the people on the registry would be killed. From then on we bandaged handicaps to pass them off as wounds.

"Maybe we should bandage my eyes tonight. Soldiers may come upon the house," said Ingrid quietly.

"Yes, we'll do that." I reached out and patted her shoulder. "I'm going to look for some supplies."

"Be careful," said Ingrid.

I stepped between the sleeping bodies and pushed through the tall, heavy door. The old hinges let out an eerie, deep groan as they rotated. The air in the abandoned house lay cold and still, lingering dead without the family within it. Walking through someone's home and personal possessions felt not only like trespassing, it felt like a violation.

A portrait of an older man in uniform hung crooked on the plaster. Which family did the estate belong to? Prussian Junkers had the reputation of being stiff and arrogant, but that seemed an unfair generalization. I had met Prussian families in Insterburg who were lovely. Many Prussian nobles had the preposition *von* before their last name to signify "of" or "from." I looked at the portrait. If I belonged to Prussian aristocracy my name would be Joana von Vilkas—Joana of the Wolf.

An aristocratic killer.

I stared at the curving stairway of stone in the dim hall, the center of each step worn smooth by the tread of many generations. I hesitated. Should I go upstairs? I thought of our house in Lithuania. How many Soviets were in it now? Were they sleeping in my bed? Had they tossed all our books to the floor like trash? I took a few steps up the cold wide stairs. Silver moonlight shimmered through a window, revealing a gray stuffed rabbit lying on a step above. One of its ears was missing. Poor bunny. Even toys were casualties of war.

I climbed two more steps.

The supplies I needed were most likely in the kitchen or laundry. I didn't need to go upstairs, but my curiosity beckoned.

I took another step up.

A clattering sounded below, making me jump. I hurried back down the grand staircase and made my way through the dark passage to the kitchen.

The German rummaged through the cabinets, his pack near his feet. A sheet was spread on the floor with a tumble of items in the center.

"Are you following me?" he asked.

"Don't flatter yourself. I need supplies."

He motioned to the bundle on the floor. "You can tear the sheet if you need bandages. There's a sharp knife in the pile."

"Thank you."

I spied a few jars of blackberries and carrots on the counter. "Where did you find those?" I asked. "Eva said she checked the kitchen for food."

"I know a thing or two about hiding places."

I looked at the jars. "And those are all for you?"

"No, save some for the Polish kid."

"I told you, her name is Emilia," I said.

He ignored my statement.

"We're all going to Frauenburg. Come with us and she can ride in the cart. The contractions and symptoms she described speak to early labor. She shouldn't be walking for extended periods."

He seemed to consider the proposition.

I rummaged through the dark kitchen and set aside dried herbs, scissors, and kitchen twine. There wasn't enough. "I'm going upstairs to get some blankets."

"No," he said, moving quickly to block the doorway. "Don't go upstairs. And don't let the little boy up there either."

"Why not?"

He didn't answer.

I stepped in closer. "Why shouldn't I go upstairs?"

He looked toward the door. He shifted his weight, hesitating. I stepped closer to him. He pulled in a breath and his eyes latched on to mine.

"No one should have to see that," he whispered.

emilia

The pressure woke me from a shallow sleep. I had to go to the bathroom. Again.

I adjusted my hat. The pretty house was warm inside. The fire still crackled and glowed, throwing shadows across the bundled heaps on the floor. How funny some people looked and sounded when they were asleep.

But not the knight.

He was strong, handsome and fine-featured, even as he slept. I watched him from my corner, his face relaxed. Did he ever laugh or smile? The blind girl had bandages over her eyes. What did blind people see in their dreams? Could she dream of a flower if she had never seen one in real life?

The nurse, Joana, was kind. I had been certain she would be angry or disgusted by me, but she wasn't. Her hands and voice carried a gentle calm, like my mama's. When she touched my stomach she smiled and nodded. She often looked directly into my eyes and that made me wonder if she saw everything. But when she sat alone her face looked cheerless and forlorn, full of tears waiting patiently to fall.

And then the noise erupted.

Screaming.

It filtered from above, shadowed between the walls. And

then it descended, clearer, sharper, drawing closer. The sound lifted the latch of memory. My shoulders began to tremble.

The wind howled down the hallway. A door slammed. The knight was awake, on his feet, gun drawn. He looked first to Joana and then to me. He moved quickly to the door but before he reached it, Eva burst into the room, wild with panic.

"Dead in their beds! They're all dead in their beds!" she shrieked.

Eva's face was so white it looked blue. A stuffed rabbit dangled from her massive hand. One of its ears was missing.

florian

There were many possibilities. I pieced together this one.

The family had been eating their dinner. They were alerted of a Russian approach—maybe someone at the door or a sound from outside. The older gentleman, probably the grandfather, instructed everyone to go upstairs and get in bed. He then walked to his room and dressed in his uniform from the Great War. Honor lost was everything lost. He would not allow his family or legacy to be stripped from their land. They would die with dignity. Shoulders square, rows of medals adorning the left side of his chest, the old man walked in and out of each bedroom, taking life yet sparing honor. He then marched to his own room, stood by the window watching the hills beyond, and pulled the trigger.

And now they lay lifeless, their legacy frozen with cold.

No one could go back to sleep. We left the estate before the first morning light appeared.

The shoemaker held the little boy's hand.

The boy held the earless rabbit.

What a sorry group we were, brutalized and bandaged, yet luckier than most; certainly more fortunate than the dead family upstairs. The giant woman wouldn't stop talking about it, describing the scene in morbid detail for the others. I wanted to hit her with a brickbat.

"Sorry, but you didn't see it, the blood, the children," she said. "Thank God it was so cold up there. Even so, the smell."

We walked down the long drive and just before we reached the road, the giant started in about the Polish girl. "Get her out of the cart. She can't come with us. We can't be caught with a runaway Pole and a deserter. We'll end up slaughtered like the family upstairs."

"Shut up," I told her. "I'm not a deserter."

"Eva, she's showing signs of early labor. She should rest," said Joana.

"Well, she made it this far, I'm sure she can make it the rest of the way. We don't want her in our group, Joana. The others just aren't brave enough to tell you."

The Polish girl looked to me from the back of the cart. I wanted to give the annoying woman a piece of my mind. The nurse stepped in front of me.

"All right, Eva. Perhaps you've forgotten that the horse is mine? I'll take Emilia on horseback and ride ahead on my own. You can all pull the cart yourselves."

The nurse girl was even prettier when she was stubborn.

"Joana, please don't leave us. Please," begged the blind girl.

The small boy clutched the maimed rabbit and began to cry.

"Really, Eva, at this point it makes no difference," said the shoe poet. "We'll reach the ice soon and—"

The blind girl threw her hand in the air. The arguing ceased.

SALT TO THE SEA   97

Noise, voices, and other sounds slowly emerged through the trees.

Someone was on the road.

I darted through the snow and peered out from behind a tree. A massive procession of people and carts created a long column, as far as the eye could see.

So it had happened.

Evacuation orders had been issued. Germany was finally telling people what they should have said months ago.

Run for your lives.

alfred

Hello, my Lore,

I woke this winter morning with memories of sweeping your sidewalk at springtime. Perhaps you noticed the vigor I applied toward your walk in particular? I smile and must bite my lip when I think of how often I overexerted myself on your behalf.

I'm really much too busy to be writing such a letter today, but I know you are probably thinking of me. You see, Hannelore, I am generous with my spirit, not only my broom. Your father could have used a good man like me at his furniture factory. I believe I once mentioned that to him, but he ignored me. No matter, I haven't time to dwell on such inconsequence.

The port, you see, is in imminent danger of attack by Allied planes. Evacuation orders were posted last night and millions of people in this region of East Prussia will now flee to me for help. The refugees will line up at the port and I will assign them to a ship that will take them to safety. Yes, it's a very important task, but I am supremely capable. You might recall my keen evaluation ability. I am the cat who contemplates both the mouse and the cheese. I know instantly which one will satisfy the craving.

These months mark the longest we have ever been separated. Perhaps you are marking each day on a calendar with a large red

X? I see you on the front step, waiting and longing for my letters. I express myself to you as I express myself to no one. Perhaps through these letters we might share our secrets. After all, war births litters of them. I suppose it is no secret, however, that my private thoughts of you soften the clutch of combat.

Sadly, Heidelberg feels quite far away now. To bring you closer, I picture the dark evenings in my mind. I see the warm, honey glow behind your bedroom curtain, your shadow dancing on the wall as you gently fold your red sweater and bend to lacquer the small nails on your toes.

Yes, the nights at home were dark and still. It was in that darkness that duty called and I made my decision. But really, my sweet, what choice did I have?

joana

Where had they all come from? This endless stream of humanity clogging the small field road—did they suddenly crawl out of a hole? Had they been waiting in the forests as we had? Young women, elderly grandparents, and too many children to count. They dragged sleds, drove carts with mules, and walked with belongings slung over their backs in sheets.

A little boy and his sister straddled an ox, gripping a frayed piece of rope tied around the animal's neck. "Please, Magnus, hurry!" coaxed the little boy, thumping his heels into the ox. His sister's thin ankles were exposed and black with frostbite.

"Let me help you," I called to them, but they didn't hear me. He slapped the ox and trotted away. A few carts, with well-rested horses, clucked by us quickly, leaving only a glimpse of the prominent family name painted across the back of the carriage. Some people were tired, despondent, others panicked and full of terror. An old man with a wooden leg thumped back and forth across the road, clutching his temples and announcing to everyone who passed, "They shot my cow."

Eva lumbered through the crowds, badgering people for information and updates. "Which way did you come from? What have you heard?"

Reports were that Germany was buckling. Although they

had finally allowed people to evacuate, for many it was too late.

"Joana!" Eva called out to me. "This one here is Lithuanian."

I made my way through the mass of people to the old woman.

"*Labas,*" I said. "Where are you from?"

"Kaunas," she said. "And you?"

"Biržai, originally. I've been gone for four years. But my cousins are from Kaunas. How are things there?"

She shook her head, barely able to speak. "Our poor Lietuva," she whispered. "We shall never see her again. Hurry child, keep moving." She patted my arm and walked off.

What was she talking about? The war would end. We would all go home.

Wouldn't we?

The temperature plunged well below zero. I thought of the warm fire back at the estate and the cold bodies upstairs in the beds. As we left the property I had taken one last look. I couldn't shake the image of the upstairs corner window, pierced with a bullet hole and covered in blood. Zarah Leander's voice lived in my head, whispering the words, *It's not the end of the world.*

I hoped she was right.

The wandering boy and the shoe poet marched in front of our cart. Poet entertained the boy by assigning shoe types.

"That one there, he has narrow feet. We would put him in an oxford. But that man, the one with the short boots, he'll have a heel bruise within the next kilometer. We'd put him in a loafer, to be sure. You know, Klaus, if you can't get a fingerprint, you would do just as well to get a foot draft from a man's shoemaker. It will tell you more than an identity card."

I stood next to Ingrid, whose eyes were bandaged. She insisted on walking and gripped the rope that hung behind the wagon. Emilia sat nestled in heaps of bundles on the back of our cart, her pink hat a blink of color among the endless blacks and grays. Emilia's eyes stayed fixed on the German boy who walked behind me, his cap pulled low over his eyes. I slowed my step and allowed him to catch up to me.

"Ingrid thinks we'll reach the ice tomorrow. She smells the coast," I told him.

"We should try to reach the ice tonight," he replied.

"Everyone will be exhausted and it will be too dark. We won't see a thing."

"Exactly. If it's dark, the Russians won't be able to see us. We'll be open targets during the day. Sort of like we are now," he said.

I hadn't thought of that.

"The ice will be stronger at night, when it's colder," he whispered. "Look at all these people. When they march across the ice, it will weaken it. They shouldn't be carrying so much baggage."

"It's precious to them; it's all they have left. Just like that pack of yours. It seems pretty important to you."

He said nothing.

"How are you feeling?" I asked.

SALT TO THE SEA   103

"I'm fine."

We trudged on in silence. I stared down at the icy road.

His breath was suddenly close. "The girl. She doesn't have papers."

Papers.

He was right. Emilia had no identity card. I had forgotten that. Germany required all civilians to legally register and carry documentation that contained our name, photograph, nationality, race, birth, and family details. The regime then assigned identifiers on the cover of the cards. My identity card said *Resettler*, indicating that Germany had allowed me to repatriate from Lithuania. We were required to show our identification to any official or soldier who requested it. Our papers determined our fate.

I looked up at her, balanced in the bundles. She smiled and gave me a small wave.

Emilia had no papers.

No papers, no future.

emilia

It was nice to sit in the wagon, but it felt unfair that I got to ride while the others had to walk. From my place in the cart I could see a long string of dark coats, farm carts, animals, and sleds behind us. The line snaked far back, until the people were just tiny specks.

Joana walked alongside the knight, her pretty brown curls peeking out from beneath her hat. He wouldn't look at her when she spoke. But whenever she looked away, his eyes quickly shifted to her.

He wanted to tell her things.

She hoped he would tell her things.

But he would not.

I could feel the blackberry seeds still stuck in my teeth from the preserves he had given me. Blackberries and black currants reminded me of Father. When I was a tiny girl, he would send me out to the bushes on the edge of our property with a small tin pail to collect them. Each time I returned with a full bucket he greeted me with hugs and smiles. There were no hugs or smiles on the farm he sent me to in East Prussia. There were stables, cowsheds, a piggery, a chicken house, and two large barns with haylofts. And then there was the cold storage cellar, standing quiet, alone behind the barn. Steps led down into the dark underground room. That's where I would take the beetroots, turnips, dried mushrooms, and barrels of soured cabbage. I blinked and rubbed my eyes.

My stomach twitched. It used to feel like a butterfly flapping or big bubbles popping in there. But now, when I put my hand on my stomach, I could feel a bumping against my palm. That bumping. It grew stronger.

florian

Dawn became day and soon became afternoon. We traveled faster knowing evacuation was permitted.

The road clogged as we neared Frauenburg. Up on a hill sat a redbrick cathedral. As we approached, so did a frenzy of activity and a number of German soldiers.

I shifted my pack. Another test. I would have to register at the checkpoint without raising suspicion. My father's words hung heavy on my conscience:

"Don't you see? Lange doesn't want to train you—he wants to use you, Florian."

"You don't understand," I had argued. "He's saving the treasures of the world."

"Saving them? Is that what you call it? Is that how easily he's duped you? This greedy imposter fills your head with rubbish and you become a traitor?"

"I am not dishonoring Germany. Just the opposite."

"No, son," pleaded my father. "Not a traitor to your country. Much worse. A traitor to your soul."

A traitor to your soul. Those were the last words my father said to me. Not because he was finished, but because I stormed out of the house and refused to listen. When I returned months later, panicked and in need of his counsel, it was too late.

SALT TO THE SEA   *107*

So now I risked everything, confronting fate and the knowledge that I had authored my own demise. But only if I failed.

A young German soldier stopped our group. I pretended to be on my own and continued walking. The Polish girl tried to scramble out of the cart after me.

"Halt!"

I stopped.

The soldier marched toward me. "You. Papers."

A muscle tremored just below my ear. I slowly unbuttoned my coat and withdrew my identity card from the pocket. He grabbed it. I moved close to him and discreetly displayed the folded paper. He snapped it out of my hand, impatient. I turned slightly. The eyes of our group were upon me, closely watching the interaction.

The soldier scanned the papers. He handed them back to me, quickly snapped his heels together, and saluted. "Heil Hitler!"

Relief flooded my every pore. I returned the salute. "Heil Hitler!"

The soldier caught sight of my shirt through my open coat. "Are you injured, Herr Beck?"

"I'm fine. But I have to keep moving."

"Are you traveling with this group?" he asked, looking over our ragged assembly. From the corner of my eye, I saw a dot of pink wool slide behind the front wheel of the cart.

The shoe poet stared at my boot. The wandering boy smiled and gave me a salute.

"Are they with you?" the soldier asked again. His gaze traveled back and landed on the nurse. His eyes widened.

"She—"

My words were clipped by shrieks amidst the crowd. The searing buzz of aircraft echoed from above.

"Off the road!" yelled the soldier.

A cluster of human beings behind us exploded with a bomb.

joana

The sound of children screaming, wood splintering, and life departing roared from behind. I tried to run toward the crowd but the soldier grabbed me and threw me off the road. I crawled through the snow toward the pink of Emilia's hat and draped my body over hers.

The explosions finally ceased and the soldier yelled at us to move quickly into the village.

"But I can help them back there. I have medical training," I argued.

"It's no use. Move along, Fräulein, now!" the soldier commanded, waving us forward. Our group reassembled and trudged toward Frauenburg. But one person was missing.

The young German was gone.

Who was he? Whatever was written in the letter commanded great respect from the soldier on the road.

Emilia was inconsolable, turning in all directions to find the German. She wailed and tried to leave. It took four of us to get her back into the cart. The bombing propelled everyone forward at a quicker pace, anxious to reach Frauenburg and possible shelter. I didn't want to move forward. I needed to go back, to help the injured. But they would not allow it.

"What good will you be, my dear, if you are injured?" said

the shoe poet. "You must preserve yourself in order to help others."

Poet didn't know the truth. I had already preserved myself. I had left Lithuania and those I loved behind.

To die.

alfred

What an enormous vessel, the *Wilhelm Gustloff*. Walking her length was more exercise than I cared for. I found it preferable to conserve my energy. Sometimes this conservation involved stealing away to the lavatory to sit for an hour. Maybe two. On occasion, while sitting, I'd remind myself that fitness was important to a healthy physique. I wanted to quell my crawling rash. After all, I had been told that a squad of Women's Naval Auxiliary were on their way to join the voyage. More than three hundred young naval cadets. They would of course require my assistance.

I'd tell the pretty ones they could call me Alfred. But just the pretty ones.

I stood in the ship's stately ballroom, imagining the dancing figures it used to hold.

Oh, hello there, Lore! Lovely to see you. Would you care to dance?

"Come on, Frick, all of this furniture has to go," instructed my superior. "Everything must be removed to create space. Carry the furniture out onto the dock. Take the tablecloths up to the arbor on the sundeck. They're organizing a hospital ward up there."

"What will this ballroom be used for?" I asked.

"For refugees. Once we remove the furniture, we'll line this ballroom with mattresses."

I looked at the dance floor, trying to imagine it covered with spongy mats.

Hannelore was a very good dancer. How I enjoyed the private recitals through the window.

My rash began to itch, chasing away my one weakness that was Hannelore Jäger. Somewhere inside, I reminded myself of the necessary truth.

Hannelore might be dancing for someone else now.

emilia

He was gone.

I tried to look for him but Joana demanded I stay in the cart.

"Let her go," said Eva.

Big Eva was scared of me, more concerned with her own survival. But Joana had won. Her importance to the group was evident. She was trusted. She was wanted.

"We'll approach the checkpoint and register," instructed Joana. "We can't cross now, the planes shot through the ice. It will refreeze overnight. We'll wait here in the village and cross in the morning."

The German Empire had renamed the cities. They called the village Frauenburg. The old name had been Frombork. Father told me it was once the home of the astronomer Copernicus, who proved that the earth rotated around the sun.

"*Per aspera ad astra*, Papa," I whispered. Through hardship to the stars. It was a Latin phrase he used whenever I complained that something was difficult. Where was my father now? Could he ever have imagined things would be this difficult? I looked up at the sky, wondering if the stars would be pretty here.

Joana whispered with Eva. I heard her say something about

refugees in the ice. She was trying to be stoic, a medical woman, but I could tell that she was upset because the soldier hadn't allowed her to help the injured on the road.

Joana climbed up into the cart. "Here," she whispered. "Take this." She handed me an identity card. "It's from a young Latvian woman who died on the road," she explained. "I was going to give the papers to the Red Cross for their registry. This woman was slightly older, but she had blond hair. Take your braids out and keep your hat pulled down."

I quickly began to unthread my braids.

"Open your coat so your pregnancy is revealed. They will assume you're older. I'll explain that you are Latvian and don't speak German."

So that was the plan. Would it really work? What would happen if they realized I wasn't a dead Latvian woman, but a young Polish girl with no papers?

Birds squawked overhead, issuing a warning.

I knew the legends of the birds. Seagulls were the souls of dead soldiers. Owls were the souls of women. Doves were the recently departed souls of unmarried girls.

Was there a bird for the souls of people like me?

florian

I held the paper, waiting to approach the checkpoint. I stared at the type.

Sonderausweis.

Special pass. It looked real. Perhaps my best work ever. The soldier on the road didn't question. He saluted me for the special mission that the pass defined. My attitude had to match the level of the forgery. If I appeared confident, they wouldn't inspect. But if Dr. Lange had discovered the missing piece, he may have wired ahead. If so, they would be waiting for me. My confidence would hold no currency.

I looked at the ledger in front of the soldier. Did the book include an arrest order for treason? I had used my real name on the pass. There wasn't time to forge new identity papers.

It had started as a dare. My friend Kurt wanted to attend a soccer match with the rest of our group, but all tickets had been sold. "Come on, Beck, use those skills to create some tickets," chided Kurt. I accepted the challenge. Using a friend's ticket and restoration supplies, I forged a couple.

"I guess we'll need your special tickets for the finals," Kurt joked on our way home. But we didn't make it to the finals. Kurt was a few years older than I and was drafted. At

Christmas, I went to visit his mother. She opened the door dressed in black, her eyes pillowed and heavy with grief. Kurt had died in service, an honorable death.

If I died, who would say the same of me?

The woman in front of me left the table. I was finally alone, no longer burdened by the young Pole and the pretty nurse. I approached the soldier with an air of superiority and thrust out my papers. "I need to cross now."

"No one's crossing now. Unless you want a cold bath," said the soldier as he opened my papers. He read the special pass and looked up at me. He lowered his voice.

"My apologies, Herr Beck. I can get you across first thing tomorrow morning." He logged my details in the registration ledger. "We can find lodging for you this evening here in Frauenberg," he said.

"No, I have arrangements," I told him. I didn't need any eyes on me.

"You may cross in the morning, then. As long as there aren't any further attacks. Heil Hitler!" he said.

"Heil Hitler," I responded, swallowing the bile that rose when I spoke the phrase.

joana

Our group approached the village registration point and the soldiers. Emilia pulled her pink hat low over her eyes. Eva clenched her jaw and the wandering boy held Poet's hand.

How closely would they inspect our papers? Could they assess refugees like I diagnosed patients? If so, they'd note the following about me:

Homesick.

Exhausted.

Full of regret.

It wasn't fair to think of myself. The stakes were so much higher for the others.

What would they do to Emilia if they discovered the truth? And Ingrid? She'd be sent to one of the walled-in killing facilities in Germany or Austria.

"Tell me something about the inspection soldier," whispered Ingrid.

"He's our age. Blond. His left foot is propped on a wooden box. Blue scarf."

The soldier rubbed his gloved hands together, suffering in the cold. He scanned our group and cart as we advanced toward his table. His eyes stopped on Ingrid.

"What's wrong with your eyes, Fräulein?"

"Glass shards from an explosion," recited Ingrid.

"Come closer," he commanded. "Approach the table." His eyes journeyed from her face to her feet.

Panic pounded at my throat.

"Joana." Ingrid smiled. "Help me forward so I don't fall and embarrass myself in front of the soldier."

I steered Ingrid forward.

"My eyes are improving," Ingrid told him. "Today I can see through the gauze a bit. I . . . like your scarf," she said quietly. "Blue is my favorite color."

The soldier stared at Ingrid. His silence was elastic, slowly curling a rope around her neck. He looked at our group and put a finger to his lips, demanding silence. He reached up and pulled the scarf from his neck.

He then held the scarf out to Ingrid.

He waited.

The ends of the scarf fluttered in the freezing wind.

I couldn't breathe.

Slowly, Ingrid's gloved hand lifted, trembling, tentative.

"Yes." He smiled, nodding. "Take it, Fräulein." He quickly pushed the scarf into her hand. His voice dropped in volume. "You're lucky. My youngest brother was born blind."

"I see your left foot is hurting, isn't it, lad?" interrupted the shoe poet.

"Like the devil," replied the soldier. "That's why I'm sitting at this stupid table."

SALT TO THE SEA   119

"I'm a shoemaker. Let me have a look." Poet was a star, with skills as good as any cinema actor. He examined the soldier's foot and ankle.

"You need a heel cup," said Poet. "Finish up with our group here and give me your boot. You'll feel better in no time."

"Really?" asked the soldier.

"Why, yes, it's the least I can do for the Reich, isn't it? But I don't want to hold up my group. That wouldn't be fair." Poet chatted to him nonstop about the relief he would soon feel. The soldier scanned our papers and logged our registration quickly, barely looking at Emilia. Poet and the wandering boy stayed behind for the boot adjustment. "We'll catch up with you," Poet said with a wink.

Ingrid stood facing the soldier, clutching his scarf to her chest. She smiled. He smiled back. I gently steered her away by the elbow. She was shaking.

We settled into the crowded cathedral on the hill with the other refugees. I walked through the clusters of people, trying to help where I could while also looking for supplies. An old woman offered to trade some herbs for a pair of socks. I reorganized my suitcase after the transaction, looking for paper to write a letter to Mother. I was one step closer to her, closer to finding out where my father and brother were. I sorted through the personal items in my case, reflecting on how much I had left behind. I used to complain that family dinners lasted too long, that we were forced to sit at the table when I needed to study for exams.

"Enough studying, Joana. Sometimes living life is more instructive than studying it," my father used to tease.

War had rearranged my priorities. I now clung to memories more than goals or material things. But there were a few irreplaceable items that buoyed my spirit and fight for life. It was at that moment that I realized.

Something was missing from my suitcase.

alfred

Dearest one,

Your tender ear is probably full of news now, listening to reports of the Russians plundering this region. So vulgar, those Bolsheviks, interested in nothing but schnapps and wristwatches. "Urri, urri," they say, demanding men surrender their timepieces. Do they report that in Heidelberg, Lore? Likely not. Many fine points of detail are overlooked by the average man. It is up to people like me—documentarians of the military—to report them. Yet I fear I will upset your fragile nerves by telling you these truths of atrocities, like the fact that six hundred Russian babies were born in Stolp alone last month, after the Russian barbarians invaded last year. Such an insult to our Führer. Yes, best to avoid mention of such things.

Instead I shall direct your attention to this marvel of a ship, the Wilhelm Gustloff. I know you enjoy the undisclosed details we share, so I shall risk including them. Of course secrets are safe with you, dear Hannelore. How you do love keeping secrets. But perhaps you had best throw this letter onto the fire after reading it.

The ship's chimney, or funnel, as sailors call it, is thirteen meters high. But we both know appearances can deceive. The impressive-looking chimney is false. It is not a working chimney at

Ruta Sepetys

all. How do I know, you ask? Well, a man of my status has access to these special details. I discovered the chimney just this week while on patrol. The inside has a nice iron ladder to a ledge where I can sit and peer out over the decks. While looking out, I have observed some of the soldiers doing things they should not. I note this information and keep it at hand in the event I need to use it to my advantage later. I quite enjoy the feeling of finally being the one who holds the cards.

We have removed all of the furniture from the ship's common areas, every last chair and table, in order to accommodate refugees. I am told they will sit shoulder to shoulder on mattresses in every room and corridor. U-boat officers and Germans of priority will of course take lodging in the ship's passenger cabins.

My Mutter always lamented my lack of friends in Heidelberg, but here each day I am introduced to someone new. Just today I met Eugen Jeissle, the ship's head printer, responsible for creating the boarding passes, the coveted pieces of paper that will allow passage to freedom.

"These will be more valuable than bars of gold," Jeissle told me.

When he left for the toilets I decided it would be best to take a stack of the passes for posterity. I'm sure he wouldn't mind.

So, dearest, that is the news of the day. Hopefully these details of consequence will soothe the strain of my absence.

I ended the mental letter but left out one detail.

The *Gustloff* only had twelve lifeboats. The other ten were missing.

florian

I crouched near the cathedral altar, carefully watching the Polish girl. She was looking for me. When she turned her head I made my move, quickly darting to the small entry. I crawled inside and pressed my back against the tiny door to keep anyone from entering. As a small boy in Tilsit, I once found my way inside the pipe organ of a local church. It was a perfect hiding spot. The organ was my target as soon as I saw the cathedral. Adults wouldn't bother me, only bored children who might be exploring.

The cramped space left little room to move, but I didn't care. I was alone, out of the cold, and one step closer to completing my mission. I watched the group from behind the pipes. The Polish girl's pink hat bobbed like a candy egg amidst hundreds of gray faces all so tired and drawn, they looked like boiled meat. The nurse continually scanned the cathedral. Was she looking for those who might need help? Was she looking for food? Or maybe, was she looking for me? I tried not to care.

Protected by privacy, I was finally able to open my pack. I took out the art supplies and my notebook. The small box was undisturbed. Had Dr. Lange peeked in the crate yet? At times, to fuel his artistic euphoria, Dr. Lange would open a crate to admire a panel from the precious Amber Room, savoring the experience as others would enjoy a vintage bottle of brandy. Initially, I was so impressed by his emotional reaction. I thought it was passion for art. It wasn't. It was greed and power that excited him in a perverse way.

Originally created in Prussia and gifted to Peter the Great, the Amber Room was a glittering chamber of amber, jewels, gold, and mirrors. In 1941, the Nazis stole it from the Catherine Palace in Pushkin, near Leningrad. Packed into twenty-seven crates, the Amber Room was the culmination of Hitler's artistic dreams. He carefully strategized its safekeeping and after much deliberation the twenty-seven crates were secretly shipped to the castle museum in Königsberg.

Dr. Lange was responsible for its protection.

I worked for Dr. Lange.

Some in the art world claimed the Amber Room carried a curse. Dr. Lange wouldn't hear of that. He said the Amber Room was the greatest of the world's treasures. I was the only one he trusted to touch the treasure. He gave me special tailored gloves, fitted to my fingers.

"Can you even comprehend what we have here, Florian?" Lange's breath fluttered while admiring the sparkling jewels amidst the golden stones.

As the Russian forces approached, Dr. Lange assured me that moving the twenty-seven crates containing the Amber Room meant preserving the riches of the Reich. In reality, he and Koch had plans of their own. They were hiding the room for themselves and, in the process, implicating me in the biggest heist of all time. It was calculated and clever, putting an unknowing young apprentice in the middle to blame later, if necessary.

When we sealed the crates to move them, I noticed that one was unlike the others.

"Why is this crate marked differently?" I had asked Lange.

He was all too eager to tell me. "Inside that one," he breathed, "is another very small box. It contains the crown jewel of the Amber Room."

"What is it?"

"A tiny amber swan." Lange put his hand to his chest, practically over his heart. "It is the Führer's most favorite."

We dug a secret bunker deep beneath the castle and locked the crates inside. I then painted the stone floor above the cellar to look aged. The door to the cellar was undetectable.

But I knew where it was.

I also had the key.

Hidden behind the organ, I carefully pulled the lid from the small wooden box and removed the top layer of straw. Even in the low light, the amber swan glistened and shimmered. People had fought for it, killed for it, died for it.

And I had it.

Had Dr. Lange gone looking for the key? Had he discovered my betrayal?

I carefully arranged the straw over the swan and slid the top of the small crate back into place. The key was my revenge against Lange. But the tiny crate with the swan was more important.

It held my revenge against Hitler.

Ruta Sepetys

emilia

The shoe poet woke early, rapping our feet with his walking stick.

"It is time to cross the iced lagoon," he announced. "If it were summer, I would swim across. I am a very strong swimmer," he told the wandering boy.

Poet said once we crossed the ice, we could walk down the narrow strip of land to one of the ports. There was no other option. The Russians surrounded us on all sides. But where was the knight? Had he walked across the ice alone?

I overheard Joana talking to Eva. "Do you have any cosmetics? It might make Emilia look a little older, like the Latvian in the papers. I can tell them she's on her way to meet her boyfriend."

Boyfriend.

I thought of August and how hard he worked the family's land. He was so kind to come into the kitchen and apologize for his mother's cruel behavior.

"Don't pay any attention to her, Emilia. Someday she'll get a dose of her own medicine," he'd said.

I learned things about him, just by watching. I knew which section of rabbit pleased him most, that he preferred autumn to spring, and that he would rather take his breakfast bread alone in the stable than with his parents in the dining room.

I watched intently, remembering Mama's words: *If you observe carefully, dear, you won't have to ask.* Mama observed too. Visitors never had to ask for cream with their coffee or jam for their tea. She had noted their preferences long before.

Joana knew who was hurting and I knew secrets about the knight. But I felt certain that no one knew my secrets, except maybe the ravens that nested above the cold cellar.

joana

My hips and back ached from sleeping on the cold stone floor. I had woken in the middle of the night and imagined I saw the German standing above me in the dark. When I blinked he was gone and I realized it was a dream.

I was concerned about his wound. That's what I told myself. But the truth poked at me. Why was I looking for him? His wound was healing well; he was stronger than most. I was embarrassed to admit it: I wanted to see him again, not to evaluate his wound but to discover his name, his mission, and why he had taken the drawing from my suitcase. Ingrid said he was a thief, but she thought he was stirred to know me, not to hurt me. I wanted to believe her. The war was full of brutality. Were there any nice young men still out there?

"He's probably here somewhere." Ingrid smiled. "Watching."

I had glanced around the crowded cathedral many times the night prior, wondering if she was right.

"Joana," whispered Ingrid, reaching for my hands. "The Russians draw nearer each day. Without you . . . I can't bear to think what would have happened to me."

"We just need to cross the ice," I assured her. "We're close. The crossing point is only a short walk down the hill."

We gathered our belongings. Ingrid spooled the soft scarf from the German soldier around her neck.

Emilia smiled at me behind red lipstick as we left the cathedral.

What a group we were. A pregnant girl in love, a kindly shoemaker, an orphan boy, a blind girl, and a giantess who complained that everyone was in her way when she herself took up the most room. And me, a lonely girl who missed her family and begged for a second chance.

We were among the first to cross. The expanse of ice looked enormous. "Fifty meters between each group," instructed the soldiers. "We must not stress the ice all at once. Hurry."

How could we hurry? The walk was kilometers long and the ice was slippery.

"Let me go first," said Ingrid, her eyes still bandaged. "Alone."

"Absolutely not," I told her. "We'll go together."

"I'll go with Ingrid," said the shoe poet. "My walking stick can test more than soles."

"No," insisted Ingrid. "If I'm alone, I'll truly feel the ice. I'll let you know if it's sound. Then you can bring the cart along with the others."

Ingrid walked several meters out onto the ice, eyes bandaged, hands in front of her. She took a step and stopped, listening.

She took another step.

The sun made its first appearance, throwing light onto

the lagoon. The ice in front of Ingrid was red, frozen with blood. She advanced, then snapped her foot back, as if sensing the stain. She stood perfectly still and breathed, alone on the frozen water. She took a careful step forward, over the icy blood. She took a few more steps, leaving at least twenty meters between us. I could not bear to see her, bandaged and by herself. I walked out to join her.

"I'm coming, Ingrid."

"Yes, the ice is strong," she called. "Come along."

I stepped toward her. The rest of our group advanced slowly, carefully, yet desperate to move quickly across the jaws of ice.

Ingrid's body suddenly stiffened. Her back arched. "*No!*" she screamed. "Go back!"

Our group retreated. I was too far out to return quickly. And then I heard them: Russian planes strafing overhead. Desperate refugees on the bank erupted in terror. Soldiers dove into snowbanks. I dropped facedown onto the frozen surface. The sun brightened, shining through the ice to reveal the horror below. A dead horse and a child's mitten glared at me from beneath the frozen glaze. I closed my eyes, choking on the gruesome images.

High-pitched whizzings flew by my head, cracking and popping. Bullets tore through the ice. Frozen shards peppered my coat as screams filled my ears.

The firing ceased. I opened my eyes. Streaks of blood surrounded a solitary hole in the center of the ice.

"Ingrid!" I screamed.

Ingrid was gone.

SALT TO THE SEA   131

Her gloved hand suddenly appeared, reaching out of the black water.

I crawled toward her.

Her hand bobbed and grasped frantically at the edge of the ice.

"Ingrid!" I wailed.

The ice broke.

The hole in the ice spread farther, sending a deep crack running directly toward me. Ingrid's hand flapped desperately.

A pair of hands tightened around my ankles. I began sliding backward along my belly to the frozen bank.

"Let me go!"

The gap in the ice widened. Water rolled toward me. Panicked screams roared from behind. "It's all cracking!"

Someone pulled me away. I tried to free myself, to fight my way back across to Ingrid.

"*No!*" I pleaded. "Ingrid!"

I looked out toward the dark watery hole. Ingrid's frantic hand suddenly went slack. Her fingers softened, slowly curled, and disappeared beneath the ice.

florian

I followed secretly behind.

When the planes appeared, the Polish girl dropped from the cart and tried to scramble to the women on the ice. I pushed her away, then ran to the nurse, pulling her back toward me. The little boy grabbed my leg, trying to yank me to safety. He had the weight of a dry twig yet heaved with the ferocity of a bull. I dragged the nurse onto the bank, restraining her, fighting her.

"Let me go!" She kicked and screamed, desperate to save her blind friend. We fell in a heap. I pulled her onto my lap. She reached out to the ice.

"Ingrid," she whispered, trembling. "Please, no."

The nurse's neck fell limp, like a broken doll. Her chin dropped against my chest. She began to cry.

The broken shards of ice shifted. The blind girl's blue scarf suddenly appeared on the surface of the water.

The little boy buried his head against Poet's leg. "Make it stop! Please, no more."

"Shh. There, there, Klaus," said the shoemaker.

The nurse sobbed, clinging to me.

I sat, paralyzed, wanting to put my arms around her, but knowing I couldn't.

The Polish girl knelt beside us. She spoke quietly, stroking the nurse's hair and wiping her tears. Then, without a word, she lifted my arms and placed them around the nurse.

alfred

Dearest Hannelore,

Good morning from the port! It has become overwhelmingly crowded in Gotenhafen. Those fleeing from the region stand in line waiting for ship assignment. We must be cautious with registration, as there may be deserting German soldiers hiding among these refugees.

I pity the man who cannot overcome his cowardice, who cannot step on the neck of his own weaknesses. I know you saw the group of Hitler Youth come to my door, Lore. The boys teased that I was a coward, not strong enough to serve our country, but how wrong they were. I'm so pleased you know that. Yes, initially I was not part of Hitler Youth and my critical father was ashamed. But now here I am, called a bit later than most but only because they have finally realized that it takes a man to succeed where boys have failed. It is so gratifying. And where are the bullies of Hitler Youth? Perhaps dead, imprinted by the tread of a tank. Death, it seems, has a mind of its own.

Yes, I know it must all sound hostile, but this is war. Brave men are reduced to numbers. These numbers are engraved twice on an oval metal disc we wear around our neck. In the event of death, they shall snap the disc in half. Half will be buried with my body, the other half turned in to Command with my papers and personal effects.

I am 42089.

I couldn't help but wonder: Did Hannelore have a number?

emilia

We waited on the bank for several hours but the planes did not return. The water froze again. So did our hands and feet.

The soldiers returned to their stations. They insisted we cross a different section of the ice. They rushed the groups of people, all eyes intent on the sky. I resumed my place in the cart. The knight held Joana by the elbow, worried that she might jump into the hole that had taken the blind girl from us. He was scared to touch her, but wanted desperately to touch her.

I held my breath as we crossed, quivering at the thought of our Ingrid frozen beneath. The ice ached and groaned, like old bones carrying too many years, brittle and threatening to snap at any moment. My nerves lurched with each sound. I held my hands across my stomach. The shoe poet walked ahead of the group, tapping the ice with his stick and nodding.

"The ice is arthritic, but no fractures yet," he reported. "Hurry along, the top is melting slightly. We have kilometers to go."

Kilometers to go.

The cramping and pressure resumed below my waist. I couldn't watch any longer. I lay back in the frigid cart, closed my eyes, and thought of August. In my mind, the warm sun burned bright. The unfenced pastures rolled soft, like worn velvet. The window boxes puffed with flowers and the tree branches stooped heavy with ripe plums. August returned to the estate, slick with sweat after a long ride with his horse, Tabrez.

I heard the wheels of the cart churn and scrape beneath me. No one had asked, so I didn't mention it.

I did not know how to swim.

joana

After several hours, we reached the other side of the lagoon. No one celebrated. Instead, we trudged quietly and slowly onto the bank. Finally, Eva spoke.

"I was sure we'd all drown, like cats in a bag."

The wandering boy looked up at Eva. Tears, like slender icicles, were frozen to his cheeks.

"Sorry," she said.

Anger suddenly consumed me. I yanked the German by the arm, pulling him aside. "I could have saved her."

"No, you couldn't. They not only fired through the ice, they shot her."

"You can revive someone who drowns! It's possible. You kept me away."

"Yes, I did. The temperature of the water alone was enough to kill her. It would have killed you too."

"You don't know that!" I yelled.

"Now, now," interrupted the shoe poet. "Let's not soil the memory of Ingrid with arguing." Poet gestured to the German. "He quite possibly saved both you and Emilia. Emilia also scrambled to Ingrid. I saw it. He stopped her too."

Emilia had also tried to save Ingrid? "Emilia, are you okay?" I called up to her in the cart.

Salt to the Sea   *139*

"Yes, okay." She nodded.

"We could have lost all of you girls," continued Poet.

"Not her," said the German of Eva. "Her big feet grew roots. She didn't move to save anyone."

"Feet with roots, that's called a fungal infection," Poet told the wandering boy.

A soldier approached our group. "Papers!" he demanded.

I pulled the German toward me. "You owe us," I whispered.

florian

Owed her? Why did I owe her? I saved her life.

I tried to distract the soldier while he looked at my papers. "A lot of hysteria back there. Their friend fell through the ice," I said.

"Lucky it was just one," said the soldier. "Yesterday we lost dozens. Damn Russians." He scanned my papers. He looked up at me, eyes sharp. "Do you still have the parcel?"

"Yes."

"This is signed by Gauleiter Koch," said the soldier.

I couldn't read his expression. Was he questioning or was he acknowledging? "Yes, I'm in a hurry," I told him.

"Wait here," he said. He turned and walked to another soldier. My pulse quickened.

The rest of the group overheard the exchange. "Come along," said the shoemaker, corralling the others. "Let's leave the boy to his business."

The Polish girl stepped away from the group and stood by my side.

It could have been so easy. I could have walked across the ice myself, without the burden of the group. They could have tried to save the blind girl. Maybe they all would have drowned in the process. That would have been so much easier.

SALT TO THE SEA   *141*

And so much harder.

"*Bitte.*"

The word was so quiet, I wasn't even sure I had heard it. I looked down at the Polish girl. She wore red lipstick. Her blond hair was released from the captivity of her braids. She pulled her pink hat down over her eyes. "*Bitte,*" she whispered again. "Please."

The soldier and a superior were discussing my papers. Had Dr. Lange and Gauleiter Koch made the discovery yet? Did the soldiers have my name on a list of traitors? If so, I'd soon feel the shadow of a gun on the back of my skull.

The soldier returned, staring at me. "I assume you're going to Pillau?" he asked.

"You assume?" I said with an air of authority, needing him to reveal more.

"I am told Gauleiter Koch may be on his way to Pillau."

"No, I am not going to Pillau," I said.

"To Gotenhafen, then?" he asked.

Gotenhafen was in the other direction. "Correct. Gotenhafen."

"Yes, Herr Beck. But it's quite a walk to Gotenhafen. There may be a small boat that can take you." He suddenly saw the Polish girl at my side and raised an eyebrow.

"Yours?" he said with a grin.

"Mind yourself. She's with that group. They helped me when I was injured. In turn, they have helped Gauleiter Koch and the Führer." I snapped my papers out of his hand. "Have you met Gauleiter Koch?" I asked.

The soldier shook his head. "No, but I've heard about him."

Of course he had. Koch's murderous reputation had made him known. And feared.

"Why doesn't Koch have you in uniform?" asked the soldier. "It would be safer for you."

"Maybe, but then I'd be dragged by some unit into the field. As you know, Koch doesn't like his affairs broadcast. This is private business," I said, staring him down.

He nodded.

"Listen. I need that boat to Gotenhafen. Now."

alfred

"Beeil dich!"

Hurry, hurry. Always hurry. Hurrying made my hands itch.

I had been assigned to the *Gustloff*'s enclosed sundeck for the day. It was being outfitted as a maternity ward. How inconvenient for women to become pregnant during a war. Quite thoughtless of them. My Mutter certainly would not have done such a thing. I thought of Mutter's bedroom, separate from my father's. But then I dismissed the thought. I preferred not to think of my father at all.

"Which cabins will the doctors stay in?" I asked as I hauled wooden cots into a line.

"You say 'doctors' as if there will be many," replied the soldier. "I think there will be one doctor who tends to both the women and the injured soldiers."

One doctor for all the patients? But then I realized my error. "So the nurses will do most of the work. Oh, yes, that's much better."

"Nurses? It won't be easy to find nurses. There's a war going on, man. If someone has a baby, you'll be the midwife."

Revolting. If women were so careless to become pregnant

144   *Ruta Sepetys*

at such a time, let women sort it out. It was not a job for one of the Führer's finest.

"Well, they'll need more medical personnel. We're already worn too thin," I complained.

"Sure." The other soldier smirked. "Folding tablecloths and laying mattress pads. That really wears you thin. I'd rather be at the front, killing Russians, but I destroyed my knee, so I'm here"—he looked at me—"with guys like you."

"This is a most important assignment," I corrected him. "We're going to be commanding two thousand people."

"Two thousand?" He laughed. "You think this tub's going to carry only two thousand people? Who told you that?"

emilia

We sat on the bank, shivering, my abdomen seizing. I watched refugees cross the ice and continue their trek down the narrow strip of land between the lagoon and the Baltic Sea. To the left—Gotenhafen. To the right—Pillau. Either way, the journey would be another long one.

Our group argued, but finally chose Gotenhafen. They thought a voyage from Gotenhafen would be shorter. The next argument was how to get there.

"We can walk," said Eva.

"It's much too far. A boat will cut across the inlet faster," argued Joana. "The Russians are on top of us. There's no time to waste."

"This is what we shall do," counseled Poet. "We will lend our cart and horse to a family on foot. They will be grateful for the transportation. We will try to hire a small boat, meet them in Gotenhafen, and retrieve our belongings. That will suit all parties."

I didn't have any belongings, just a rotten potato in my pocket that I gnawed on when no one was looking. That was all I had.

It made me think of my father. *You're all I have,* he would say. Mama's death changed my father. One day a tuft of pure white hair appeared on the back of his head. When I mentioned it, he said it was special—angel hair. But other things changed too. His skin clung to his bones like drenched clothing. He often held his face in his hands.

I quickly realized that what pleased my father the most was my happiness. So I learned to appear happy, even if I wasn't.

Father constantly worried about me. He cried when he told me that he was sending me away to the Kleists' farm in East Prussia for safety. I wanted to cry too. I wanted to scream and refuse. But it hurt so much to see him sad, losing all that he loved. So I assured him that he was right, it was for the best, and that I was not upset. I told him that we would see each other in a couple of years, when the war of winter turned to spring.

I became good at pretending. I became so good that after a while the lines blurred between my truth and fiction. And sometimes, when I did a really good job of pretending, I even fooled myself.

florian

The Polish kid would not give up. She was fifteen, pregnant with her boyfriend's baby, pregnant with a vision of freedom. And she was brave. I couldn't deny that.

There was something else I couldn't deny. Time was running out. I had bullied my way through a couple young guards in rural outposts, but Gotenhafen would be altogether different. Gotenhafen was a major base for the Kriegsmarine, the German navy of the Nazi regime. The military presence would be thick and constant. The naval base and port were also a prime target for Russia's Red Army. They said that Koch himself had left Königsberg. When had he left and where exactly was he now?

Heavy snow fell. I didn't mind the freezing temperature. The cold lowered the risk of infection in my wound. It kept me alert.

"Beck," the soldier called out. "That one's yours." A small boat sped up to a rotting pier. I said nothing, just turned and walked toward the pier, the pink hat following close behind.

If I had to take the Polish girl in the boat I would. She would be lost amidst the chaos in Gotenhafen. She'd have to deal with her Latvian papers and her pregnancy by herself. A sense of relief washed over me. I would soon be back on my own. I stepped onto the pier and nodded to the driver of the boat.

"Wait, all of you?" he asked.

I turned to find the entire group standing behind me on the pier. The little boy approached and held up the earless rabbit, asking if he too could come to Gotenhafen.

The nurse's eyes found mine. *Yes, you owe us,* they seemed to say.

alfred

Good evening, sweet Hannelore,

I'm taking a bit of air on the deck of the Gustloff. Although it is minus ten degrees centigrade and the wind is howling, it is nice to breathe freely. Everyone seems to smoke. You know how cigarette smoke bothers me. It would upset me greatly to see you defile your candied mouth with foulness like so many young girls I see. Have you done that, Hannelore? Of course you haven't.

From up on deck I can see into the port and its surroundings. There must be thirty thousand people in the sea of humanity down there. And they say the operation hasn't even truly begun.

We are kept company by other ships here in the port. I can see Hansa, merchant ships, old fishing boats, trawlers, and even dinghies that have brought fleeing people from the nearby lagoon. I am told that the Gustloff will sail for the German port of Kiel, an expected journey of forty-eight hours. I am wondering how she will fare as a heavy-weather boat, considering she was built for calm voyages under sunny skies and has not sailed for four years.

One of our captains in charge is Captain Petersen. He is a pleasant white-haired fellow in his mid-sixties. Many of the other naval personnel have gone ashore to defend the port. They have been replaced on board by a Croatian deck crew. It is annoying to have to share everything with the personnel, but fear not. I have devised clever alternatives. Today I marked one of the toilets as inoperable. So from now on I will have it all to myself. Quite clever of your Alfie.

Some at home did not appreciate my cleverness or abilities. They saw me as a birdie with a troubled wing that should remain close to the nest. They didn't know the truth.

I am quite confident that no one is aware of my ingenuity and objectives. I just might surprise them all, Hannelore. War is full of duty and decision. You know I have made that commitment.

Yes, life can be lonely for the truly exceptional, darling. So I build my own nest and feather it with thoughts of you.

joana

We arrived in Gotenhafen at dusk, our faces red and chapped from the wind on the water. Emilia had been sick through most of the boat trip, but insisted she was fine. Her face was the color of phlegm as we walked into the port. She held on to the sleeve of the German to steady herself. We needed to find a place for her to rest, something for her to eat.

For weeks we had trekked to get to the port. Nothing could have prepared us for what we found there. Horses and animals, lost or abandoned by their owners, roamed helpless in the streets. Gray naval supply trucks zoomed about. Crates, boxes, luggage, and provisions lined the quays.

"Meta!" a woman screamed, running toward us. She grabbed my arm. "Please, have you seen my Meta? She's only five years old."

A lady with a blue bundle drifted by, crying. "His wet diaper's frozen solid. Should I tug it? Will it tear his skin off?"

People screamed out for food and lost family members.

"My God, look what this war has done," said Eva.

The wandering boy clung to the leg of the shoe poet. Even the German seemed startled.

Poet looked around. "There are so many, it could take days to secure passage. We must stay together. Let's agree that if we get separated, we shall meet under the large clock on that building." He motioned to the distant clock with his walking stick.

Eva stopped a shawled woman pushing a baby buggy through the snow. "What are the reports? What do you know?" she said.

"What do I know? They say Hitler's in a bunker in Berlin." The woman's voice was deep, husky like a man's. "And we're here. Where are the bunkers for us?" She looked up at Eva. "Boy, you're a big one, huh?"

Eva's face clouded.

"Excuse me, is there any organized lodging?" I asked.

"Organized?" The woman laughed. "Take a look around. Nothing's organized. It's bedlam, stupid girl. Grab space where you can and fight for a boarding pass like the rest of us."

The group moved closer to me. The wandering boy approached the baby carriage. His eyes widened.

"And how is your child faring?" I asked, peeking into the buggy. Tucked into the buggy was not a child. It was a goat.

"Don't judge me," said the woman, stepping in front of the buggy. "If I don't take it, someone else will. I've got kids who are hungry."

"I'm not judging. We're all hungry."

"Well, this goat's mine. Find your own." She then looked us over and motioned me closer. "I'm told the roof of the old movie house doesn't have holes. Might be warmer there."

"Thank you," I said.

She stood, waiting. "I could have sold that information,"

she told me. She snorted and shoved off, thrusting the buggy across broken stones and ice. The sound of a bleating goat echoed behind her. We stood silent in a circle, staring at one another.

Eva finally spoke. "I'm sorry, but that was the ugliest baby I've ever seen."

"And for heaven's sake, Joana, find your own goat," Poet chimed.

"Movie house has no holes," said the wandering boy, imitating the deep tone.

And then, from behind the group came his voice: "Careful, Klaus, you could sell that information," said the German.

I tried not to, but I couldn't help it. I laughed. The wandering boy started to giggle. Eva burst out laughing. And then the most amazing thing happened. The German smiled and laughed. Hard.

"Let's find the movie house," said Eva once we had regained our composure. We walked away from the harbor and the enormous ships. Would we be able to secure passage on one tomorrow? If so, which ship would ferry us to freedom?

Snow fell as we walked, piling atop our heads and shoulders. The German grabbed my hand and pulled me toward him.

"I'm sorry," he whispered. "About Ingrid."

I looked down. Before I could respond, he dropped my hand and walked away.

emilia

He was beautiful.

The knight was beautiful, handsome when he smiled.

He didn't want anyone to see it.

He didn't want to acknowledge it himself.

But for a brief moment, I saw him. The real man inside of him, not the one tortured by secrets and pain.

And he was beautiful.

I wanted August to meet him. They were so alike. Quietly strong.

I wished Mama could meet August. She would seat him at our dining room table and serve him thick cuts of bread with sticky marmalade. The belly of the teapot would be warm, full of raspberry tea. Red poppies in the center of the table would give a friendly wave from their glass jar. Mama would remove her apron before sitting down next to August. Then she'd reach across, put her hand on top of his, and tell him—*Tak się cieszę, że tu jesteś.* I am so glad you are here.

Joana still had her mother. Reuniting with her mother was her motivation. She would slay dragons to get to her. Mother was anchor. Mother was comfort. Mother was home. A girl who lost her mother was suddenly a tiny boat on an angry

SALT TO THE SEA   155

ocean. Some boats eventually floated ashore. And some boats, like me, seemed to float farther and farther from land.

I forced my mind toward happy thoughts—August, warmth, storks, home—anything to distract myself from the swelling pressure inside me. I walked with the others in search of the movie house. With each step, the truth drew closer.

I could not make it much longer.

florian

The military presence in the harbor was even heavier than I expected. That meant the Red Army was close. For once I was grateful to be within the group. I kept my head down and walked with them surrounding me. The scenes were agonizing.

A woman nearby fell to her knees, sobbing. "They say I can only choose one child for the ship. How can I choose? Please don't make me choose."

The feeling of desperation was so physically present I could have shoveled it off the dock. Germany needed any and all men for service. SS squads would be on patrol. I had forged courier papers, but an officer could easily ask me to abandon my mission and drive a tank instead.

The woman with the goat had said everything was disorganized. She was wrong. Things were chaotic, yes, but the Germans were always organized. Meticulous. They had systems for everything.

Nazi Party officials, local leaders, and their families would have priority passage on the departing ships. Officers and wounded soldiers would also be granted passage. After the priority travelers and military personnel were loaded, the Germans would choose refugees. Women with children would

SALT TO THE SEA   157

be allowed first. Young single men like myself would not be allowed. At all.

I might finally be forced to reveal that I was hiding a wound greater than a piece of shrapnel. If so, I would need the nurse's help. The strategy was one I had hatched days ago. But it wouldn't work if she was mad at me. By grabbing the nurse I had saved her life. Why was she angry? It bothered me that she was mad. It bothered me even more that I cared.

But I needed her help.

So I had to say I was sorry.

But I didn't have to hold her hand.

alfred

Darling Lore,

The tension grows with each hour that passes. Tomorrow morning, ambulance trains will be arriving from the East, full of wounded soldiers. I was initially assigned to the hospital ward but I will find a replacement, of course, as they will surely discover my talents are better suited in other areas.

As a child my Mutter would shield my eyes from sickness and deformity. She was quite right to do so. There is so much ugliness and imperfection in the world. We know it exists but we create further trauma by being forced to look at it. Some things are better ignored.

"Frick, snap out of it!"

I turned toward the voice that addressed me.

"This area will be for limbless soldiers and amputees. But we can't take all of them. Tomorrow, when the ambulance trains arrive, we will examine the wounded. Only soldiers with a strong chance of survival will be embarked."

Examining wounds? No, that wouldn't do at all.

"Excuse me, sir," asked another sailor. "You said those with a chance of survival will be embarked. What about our men who are more gravely injured?"

"They will be left behind," replied the officer.

SALT TO THE SEA   159

"Quite wise." I nodded. "Leave the browned cabbage in the basket. It makes no sense to save a head with only a few good leaves."

"Shut up, Frick," they said in unison.

joana

The town of Gotenhafen bloated with refugees and military. The shoe poet scavenged through abandoned luggage as we walked. He found two pairs of boots. The wandering boy quickly shined them. By the time we reached the movie house, Poet had traded the boots for a large bucket of hot porridge.

"Useful skills can always be bartered. You see, your expertise is valuable," he told the wandering boy. The boy beamed.

We approached the small movie house. "We'll sit down soon," I assured Emilia. She looked as if she might collapse. We walked to the back door but found it locked.

The shoe poet turned to the German. "Perhaps you can find a way in, friend?"

"Perhaps." He nodded. "Gather around me." We did as he asked. He removed a small jackknife from his pocket and within seconds had opened the door. We slipped inside and he locked the door behind us.

"We should leave it open," I told him. "Others will need a place to stay too."

Others were already inside. Sitting in the chairs, lying on the floor.

"I see the goat mother made a few coins selling her information," said Eva.

"Where shall we make our camp?" asked the shoe poet, looking around.

"We should take the projector room," said the German. "Upstairs."

"I don't want to walk up the stairs," said Eva. "I'm tired. Let's just sit and eat this porridge before it gets cold."

I agreed. The day had been so long. The boat ride, the ice, Ingrid.

Ingrid.

I felt a tremor in my throat.

"So," said Eva, "who's hiding the blackberries and carrots from the dead house?"

After a quiet meal I laid Emilia down and elevated her legs on a suitcase. The wandering boy was asleep in seconds. Eva also fell asleep quickly, her huge frame the length of two wandering boys. She snored, sputtering growls each time she exhaled.

I pulled my medical bag from my suitcase, preparing for those who might need help.

"Hey," said the German quietly.

I looked over to him.

"There are several ships. Tomorrow we'll all be split up at registration," he said.

Emilia looked at me. I hadn't thought of that. "But we should try to stay together," I whispered to him.

"Well, what's your story for her?" he said, pointing to Emilia.

"I guess the same, with the Latvian's papers."

He shook his head. "It will be tougher here. Everyone wants to get on a boat."

"I'll explain that she's pregnant. She'll open her coat and they'll see."

"But she doesn't look old enough to be the Latvian. She doesn't speak any Latvian," he said. "They're strict here. There are senior officers in charge, not just young recruits."

Emilia reached out and touched the German's knee. "*Bitte*," she said.

"I'm sorry, I can't take you on," he told her. "But she can." He pointed to me.

"I can?"

"Yes. Like the old man said, skills are valuable. The larger ships will have hospital wards. They'll need you. Present yourself for work, but tell them you want to bring your patients with you."

Emilia looked at him. "You are patient too," she said.

"Maybe. I do have"—he hesitated—"a medical condition," he said.

The shrapnel. I had nearly forgotten. "Oh, I haven't even asked. You seemed well. How is your wound?"

"It's not that. It's something else," he said.

"What?" I asked.

Emilia patted her left ear and then pointed to the German.

He stared at her, shocked but laughing. "What are you, a little witch or something? How did you know?"

"What is it?" I repeated.

He leaned in, over Emilia. "My left ear has been damaged,"

SALT TO THE SEA   *163*

he whispered. "I have papers, an important assignment. I need to get on a boat. But there's a chance they'll ask me to stay and fight instead. I'd have a stronger case with a medical testimony. You could say that I'm recovering from a wound along with losing my hearing."

What was he asking me to do?

"I'm not a doctor," I told him.

"But I was your patient," he said. "Please, just think about it." He grabbed his pack and pointed up to the projection room. "I'm going to find my way up there."

He walked off. He had spoken more to me in the last five minutes than he had since he joined our group.

The shoe poet was still awake, listening. He raised his eyebrows at me, then rolled over to sleep.

alfred

I stared at the envelope from Mutter. It had arrived two months ago. I decided to open it.

> *My dear Alfie,*
>
> *I am so very worried. Despite my many letters, I have heard nothing from you. Please send a few words to let your Mutti know that you are safe. Are you eating well? How is your stomach?*
>
> *Heidelberg is fairly quiet relative to the rest of the country. I am grateful that we are insulated. I clean your room, in hopes you shall soon return home. Last week, while dusting in your closet, I discovered all of the butterflies pinned to the back wall. Imagine my surprise. So many, yet you never mentioned them. How long have you had them, Alfred, and why?*
>
> *All is the same as in my last letter. The Jägers' house is still lonesome. Frau Henkel always mentions you when she speaks of the Jägers. I think you admired little Hannelore, did you not? I wonder if there is something you haven't told me? Do not be frightened to share your secrets. I will not tell your father. When the war is over there will be a "right side" to land upon. The "wrong*

SALT TO THE SEA   165

side" could have grave consequences. Your father is aware of that. I hope you are too.

Remember to wear two pair of socks. It will protect your bunions.

With loving thoughts always,

Mutti

I grabbed a pen and paper.

Dear Mutter,

Your letter has just arrived. I am in Gotenhafen. I am fine and very busy. I am working on the ship Wilhelm Gustloff and am too occupied in duty to write often. Do not touch my butterflies and please refrain from entering my room. I know nothing of the Jägers.

Your son,

Alfred

florian

I knew it. The nurse would want to see my ear. I watched her make her way through the aisle, looking for the stairway. Would she find it? I sat down and began cleaning my nails with the knife.

She opened the door. "I'm surprised it's unlocked."

"I knew you would come up."

"How did you know?" she asked.

I shrugged. "You're exceedingly responsible. You have this terrible need to heal people." I looked up from my jackknife. "Why is that?"

"You're one to ask questions. You barely speak. I've asked your name several times and you won't reply. Do you know what I call you?" she asked. "The German."

"I'm Prussian." I looked down at my knife. Should I have told her that?

"Okay, so now you're the Prussian." She knelt in close. "Let me look at your ear." She reached into her bag, pulled out a small light, and peered into my ear.

I could feel the warmth of her face near mine. An amber pendant rested in the hollow of her throat. "Nice necklace. Do you like amber?" I asked, thinking of the priceless swan.

SALT TO THE SEA   *167*

"I'm Lithuanian. Of course I like amber. Your eardrum has ruptured. This is recent. How did it happen?" she asked.

"The explosion. Same time as the shrapnel," I told her.

She pressed around my ear. Her fingertips brushed against my earlobe. I twitched.

"Does that hurt?" she asked.

I shook my head. No, it didn't hurt. I was half-deaf but I wasn't numb. The nurse's face was inches from mine. Her mouth was close and her breath was in my ear. I closed my eyes, fighting like hell to hold off the shiver. She was testing me.

She leaned back on her heels, grinning.

"Are you satisfied?" I asked her.

"Oh, yes." She smiled. "You must be deaf in that ear."

"I know you said something. I could feel it. I just couldn't hear it."

"Well, I'd like you to hear this. I'm Joana. You should call me by my name. Not nurse, not girl. Joana."

"That might be impolite," I told her. "You're older than me. I should probably call you ma'am, or maybe madame?"

She rolled her eyes. "Lie down. I want to check the dressing on your wound."

I lay back and folded my arms behind my head. I had to ask.

"Or maybe you're a Mrs.?" I said.

"No, I'm not a Mrs.," she said, inspecting my wound. "Do you have a Mrs.?"

I flinched. "That area you're touching now. It still hurts," I said.

"That's normal. If it were infected, you'd have a fever and

discoloration." She had no problem returning to medical chat. She softly swept back my overgrown hair and laid her palm against my forehead. Her hand was warm. "You don't have a fever." She paused and cleared her throat. "So I've been thinking about what you said. We could all be split up tomorrow. I need to stay with Emilia."

"You need to?"

She peeled my soiled bandage back farther. "Yes. Her time is near and despite the brave face she's putting on, she's probably quite frightened."

Are you frightened? I wanted to ask. Was a soldier waiting somewhere for her? I thought of the song "Lili Marleen" that she had mentioned. Maybe a guy was waiting under a lamppost back in Lithuania.

"So you want to help the Polish girl. Are you like that English nurse, the one who carried her lamp through the dark to save all of those sick people?"

"No," she said flatly. "I'm no Florence Nightingale. It's just—Emilia reminds me of someone."

I realized that telling the truth might be the ammunition I needed. "She reminds me of someone too," I said. "I have a younger sister."

It worked. Her head snapped to me.

"You do?"

I nodded. "She's nearly sixteen now, like the Polish girl. My father sent her up north near the Danish border for safety. I haven't heard from her in over three years. I'm going to find her."

Her expression softened.

SALT TO THE SEA   *169*

"Are your parents still alive?" I asked.

Her hands stopped. Her fingers rested lightly on my chest. She stared off into the corner. "I hope so." She sighed.

Family. I had hit the nerve. I was exactly where I needed to be to convince her, but suddenly I felt bad. She was genuinely a nice girl. And why did she have to be so pretty? Why couldn't she have a mustache like that giant, Eva?

"I try so hard not to think negatively," she said. "My mother is in a refugee camp in Germany, but my father and brother are still in Lithuania. Mother thinks they're fighting in the forests. I've heard that Stalin has done unspeakable things to Lithuanians. And then I think of the family upstairs at that estate." She paused. "Are you absolutely sure they were all dead? I keep thinking that maybe one of the children was alive, that I could have helped."

I didn't want to describe it for her. "They were dead."

She looked straight at me. "I did something stupid."

I stared back at her, waiting. The curtain to her guard was sliding down. Her truths were there for the taking. A soft curl slipped from beneath her ear onto her cheek. That curl. It was killing me.

"I wrote the family a note, saying that I borrowed their sewing kit. It didn't feel right taking something of theirs. That was before I knew they were all upstairs, of course. I signed my name on the note and left it in the kitchen. Now my full name is in that house. What if the relatives return to find the dead family and my name?"

"Sure, you slaughtered the family and then left a borrow

note for a sewing kit. That's a real calculated killer." I laughed.

The curtain flew back up. I had pushed too far. "Killers aren't always assassins. Sometimes they don't even have blood on their hands." She gathered her bag, leaving my shirt open.

"Your stitches should be removed in a couple days. I don't know if they will accept me on a ship. If they do, I may think about vouching for your ear and your wound. But I have to know more. I can't take the risk. Either give me your name, show me your papers, or tell me what you're hiding in your pack." She stood up and looked down at me.

I raised myself onto my elbows but said nothing. I really wanted not to like this girl, but was failing miserably.

"You think you're sly," she said, shaking her head. "I know you took something from my suitcase. I want it back, by tomorrow."

"I don't know what you're talking about. Maybe you'd better check your suitcase again."

"Oh, you're good, but you're not that good," she said. "And trust me, you're not the only one with secrets. Good night, Prussian." She closed the door.

I lay back down on the cold tile floor. I reached into my pocket and pulled out her note about the sewing kit. What sort of girl leaves a promissory note in the midst of a bloodbath?

An honest one.

I stared at her pretty handwriting, memorizing it and tracing over her signature with my finger. I had slipped the drawing back into her suitcase. Yes, I was that good.

Good night, Joana.

SALT TO THE SEA   *171*

alfred

Good morning, Hannelore!

Today shall be a busy day. In a few hours we will begin registration for all of these fine ladies of the lake, the ships that will save thousands. There is quite an armada assembled here at the naval base. But my boat, the Willi G, as we navy men call her, is a real mackerel amidst the minnows.

A letter arrived from Mutter. She informed me that nosy Frau Henkel has been gossiping untruths on our doorstep. Indeed, I saw the old swollen Frau peeking from beneath her curtains when those Hitler Youth irritants arrived at my door and insisted on coming inside. They were so arrogant and aggressive. I am thankful that Mutter was on an errand to the baker during their visit. Of course I didn't mention the episode to her. The war had already disrupted her nerves to the point of exhaustion. But apparently old sow Henkel has brought it up, so I now feel compelled to make comment.

After the pests left our home I happened to be in our bathroom. I noticed that you promptly left your kitchen and walked toward the foyer when the boys of Hitler Youth came knocking. I still wonder why you moved so quickly to the door.

We cannot be too cautious, Hannelore. Just because someone knocks on the door doesn't mean you have to open it. Sometimes, sweet girl, there are wolves at the door. If we are not careful, they might eat us.

joana

We left the movie house at dawn and walked to the port. The energy in the harbor had escalated to a frenzy.

Refugees hauled possessions however they could. Eva dodged a man on a bicycle and pointed across the road. "Is that a dining table?" A tired horse dragged an inverted table loaded and strapped with belongings. "Talk about a last supper. Sorry," said Eva.

A few hundred yards away sat Oxhöft station. Eva threaded through the crowd, collecting information.

"They say wounded soldiers will be brought via train if the railways are still operating. Several claim the Russians have already bombed the entire track."

Rumors spread like infection. Some said Berlin didn't care about the Germans in East Prussia. Others said boys as young as twelve were being conscripted, carrying guns taller than they were.

"Why are you so nervous?" said Eva. "You know you're getting on a boat. You told me you've got a letter."

"Shh." I looked behind me to see if anyone was near. "I don't want the others to know."

"Why the secrecy?" whispered Eva.

"I don't want them to think I'll have preferential treatment or opportunity."

"It's a letter from the doctor in Insterburg saying you're good at dealing with blood and guts, Joana. I'm sorry, but I don't call that an opportunity," she said.

"The whole thing's unfair, Eva. You know that. Hitler allowed me into Germany. He thinks some Baltic people are 'Germanizable.' But for every person like me that Hitler brought in, he pushed some poor soul, like Emilia, out."

Eva shrugged. "Life's not fair. You're lucky."

I didn't feel lucky. I felt guilty.

"Do you think you have time to be moral?" snapped Eva. "The Russians are right around the corner. If you wait, they'll be under your skirt and you'll be dead. Sorry, but don't waste your time with some goodwill gesture for a lost Polish kid. Get in line and get on a boat. It's been nice to trek with everyone, but now we're here. I don't need a group. I need my belongings and I need a ship."

I saw a young sailor digging through a pile of luggage.

"Excuse me," I said.

The sailor stood upright quickly, trying to conceal a crystal butterfly behind his back.

"Good morning, ladies. Alfred Frick, at your service."

florian

I stood behind the shoe poet and the Polish girl, straining to hear the exchange between Joana and the sailor. The Polish girl did her best to conceal me.

The sailor rambled. "I was sent to meet a train that's due in. I thought I would make use of the valuable time and perhaps reunite some precious items with their owners."

Instead of questioning us, he was explaining himself. His rank, *Matrose*, was the lowest for an enlisted seaman in the German navy.

"Certainly," said Joana. "I won't take but a minute of your time. Could you tell us where and when registration begins?"

"Ah, yes, that is the question of the day, isn't it? Registration will begin at oh seven hundred hours on the eastern side of the quay. Of course, as you can see, there are many vessels. But that one"—he pointed to the largest ship in the distance— "that, ladies, is the *Wilhelm Gustloff*. That is my ship."

Joana looked carefully at the young man. "Forgive me for asking, but what happened to your hands?"

He stuffed his hands in his pockets. "Oh, it's nothing. Just a little skin irritation. Sailor's hazard. A small sacrifice for Germany."

Eva rolled her eyes.

"I have a salve that will protect your hands and calm the irritation," said Joana.

The sailor looked down and mumbled something.

"I have medical training," said Joana. "I used to work in a hospital."

The sailor's eyes brightened. "Are you assigned to a ship?"

"No, that's why I was asking about registration," said Joana.

"Well then, consider this your day of good fortune, Fräulein. I'm waiting for a convoy of hospital trains and field ambulances. We're boarding our wounded men onto the *Gustloff*, you see. We have just one doctor. He's walking this way and I will introduce you."

This wasn't Joana's day of good fortune. It was mine. This guy was a first-class booby. I stepped from behind the Polish girl to make my move, but Joana spoke first.

"Oh, my. Thank you, sailor. But you see, I have some important patients that I've been supervising. I'd have to take them with me."

"Well, if everyone's papers are in order we can make a request. Wounded soldiers and members of the Party will of course be boarded first. But I'm told that we will be evacuating many fine ladies . . . such as yourself." He gave Joana a strange smile, his top lip curling over filmy teeth.

Eva turned to me, annoyed. "Is he the best that's left? I'm sorry, but I'm not putting my future in the hands of this heavy breather."

alfred

The fates of fortune had found me. I had stumbled upon a qualified nurse just minutes before the trains carrying mutilated men would arrive.

I grabbed the young woman by the sleeve and dragged her through the crowd. "Dr. Richter!" I shouted through the hordes of people. "Dr. Richter! I have your nurse." I shoved the girl in front of the doctor. She nearly toppled over him.

"Stop right there. What are you doing?" asked the doctor. He offered a hand to steady the nurse.

"I'm sorry, sir," said the girl. "This sailor thought you might need assistance." She pulled out her papers and handed them to the doctor. "I was a surgeon's assistant in Insterburg. There's a recommendation among my papers."

"A surgeon's assistant." I grinned. "Outstanding qualifications."

The doctor quickly scanned through her papers. "Are you registered yet?" he asked.

"Not yet, sir," she replied.

"I have a convoy of wounded on the way. We don't have room for all of them. We need to quickly evaluate their condition. Those who are strong enough to make the voyage will be boarded onto ships."

178   Ruta Sepetys

"I'm traveling with priority patients," said the nurse, "including an expectant mother who—"

"Do you have maternity experience?" interrupted the doctor.

"Yes, I do."

He handed back her papers. "Help me here. We'll register you for the *Gustloff* after we sort the wounded."

"And my patients, sir?" she asked.

The doctor became annoyed. "I don't have time." He then looked to me. "You. The one who brought the nurse. What's your name?"

"Frick, sir."

"Take her people to registration. Maybe one of the ships has space."

The nurse removed a stethoscope from her bag and put it around her neck.

The doctor nodded at me. "Thank you, Frick."

"Happy to be of service."

I stood tall, pleased. When given the opportunity, Alfred Frick rose to the occasion and seized the path of the hero's journey.

SALT TO THE SEA

joana

Part of me felt drawn to the doctor and the opportunity to help the incoming patients. But I did not want to leave our group.

"Go, my dear," said the shoe poet. "Help others if you can. This young sailor will take us to registration. We'll come back and find you."

I knelt down to the wandering boy. "Now, Klaus, you stay close to Poet. Hold his hand." The boy nodded. I gave him a kiss. He held out his one-eared bunny for a kiss and I obliged.

"Take care of him, Poet," I said as I hugged the old man. "Make sure you find me before boarding a ship."

"The clock," reminded Poet. "We can meet under the clock."

A panting, soot-covered locomotive appeared in the distance.

Emilia stepped toward me, eyes wide with fear.

"Don't worry," I told her. "I have to help these people. But I'll help you too." I tugged her pink hat down and straightened it. "Put on the lipstick," I whispered. I set my hand on her belly. "I'll see you both tonight."

Even from afar, I could see the train cars were stuffed with wounded and refugees. Passengers leaned out of the compartments, screaming for help. Sailors rushed in, prepared with gurneys and pallets. The doctor began shouting instructions.

And then amidst the pandemonium I heard him.

"Joana."

I turned toward the voice.

The Prussian pulled me aside.

"You wanted to know something," he whispered, moving in close. His eyes found mine. "I'm Florian. My name is Florian." He reached out and took one of my curls between his fingers. A blush of heat washed across my face.

I grabbed the young sailor who had brought me to the doctor. "What's your name?" I asked him.

"Frick. But you may call me Alfred."

"Alfred, these people are very important. They have papers. I'm going to help the doctor, but these people must be taken to the same ship I will be on. Do you understand?"

"Yes, Fräulein. Certainly."

The train, battered like a bruised fighter, hissed in the sidings.

The doctor handed me a clipboard. Could I trust the sailor?

"Alfred, will you promise to take care of my group? This young mother is very important."

"Leave it with me, Fräulein."

Urgent shouts came from the train.

"Let's go!" said the doctor.

I grabbed the Prussian and whispered in his good ear.

"Nice to meet you, Florian."

emilia

She was leaving. Why did everyone leave me? But Joana was special. A doctor had chosen her for work. A flurry of commotion erupted when the train arrived. We turned away from the tracks and followed the sailor toward the port.

The sailor concerned me. Something shadowed lay beneath his surface. Ingrid would have felt it. As the group was talking to Joana, a starving dog approached the sailor. The poor animal, too weak to even bark, sniffed plaintively at his feet. The sailor kicked the suffering creature away with his boot, annoyed and disgusted.

"Remember, don't speak," the knight whispered to me. "You're Latvian."

My knight hadn't left me yet. He was happy about something. The sailor or Joana. Maybe both. But he would probably have to leave me too. Father hadn't wanted to leave me. I had felt his struggle as I eavesdropped from behind the door.

"Promise me, Martin," Father had said to Mr. Kleist. "Promise me you'll protect her, take care of her, love her like your own. She's all I have." I couldn't erase the memory of choked emotion in my father's voice.

Mr. Kleist had promised. "Yes, Michal, we'll take good care of her. She'll love the countryside and the farm. Else and August will be happy to have another young voice in the house."

"And what about Erna?" asked Father. "Are you certain she will welcome her?"

"Erna . . . yes," said Mr. Kleist.

I continually returned to the conversation in my mind. He had spoken the word *yes* but something screamed *no*. And then I revisited the truth:

Martin Kleist welcomed me.

Else Kleist welcomed me.

August Kleist truly welcomed me.

But Erna Kleist, she did not welcome me.

Ever.

florian

Hundreds of thousands had descended upon Gotenhafen from the depths of East Prussia and the Baltic countries. They now pushed and floated, like human driftwood, near the harbor. Vehicles shrieked their horns, carving a narrow path through the sea of refugees. A crowd gathered around a small girl who had been hit by a car. Hooded crows feasted on the innards of a dead horse in front of an overturned wagon. People wandered, looking constantly to the sky in fear of the Black Death. On the side of the road, where the earth had been turned by tank treads, an emaciated cow wailed. Its udders had frozen and burst overnight.

"You will step aside, please. I am an official escort!" announced the sailor who accompanied us.

The Polish girl tugged at my sleeve and gave me a concerned look. The sailor was drawing attention unnecessarily. He was more than a booby without experience; he was desperate to feel important. I knew the type.

In the distance I saw a group of Party officials with their wives. The women wore thick fur coats and expensive jewelry. They were flanked by parlor maids carrying trunks and hatboxes. These were the privileged passengers who would have priority boarding with the officers and wounded. They were also the type who could give me trouble.

"Say there, sailor. Hold up a minute." I clapped him on the shoulder and he turned. I pulled him aside from our group, allowing the blistering noise to cover our conversation.

"You strike me as a man of confidence," I told him.

"Well, yes."

"What I really mean is, a man of discretion," I clarified. "As the nurse mentioned, some of us are on important missions." I lowered my voice. "Perhaps even for the Führer himself." I removed the folded sheet of paper from my interior coat pocket.

"Oh, yes, I am quite discreet," he assured me, looking curiously at the paper.

"Then I can trust you to read this letter and speak of it to no one." I handed him the letter and he began to read. The tops of his hands were baked in crusty red blisters. Just the sight of them made me itch. I scratched the back of my neck.

The sailor looked up and started to salute.

"Don't do that. You'll draw attention."

"Oh, yes, Herr Beck. I understand. Yours is a secret mission." His face glowed with conspiratorial excitement.

"I can't be diverted with other work or inquiries," I told him. "I have to board a ship and preferably somewhere out of sight. But some of these officers, they might want to recruit me for their own efforts, to pull me off my assignment. The others here, you can take them to registration. But if you can

SALT TO THE SEA   185

assist me with a discreet registration, I will recommend you to Gauleiter Koch for commendation and even—to the Führer."

I had his attention.

"I see that the Reich has very efficient and organized practices here, sailor, but perhaps a man of your talents can provide options?"

His lips twitched into a grin. "I might have some extra boarding passes. Taken only as mementos of course."

"Very smart of you," I assured him. "And you have these passes with you?"

"Alas, I do not. But I can get them. They are under my bunk."

"Then take these important people and get them registered for the nurse. Come find me at the movie house just into town. Knock three times, twice, and I'll open the door."

His fingers began to flutter. "Knock three times, twice. Yes, Herr Beck. I'll do it."

I gave him my best serious look and lowered my voice to a whisper. "Heil Hitler, sailor."

"Heil Hitler, sir."

alfred

I had read about these young recruits in spy journals. The Party identified them early and bestowed them with important missions. And this one—sent by Gauleiter Koch himself. He was worthy of my favor.

The knobby white-haired man with the little boy asked me to stop. "Please, wait for the rest of our group."

The expectant mother, quite young, with tawdry lipstick, was crying and clinging to the young recruit.

"Don't cry," the recruit told her. "I'll be on the ship later."

"Ah, I see. She is carrying your child," I said to him.

"*No,*" they both replied in unison.

"She's Latvian," said the recruit. "A friend of the nurse. She's concerned because she doesn't speak German. She understands a bit, but is not able to speak."

"Many in this evacuation share your handicap," I assured her. "We have Croatian deckhands on the ship. They don't speak our language either, but somehow we communicate."

"Remember, her condition is fragile. The doctor gave you specific instructions to get her on board," the recruit said to me.

"We will watch over her," said the old man, putting his arm around the young mother. He gently pulled her from the recruit, who disappeared into the crowd.

SALT TO THE SEA   187

Tears streamed down her face. Such weakness. What was I to do with this crying woman? The little boy stood on one side, the old man on the other. The boy offered her an ugly stuffed rabbit. A feeling of pain and misery surrounded her entire spirit. It then occurred to me that this besotted and hormonal creature could present an opportunity.

Despite her tears, she was Aryan, a fine specimen of the master race.

She could be saved.

Yes, Hannelore. Amidst the grips of war, the beast of man emerges to conquer the ever-lurking infidel inside. My sword is drawn. Death to the man who tries to harm this Dulcinea.

joana

Throngs of wounded were emptied from the cars. As the trains unloaded, a convoy of ambulances arrived. Soldiers, still wrapped in mud-encrusted field coats, had been brought straight from battle. They howled with pain, reaching for me, for anyone, with desperate eyes.

Some I could identify quickly—typhus, dysentery, pneumonia. Others required the opening of their coat to discover missing limbs, gunshot blasts, and tank treads.

Dr. Richter's instructions were explicit: "If you are certain they can survive the voyage, log them for registration. Only if you are certain."

Many would not survive the voyage. They wouldn't survive the hour. Their bodies and voices trembled with the delirium of death.

"My son wants the book *Max und Moritz* for his birthday," a soldier repeated, eyes closed, blood leaking from the sides of his mouth. "Please, *Max und Moritz* for his birthday."

"How many do you have?" asked the doctor following our rapid examinations.

"Seventy-three to register. Two hundred and twelve unable."

"Seventy-three? Then with my list, we're full. Are you sure they all have a chance?"

SALT TO THE SEA *189*

"Yes."

I spoke without hesitation. I wasn't sure, but I was sure I wanted to try. I leaned down to tell the soldier that he would see his son and give him the book. He was already dead. The condition of the soldiers spoke to the fate of the Reich. The voice was clear.

Defeat.

But I would get these wounded men on the big ship.

The *Wilhelm Gustloff* would save them.

emilia

The knight was gone.

Joana was gone.

The sailor marched us to registration, quietly chanting the phrase *Yu-go-slav*. He was fidgety and blinked constantly. The knight thought he could dupe the sailor. Maybe he could. But what would that mean for me? We approached the registration area near the water. Lines of applicants snaked in endless turns. Wealthy Germans in luxurious clothing stood in one line, military personnel in another. The remaining lines were full of weary refugees and families.

"I'm not getting in line," announced Eva. "I want to wait for our cart. All of my valuables are on that wagon. I don't want to leave without them."

"But, Eva, dear, your shoes are carrying your most valuable possession—your life. Do not delay. Everything else can be replaced," said the shoe poet.

"My mother's silver is on that wagon. I'm waiting," she insisted.

The sailor continued on, completely unaware that one in our group had departed. He brought us into the line for Party officials. He then changed his mind and took us directly to the front of the refugee line. Others, who had been waiting, protested.

Despite the bitter cold, I began to sweat. I opened my coat and took a deep breath. The soldiers in charge stopped the sailor and demanded an explanation for our jumping the line.

"I have four passengers, direct request from Dr. Richter."

"I see only three," noted the soldier. "Can't you even count?"

"I am quite good at math." The sailor turned around. "Where is the huge gorilla woman? Well, I have three passengers. Direct request from Dr. Richter. And this one is with child." He turned to the soldier and sneered. "So that makes four, doesn't it? Can't you even count?"

He pulled me up to the counter, squarely in front of the registration officers.

"There we are, Frau. Show them your papers," he commanded.

florian

I sat inside near the back door of the movie house. Had I pegged the sailor correctly or had I judged too quickly? Was there really a desperate hero inside of him or just a nervous skin condition? My mistake in trusting Dr. Lange plagued me; perhaps my judgment was unreliable.

From the very first day, Father saw Dr. Lange for the manipulative and evil human being he was. I made excuses for him, desperate to validate the reasons he chose to work with me. I wanted to believe his motivation was to save and preserve the treasures of the art world.

One stormy night last July, a large painting arrived via truck with armed guards. Dr. Lange was dining with colleagues and I accepted the arrival from the soldiers. I unpacked the piece to display for Dr. Lange, inspecting it to see if restoration or repair would be necessary. I recognized the winter hunting scene immediately. The artist was Julian Falat, a Polish painter. Falat's art was featured in books at the institute.

The painting was treasured by the Poles. It was the property of Poland.

The Nazis, under the greedy direction of Erich Koch, had stolen it.

A few days later, I found my letters unopened in Dr. Lange's

SALT TO THE SEA   193

drawer. I felt ill. He had claimed we were a team, yet never bothered to open my letters, didn't care what I had to say. I sat on my bed for a full day, sick with dread that Father was right about Lange. I replayed every interaction in my head, analyzing them from all angles. The pieces of art cloaked under tarps, the whispers, the handshakes, the deliveries late at night. I wanted to be wrong, but I always came to the same conclusion: Koch and Lange weren't saving the treasures of Europe.

They were stealing them.

And, unknowingly, I had been helping.

The following day I left my small apartment near the museum and took a train to Tilsit. My father would know what to do. Together we would figure something out. I arrived home to find our front door hanging by one hinge. The house was ransacked. Our neighbor quickly emerged and whisked me into her cottage.

"I'm so sorry, Florian," she said, crying. "Your father . . . you're too late."

emilia

"Show them your papers," commanded the sailor.

They weren't my papers. They were hers, the Latvian who had lost her life to winter and war on the side of a road. Perhaps she paused to rest and froze to death. What right did I have to pilfer her identity? And if I got on a ship, where would it go?

I wanted to go home.

"You, in the pink hat," commanded the officer. "I don't have all day. Show me your papers." He pointed to the identity card trembling in my hand.

I couldn't move.

He stood up to face me. "What's going on here?"

The shoe poet softly placed his hand on my shoulder. "Una, dear, are you all right?"

Una. How could I steal Una?

"As you can see, Una's quite far along," said Poet. "And she appears to be ill."

The sailor, Alfred, snapped the papers from my hand and handed them to the official.

The officer sighed. "I already had a kid get sick on my desk. Move her aside," he said. Poet pulled me away from the table. The wandering boy petted my coat.

"Her nurse is assisting Dr. Richter at the ambulance train," said the sailor. "She asked me to bring the expectant mother for registration."

"We're registering, but not boarding yet," said the officer. "Everyone must be inspected first."

The sailor looked toward me with an odd smile. "Oh, please do inspect her. Don't you see? The hair, the eyes," he said. "An exquisite specimen. Her offspring shall no doubt be the same."

"I can't," I whispered to Poet. This wasn't right. I had no right.

"You must." He nodded. "For your child."

The officer reviewed the papers. Heat prickled up my cold neck. The sound of muffled crying floated nearby.

"Madame," said Alfred to a tearful woman behind us. "What do you have there?"

"Nothing," said the woman, pulling a bundle close to her chest. "She's sleeping."

"Is the child ill?" he asked. "We cannot register those with contagion."

The woman's tears turned to sobs. "No, she's not ill. She's sleeping."

Alfred turned to face the woman and pulled back the blanket. He sneered. "She's not sleeping. She's dead! Officer, this child is deceased." Alfred peered at the dead baby with studious fascination.

The mother's strength was no match for her grief. Her body quaked as she tried to speak, choking breaths between her words. "No. Please. She's just asleep. I swear. Don't take her from me."

The officer whistled to a nearby sentry and motioned him over.

The woman sobbed, clutching the bundle. "No! Please. I can't leave her here. Don't take my baby. Please, don't take my baby!" Pandemonium ensued.

The shoemaker turned to me, his eyes full of tears. "Do you see, my dear? The proverbs are at play. 'I wept because I had no shoes, until I met a man who had no feet.'"

I cried out, faking labor, and fell to my knees on the dock.

alfred

Hello, my Hannelore,

Such a trying day already and it's only just begun. Against all odds, I found a nurse for our ship's doctor, Dr. Richter. It was an impossible task, but like so many other occasions, I was able to make the impossible possible.

My first assignment was to register the nurse's patients for embarkation on the Gustloff. There was an old shoemaker (with the type of grotesque knuckles that distress me greatly), a small boy, and a young, pregnant Latvian who spoke awful German but had the favored features of the Reich. Once again, I drew my sword and laid my cape for Germany, helping the woman cross my cloak to safety. Yet another saved for the Vaterland!

Something else quite astounding took place this morning. I am assisting a young recruit on a very important mission for Gauleiter Koch. Perhaps you don't understand the significance Koch has in this war. He is the regional Nazi Party leader, second only to Hitler in this area. Koch successfully obliterated Ukraine. This young recruit has papers signed by Koch himself, indicating he is a courier carrying a valuable treasure for the Reich. Of course I'm handling the matter with the greatest discretion and not disclosing even the slightest detail. After all, perhaps I shall have occasion to meet Koch myself.

My catalog of heroics is growing so rapidly I can scarcely keep track. I am enjoying a bit of quietude in my private toilet right now to strategize for the next undertaking. Duty calls as the young recruit awaits me. I have to be in my tip-top condition for such a mission.

It was so nice and warm in the toilets. I decided to stay a bit longer.

joana

In a matter of hours the crowds had doubled in Gotenhafen. The stethoscope around my neck detained me as I walked. People saw it and ran out of bombed buildings and craters, begging for aid and medicine. I tried to help a woman whose face was blackened with frostbite.

"I used to be beautiful," she whispered, her eyes vacant.

"The scars will fade," I told her.

"Can you give me a cigarette?"

I shook my head. "I don't have any." A cigarette was akin to gold.

Her fingers stroked the cracked, blackened skin on her chin. "I'm so ugly now. Do you have a cigarette?" she repeated.

I put the stethoscope in my bag and pushed my way through the swarm of people to the port. In my pocket I had the boarding pass that Dr. Richter had secured for me. Where was our group? Had the sailor registered them? If Emilia was having difficulty I needed to help her.

"Joana!" Eva's head towered above the throngs of people.

She walked toward me, alone. "Where are the others?" I asked.

"I haven't seen them."

"You didn't register together?"

"No," she said. "I walked hundreds of kilometers with that cart. My silver and dishes are in that wagon. I'm sorry, but I'm not letting some peasant family make off with all of those valuables."

"Eva, there's no time. The Russians are upon us. They could invade this port at any moment."

"Once the wagon comes, I'll register."

"No, you must register now. The doctor told me the port will soon be overrun with nearly a million people. The *Gustloff* and other boats are leaving soon. Secure your passage now. Give the cart and horse to someone who needs it."

She seemed to consider my urging.

"Have you seen the others?" I asked.

"I left them with that strange sailor." She turned and began talking to another woman.

"Eva, wait. Did Emilia get through?" I pressed.

"I don't know. The sailor took her, the shoemaker, and the boy to registration. That was the last I saw of them."

"And what about Florian?" I asked.

She looked at me, confused. "Florian? Who's Florian?"

emilia

On September 1, 1939, Germany invaded Poland from the west.

On September 17, 1939, Russia invaded Poland from the east.

I remembered these dates.

Two warring nations gripped Poland like girls fighting over a doll. One held the leg, the other the arm. They pulled so hard that one day, the head popped off.

The Nazis sent our people to ghettos and concentration camps.

The Soviets sent our people to gulags and Siberia.

I was nine years old when it started. People changed. Faces shriveled and sunk, like baked apples. Neighbors spoke in whispers. I watched them play their games. I observed them when they weren't looking. I learned.

But how long could I play this game? A ploy of war both outside and inside. What would happen if I actually made it to the West? Would I be able to reveal myself as Emilia Stożek, a girl from Lwów? Would Germany be safe for me?

Once the war ended, which side would be the right side for a Pole?

florian

Hours passed. The sailor didn't come to the movie house. My mind coursed through the possibilities: He was busy, assigned more tasks. He forgot. Maybe he wasn't as gullible as I thought.

And what about Joana? Would she look for me?

I debated whether to leave the movie house. With every minute that passed, more refugees poured into Gotenhafen. Fewer ships would be available. The Reich would grow more desperate. Joseph Goebbels, the composer of blustery Nazi propaganda, had been issuing nonsense statements for years. He tried to boost morale with lies. "Total victory will be ours. Hold strong!" But victory had slipped through their fingers. Their hands were sticky with blame. And now the Russians drew closer. I looked at the newly issued propaganda leaflet I had found outside the movie house. It was titled *Victory or Death*.

WE ARE GERMANS!
THERE ARE TWO POSSIBILITIES:
EITHER WE ARE GOOD GERMANS
OR WE ARE BAD ONES.
IF WE ARE GOOD GERMANS, ALL IS WELL.
IF WE ARE BAD GERMANS,
THEN THERE ARE TWO POSSIBILITIES:

Ridiculous. I couldn't read the rest. I folded the leaflet and put it in my pocket. Goebbels was right about one thing. There were good Germans and bad Germans. But in truth, the labels were currently applied in reverse.

Those perceived as deserters would be executed. The longer I waited, the greater the odds that Lange would discover my betrayal. Had he broken into my apartment or the secret room below the castle? Had he already searched the crates?

Or worse—perhaps Nazi leader Erich Koch was standing on the dock right now, waiting for me.

alfred

Life vests and floats. That was my new assignment. Collect as many life vests and floats as I could find. I was glad of the task outside as it would finally give me a chance to visit the movie house and the young recruit. This was becoming exciting, just like the Karl May adventure novels that Hannelore loved so well.

But where exactly was the movie house? It was bitterly cold outside; the hairs inside my nose gummed and froze. A long walk would not be tolerable. I spotted the old man and the young boy standing under a damaged building with a large clock.

My pulse raced as the crumbling theater came into view. Yes, yes, I would do this. I would be in best favor with leaders of the party when the recruit revealed that I had helped him.

I walked through the snow around back and realized I had forgotten the number of knocks. No matter. The door stood open and people moved in and out freely. The movie house overflowed with refugees. The smell was quite unpleasant. Baggage and personal articles towered on top of the seats. A shrill whistle sounded. It came from the pregnant Latvian woman. She pointed above, toward the ceiling. I supposed she was suffering the feminine hysteria common to pregnant women, but then I saw the recruit, standing in the small window of the projection booth.

SALT TO THE SEA   205

It took me quite a while to find the stairs and I was belabored of breath once I climbed them. I approached the closed door at the top of the stairway. Was this where I was supposed to use the secret knock? The door flew open. The recruit pulled me inside.

The tiny dark room smelled of cigarettes. I waved my hand in front of my face, hoping to clear the air.

"You want a smoke?" asked the recruit, pacing the floor.

"I don't partake," I told him.

"Do you have it?"

He spoke in code, but I knew what he meant. The pass. I tried to remember the terminology used in the spy magazines but could not recall any. So I just slowly whispered, "Yes." His coat shifted and I saw a pistol in his waistband. I quickly produced the pass.

"You're a good man," he told me. He then handed me a leaflet labeled *Victory or Death.*

"Have you read that one?" he asked.

"No," I admitted.

"It speaks of good Germans and bad Germans. You are a good German."

"Thank you." I felt a glow of confidence within me. "Permission to ask a question?"

He smiled. "Permission granted."

"How will you manage? The pass is blank. It will need to be filled out and also stamped officially for you to board. They will have a complete manifest."

"Yes, I know. Leave that to me. Now, friend, before boarding

206   *Ruta Sepetys*

begins and all hell breaks loose, I need you to bring me the nurse."

"The pretty nurse from this morning?" I asked.

He stopped pacing. "You think she's pretty?"

I had heard other sailors talk often of girls, sometimes in graphic detail. And of course I had my Hannelore.

"Yes." I grinned. "In my experience, the nurse would certainly rate as attractive."

He stared at the pass. "Can you find her? Tell her that her patient needs her. Make sure you use the word *need*, sailor."

"But where will I find her?"

"She promised the pregnant girl she would come for her. She's probably on her way here."

"Ah, yes, she did seem most concerned for the Latvian."

The recruit turned to me, lighting the stub of a cigarette. "The pretty nurse," he said. "Her name is Joana. And when it comes to her, sailor"—he clapped me on the shoulder, exhaling a scarf of smoke—"I've heard she's already spoken for."

SALT TO THE SEA   *207*

joana

Dr. Richter would be angry. Instead of following him to the ship, I had left him with hundreds of wounded men.

Blessed, reliable Poet. He stood under the clock in the cold, the wandering boy playing in a mound of snow near his feet.

"See," he said to the boy. "I told you she would come."

The wandering boy jumped up and hugged my leg.

"Hello, little one." I looked to Poet. "Were you able to get passes?"

"Four hours in that line. But yes, we were given passes. I was nearly conscripted to repair military boots. To be truthful, I think little Klaus was the only reason I was granted a pass. Small children are a priority."

"And what about Emilia?"

"It was a mess. That blathering sailor pushed her to the front of the line. It drew more attention." Poet frowned. "The girl, she was terrified. I had to push her, but she finally caught on and feigned contractions, lying on the ground wailing. Then the soldiers wanted to put her on the boat immediately, but she said she wouldn't go without you, her nurse. They were only too happy to be rid of her. That silly sailor was so frightened by the threat of birthing that he lost all color and nearly keeled over."

208   *Ruta Sepetys*

"But did she get a pass? Where is she now?" I asked.

"Oh, yes, the pregnant Latvian got herself a pass. She's in the movie theater. She insisted on waiting for you. Where is Sorry Eva?"

"Eva's in line for registration. We have to hurry. I need to get back. They're boarding the wounded tonight. I want to take Emilia with me. The rest of you may board tomorrow."

The young sailor suddenly appeared.

"Aha! There you are, Fräulein." He moved uncomfortably close and began to whisper. "Your patient says he needs you in the movie house. I stress, Fräulein, he *needs* you."

I looked at him, confused. What did he mean?

"He used those very words himself." The sailor stared at me, blinking rapidly.

We left the sailor and ran to the movie house.

florian

Joana pushed through the door of the projection room, flushed and out of breath.

"Are you okay?" she asked.

"That was quick," I said with a smile.

She looked at me, annoyed there was no emergency. "I have to get back to the ship. I'm taking Emilia. Poet and the boy will board tomorrow. Eva still hasn't registered."

I nodded.

She stared at me, evaluating, then crossed her arms over her chest. "I'm not to be summoned whenever you please. I don't know what you're playing and I'm not sure I want to know. But I think I deserve to know your name. Is it really Florian Beck?"

"You don't believe me?" I reached in my pocket and handed her my identity card.

"What sort of name is Florian?" she asked, looking at my identity photo.

"My mother named me after a sixteenth-century painter, Florian Abel."

She shrugged, satisfied, and handed back my papers.

I lit the remainder of my cigarette and passed it to her.

"I'm on the *Wilhelm Gustloff*," she said, taking a drag and passing it back to me.

"Are you inviting me?" I grinned.

"I have a feeling you'd find your way on if you wanted to."

I couldn't tell if she was amused or annoyed. "Can I see your boarding pass?" I asked. She removed it from her papers and handed it to me. She walked to the little projection box and looked down at the theater.

I studied her pass, taking note of every detail. "Where's the *Gustloff* going?"

"To Kiel," she responded.

Kiel was nearly three hundred nautical miles away, at the northern tip of Germany. It was close to the border of Denmark, close to where my sister, Anni, might be. I stared at the pass.

"I think I understand now," said Joana. "When you need something, you start talking to me. Is that right?"

I changed the subject. "You seem happy working with the doctor. I bet you were top of your class."

She laughed. "Yes, top of my class, but what does that mean now? Can you believe I used to study instead of going to the beach?" She shook her head. "But I do like helping people. And I like being one step closer to my mother." She stared down below. "All those children. There are so many."

I moved in behind her and looked over her shoulder. The wandering boy clutched his rabbit and waved up at us. We waved back.

"I especially like the little boy," I whispered.

Joana turned, her face suddenly close to mine.

"Why?" she asked.

"He takes care of one-eared bunnies." I grinned and touched my ear.

She let out a small laugh. "I like that," she said, pointing to my mouth.

"What?"

"You look completely different when you smile."

We stood, staring at each other. The space between us narrowed. We were close, nearly touching. Her chin raised toward me. I looked down at her lips.

"I . . . should probably go," she whispered.

I nodded slowly and handed back her pass. We waited, silent. She suddenly looked embarrassed.

"Well, good-bye then," she said, slowly stepping away from me.

I said nothing, just watched her walk through the door and close it behind her.

I exhaled, unaware that I had been holding my breath.

alfred

Ahoy there, Hannelore!

Ahoy is a term we seasoned sailors use. I am standing at this moment on the top deck of the Gustloff. Evening and darkness have arrived. Tethered to the pier around us are many ships of all configurations. Sitting opposite is Hansa, a large vessel also aflurry with activity and preparation. Two lighthouses stand guard at the mouth of the harbor, yet they are not illuminated. No need to wave at the Russian planes above, you see.

Today I progressed from my traditional excellence to something altogether more interesting.

As you may remember, the Wilhelm Gustloff was built not for luxury cruising of the privileged. Hitler built the Gustloff for the everyman—the carpenter, the postman, the locksmith, and even the housewife. But now the everyman's ship shall in fact carry very important people. The Gustloff will transport our wounded men, officers, and priority passengers whose identities I am helping to conceal. Yes, aren't you curious to hear more about the young recruit? That is all I will say today. I mustn't empty my net too quickly. I must keep you, my little fish, swimming to the top of the water for food.

You are of the fairer sex and for that I am glad. May your

SALT TO THE SEA   213

fingers never know a fist. May your ears never ring with the call of duty. Before this war is over, all men will have an opportunity to reveal their true selves. I welcome that opportunity. To be a hero requires difficult choices and sacrifice. Each man can respond only when the finger of bravery curls and beckons him forth. That finger, it beckons me, Hannelore. I feel it.

joana

Emilia wanted to wait for Florian. I grabbed her by the hand and pulled her out of the cinema, assuring the others we'd see them tomorrow.

A thick procession of wagons and evacuees clogged the road to the port. The gray stone buildings lining the cobbled street were pockmarked, missing their doors and windows. Interior rooms were now visible, like a broken dollhouse. I saw a beautiful mahogany desk with a typewriter, the chandelier above swinging in the wind. A faded and torn banner of Hitler flapped from the splintered window of a perfume shop. It said, *Volk ans Gewehr.* People Get to Your Gun.

Did Lithuania and Poland look this bad too?

Our papers and passes were checked as we entered the harbor, as we approached the ship, and then again near the gangway. The soldiers instructed us to board and report to a desk on B deck. Emilia's hand trembled in mine as we walked up the gangway through the open cavity on the side of the *Gustloff.*

Inside, the ship was a floating city. A warm one. Enormous would be an understatement. It appeared that amidst the chaos outside, the Germans were preparing and insisting on a very orderly boarding process. Signs were in place to direct

SALT TO THE SEA   215

passengers. Once we reached B deck we were told to proceed to the promenade deck where a makeshift maternity ward had been established.

Sailors and authorized personnel darted every which way as we progressed through the corridors. "Step aside, please." Two sailors ran past us with a stack of blankets. Announcements squawked through the public address speaker. We arrived on the promenade deck. Emilia dropped my hand.

"I want to leave. Want to be outside," she whispered.

"Let's get you settled. You'll feel better in a moment," I assured her.

I found Dr. Richter. He directed us to what would be the maternity ward. Cots with crisp white linens sat in uniform rows.

"You are the very first mother to arrive," Dr. Richter told Emilia. "We're hoping to have another doctor on board but we haven't received confirmation yet."

Emilia said nothing.

"It's all quite overwhelming for her," I explained. "Her condition, the trek, the language barrier, being separated from her . . . husband."

"Of course," said the doctor. "But I can solve one of the problems. Many of the passengers will be multilingual. Once boarding begins I'll find someone who speaks Latvian." Dr. Richter patted Emilia's shoulder. "Don't you worry. Soon you can tell us absolutely everything." He turned and walked out of the maternity ward.

Emilia's nails dug into my arm.

emilia

What was I going to do? Should I run? My panic seemed to increase the pain and cramping below my waist.

"Don't worry," insisted Joana. "I'll think of something."

I hated the ship. It was steel, lifeless, and hollow inside. I would rather be in a small wooden boat carved from an old tree, or even a floating nutshell. I detested steel birds and boats. These sterile boats were not made to appreciate the sea. Boats of steel were boats of war. Part of me hoped they would send me away, tell me that I didn't belong, that I should run back to the forest and the birds.

Joana said the *Wilhelm Gustloff* was a KdF ship. I knew what that meant. August had told me.

KdF—*Kraft durch Freude.* "Strength Through Joy."

KdF was a national German organization that was supposed to make leisure activities available to the masses, regardless of social class. Hitler said KdF brought opportunity for everyone, all were equal. But how could all be equal if some were favored?

Like Hitler, August's mother believed in a master race. I was Polish, so in her opinion, I was not part of it. Somewhere behind the locked door in my mind, I heard the echo of Erna Kleist's stringent voice: *Not that one. This one is prettier.*

The *Wilhelm Gustloff* was pregnant with lost souls conceived of war. They would crowd into her belly and she would give birth to their freedom. But did anyone realize? The ship was christened for a man, Wilhelm Gustloff. My father had told me about him. He had been the leader of the Nazi Party in Switzerland.

He was murdered. The ship was born of death.

florian

I barricaded entry to the projection room, wedging items under and against the door so it could not be opened. The movie house was now overrun with refugees seeking warmth and shelter. Many had ventured upstairs and I turned them away. My pistol sat loaded and ready. If I was going to forge a pass, I couldn't be disturbed.

The Polish girl knew. I approached her when she entered the movie house and she handed me her pass without a word. I memorized the Gothic style of the writing the hue of the ink, traced the stamp, and made note of the terms used. Joana's pass was slightly different from the girl's due to her assignment. It was helpful to see both.

My father was overjoyed when I showed drafting and visual memory aptitude. As a small boy I could briefly look at his maps and then draw them myself. But as I grew older, my interest wasn't in creation, but duplication. I loved the challenge of trying to precisely re-create Father's maps so he couldn't distinguish the original from the copy.

He acknowledged and praised my talent, but wanted me to produce instead of reproduce. "You are so talented, Florian, why not create something of your own, something that comes from your imagination? As the philosophers say, 'Life is short, but art is long.' Contribute a piece of art instead of copying others, son."

But I wasn't interested. I loved the idea of restoring old treasures and pieces of art. And once in a while, I liked copying them too.

The handwritten parts of the boarding pass were black. The ink stamp was black. The pass would be simple to forge.

alfred

Hello, sweet girl. How your patience must fray waiting for my letters.

There are no more leisure hours or breaks on the ship. I am told that we will work around the clock until we sail. I am carefully noting and recording all details. The temperature is steady at minus ten degrees Centigrade but the maritime office predicts it will dip even lower. The railings and decks on the top level of the Gustloff are encased in ice, which we are continually ordered to scrape. Fortunately, we will not be using the top deck during the voyage.

Hitler calls for every German to fulfill his duty and make sacrifices. Have others made as many sacrifices as I have, Hannelore? I nearly suffocated in my vapor bath while trying to strengthen my lungs prior to deployment. You will be relieved to know that the eternal thunderstorm that once lived in my chest has finally eased.

Yes, Lore, my main affliction now is simply a malady of eagerness. I feel quite empowered wearing this uniform. I am confident I shall soon receive the documentarian post I deserve. The watchman will prevail.

Following this initial voyage, I look forward to returning to my own territory. This region of East Prussia is quite strange. The

SALT TO THE SEA   *221*

East Prussians themselves are a different Germanic breed altogether, very unlike the Deutschen we know.

Some of the Prussian squirearchy are now making their way to the port. One Prussian sailor told me that his family will not come. They refuse to abandon their estate. Instead, they have sent their servants toward the ships for safety. The family members have dug graves for themselves in their garden. Should the Russians arrive, they will step into the dirt pits and take their own lives. Can you imagine? The Führer is offering a means of escape and they refuse to leave their lands. That speaks not of sacrifice but of stupidity. It is annoying, yet somehow quietly satisfying to think of them in the cold ground.

joana

The hot cloth felt glorious on my face. The *Wilhelm Gustloff* had fifty bathrooms, one hundred showers, and one hundred and forty-five toilets. Dr. Richter gave me a white pinafore apron and suggested that I "freshen up."

The woman in the mirror was frightening, especially when I realized that she was me. My face was caked with soot, my eyes ringed with grief from the things they had seen. I had lived for twenty-one years, but the recent months had changed me. I scrubbed at the dried blood and grime beneath my fingernails, thinking of the remorse I would never be able to wash down a sink.

To assist others, to help and heal, it was a good distraction. But what would I do about Emilia? In the privacy of the bathroom, alone and unseen, the weight of the experience pressed down upon me. I missed my family, questioned the fate of my country, and feared for my cousin Lina.

Survival had its price: guilt.

Vilnius, Kaunas, my birthplace of Biržai. What were the Lithuanian people experiencing? I longed to speak Lithuanian instead of German. To sing Lithuanian songs. Everything I ever loved I had been forced to leave behind.

Someone knocked on the door. I didn't respond. Some part

of me did not want to leave the small steel bathroom. I wanted to stay locked away from the pain and destruction. I didn't want to be strong. I didn't want to be "the smart girl." I was so very tired. I just wanted it all to be over.

Four awful years rose to the surface.

And I started to cry.

florian

The ink was dry. I slid my brushes and supplies into the leather case and returned them to my pack. I jotted some remarks in my notebook, where I had practiced the forgery.

I had two options.

I could board early and risk the officers deeply analyzing my pass and papers. Or I could wait until the boat was already full and board with the last rush of passengers. If I boarded early, I could find a place to conceal myself for the voyage. I would get extra sleep. But I would probably need the toady sailor to help me. Was it worth the risk?

I looked at the paper. My pass was an excellent forgery. A wave of adrenaline hit me. I wanted to try it. Would it work or would they apprehend me on the gangway?

Hitler might lose the war, but he wouldn't be willing to surrender all the art he had stolen. Especially not the Amber Room.

"The Führer is a talented watercolorist. He applied to art school"—Dr. Lange had lowered his voice—"but the school did not accept him. Oh, how they will regret it."

So instead of creating art or collecting it, Hitler stole it. Large albums with photos and lists of the items he targeted for his museum were assembled. Two such albums had been delivered to Dr. Lange. Some of the art listed was in private homes, owned by Jewish families. Other pieces, like the Julian Falat painting, were in museums. The Czartoryski Museum in Kraków had been pillaged. Masterpieces by da Vinci, Rembrandt, and Raphael now hung in the private apartments of Nazi officials.

Other stolen pieces were hidden in salt mines, abandoned factories, castle ruins, and the basements of museums. Dr. Lange estimated that over fifty thousand pieces of art would be "reassigned" from Poland to Germany alone. He found this completely acceptable.

But the Amber Room was the greatest treasure of all. Six tons of pure glistening amber, a jeweled chamber that glowed like golden fire. The panels were backed with gold leaf, the fronts inlaid with shimmering diamonds, emeralds, rubies, and jade. And in the center of the room, in a small oval alcove, sat the prized piece—the amber swan.

I looked down at the small box in my pack. Hitler would look for the swan first. I thought of the twenty-seven crates hidden far below the castle in the secret cellar. The labyrinth of tunnels would make it impossible to find the secret chamber.

Lange knew where it was.

Koch thought he knew where it was.

I not only knew where it was, I had a map to the location and a key.

They were sealed in the hollow heel of my boot.

joana

Dr. Richter evaluated Emilia's condition. "She seems a bit traumatized," he commented.

I tried to agree with him without raising suspicion. "Yes," I whispered. "I thought so too. She speaks constantly of her husband, August, a German who's fighting at the front. She's desperate to get to him since being separated from her parents. She fears he is dead."

He nodded. "You mentioned you have maternity experience?"

"I assisted at the hospital in Insterburg. I delivered several on my own without complication."

"I don't know how many expectant mothers we'll have. I have a couple of nurses and one medical orderly. I'll need you to help the wounded soldiers in the other ward as well," he said.

"Yes, of course. I was shocked when I saw the men this morning," I told him. "We didn't see injuries of that severity in Insterburg."

The doctor lowered his voice to a whisper. "I fear the condition of the men speaks loudly of Germany's fate. It's a short voyage. Let's do what we can to make them as comfortable as possible. Have you lost many?"

I've lost my family, my language, and my country. I've lost it

Salt to the Sea   227

all, I wanted to say. But I knew what he meant. "I lost a friend crossing the ice just yesterday. And you?"

"Too many to count," he replied. "Tomorrow more wounded will be the first to board. I'm told we'll also have a group from a sanatorium—German girls who fell into the hands of the Russians. I suggest you get some sleep tonight. The coming days will be long."

I dragged my cot over to Emilia's and settled in next to her. We were finally surrounded by protection and comfort. Sheltered from the snow, the cold, and Russian soldiers, I finally felt safe. The ship had anti-aircraft guns affixed to the deck. Tonight I would sleep on a cot in a warm room, out of harm's way.

I lay face-to-face with Emilia, who was still wearing her pink hat. She smiled at me. I thought of the summers in Nida with my cousin. At night we'd lie close, noses nearly touching, whispering and giggling. Emilia reminded me so much of Lina. She had the same blond hair and sea-blue eyes, deep with strength and secrets.

alfred

The temperature dropped further. I decided it was far too cold to collect life vests and floats. Instead, I marched through the passageways of the ship chanting my melody. I found that if I kept my pace at an urgent clip, no one would stop me to assign a task. So I walked and walked, oxygenating my lungs and mentally documenting all that was going on.

All furniture had been cleared from the main rooms. The floors of the dining halls, the ballroom, and the music room were lined with thin mattress pads for refugees. I ran my fingers across the smooth wood of the grand piano in the music room. I then marched down the long teak walkways of the promenade decks. They were enclosed by glass and wrapped around the ship. I made my way down to E deck, near the bottom of the ship. There was a lovely swimming area on E deck. The pool, now drained, was still beautiful. White columns surrounded the edges of the pool under an opaque glass ceiling. At the head of the swimming room was a large mosaic depicting Neptune and mermaids swimming with fish. I liked the look of those mermaids, held captive in the tile.

Hundreds of men from the U-boat service were on their way to the ship, preparing to man submarines once we reached Kiel on mainland Germany. They would be assigned to cabins on B and C decks. Party officials and important Germans would also share cabins.

I marched toward the galley to see what they might be cooking. We had been told that each passenger would receive one hot meal per day. My stomach felt full of empty gas. It appeared that pea soup was to be the menu staple.

"What do you need?" asked a sailor who was counting food supplies.

"Just observing. I am a documentarian," I said, scribbling in the air.

"What's wrong with your hands?" the sailor asked with disgust.

"Nothing really. Just a bit of an irritation."

"Is it contagious?" he asked.

"Me, contagious? How dare you."

"Watch the attitude and go to the infirmary. We don't need to be infected."

The infirmary for my hands. I could spy on the pretty nurse. Why hadn't I thought of that?

emilia

Joana fell asleep quickly.

The pain began first in my lower back and then moved up through my core. It was similar to the cramping I had experienced for the past few days, but more severe. I lay on the cot for several hours. It came in intervals. Just as I would fall asleep, I'd wake again with the intense pressure and pain.

I pulled off my hat and wound my fingers through the pink crocheted holes in the yarn. I sang through *All the little duckies* in my head. A sharp pain came. I clenched my hat and teeth to keep from crying out. The pain spread, splitting through my abdomen. And then, amidst the agony, the locked door in my mind suddenly opened and I was no longer on a cot in the ship's infirmary.

I sat on the cool wooden floor outside Mama's bedroom, a bowl of black currants resting quietly in my lap. When it was over, I would sit on the edge of the bed and feed them to her. I would finally have a baby brother or sister. I had been waiting, asking for years.

Papa paced the floor of the hallway. At times, Mama would yell, trying desperately to bring my sibling into the world. It went on for hours. I became hungry. And then, just as I raised a fistful of berries to my lips, the sounds changed. Her screams

SALT TO THE SEA   *231*

of labor became screams of terror. Papa ran into the room. I sat frozen to the spot on the floor, paralyzed by the sound of Mama's voice.

Then it was quiet. The midwife began crying.

A clatter on the roof announced the departure of the stork. And then the midwife came into the hall to announce the departure of my mama.

I didn't believe it was happening. I thought it was a dream. I closed my eyes and opened them. *Wake up, Mama. Wake up. Please don't leave me!* I screamed. The berries dropped down the front of my dress and rolled across the floor.

And now, from my cot, I spoke to my mother. "Am I going to die too, Mama?"

Joana stirred next to me. "Emilia?"

I looked above at my mother and asked again: *"Umrę, prawda?"* "I'm going to die now, aren't I, Mama?"

Joana flew off her cot and stuffed pillows behind my head and back. Her reaction confirmed my fear.

Yes, I would die now.

But unlike Mama, I would not go to heaven. My secrets padlocked the gates. I'd be a torn kite stuck in the dead branches of a tree, unable to fly.

A searing pain ripped through me. Death hacked at me with its sickle, tearing, chopping, unbearable. Then the hurt subsided. "Joana." I reached out for her, but she was hard at work below me.

She quickly looked up and put her hand on my knee. "I'm right here, Emilia."

"Listen. Please. Listen to me," I begged.

"Yes. Think of August, Emilia."

Another pain came, torturing me for my lies. It grew sharper, deeper, lynching my breath. I bit down and felt my teeth puncture the skin of my lip. The sickle was inside me, twisting and stabbing.

You must tell, Emilia.

Clear your conscience. Free your soul.

The pain retreated.

Tears fell onto my cheeks.

"Don't cry," said Joana. "This will soon be over. Think of August, Emilia. Think of how happy you will all be."

She was right. This would soon be over. A ripping slice burned through me. I screamed in agony.

You must tell, Emilia.

My conscience, my shame, it all boiled over. I looked at her and shook my head, barely able to speak through my tears.

"There is no August," I whispered. "There is no August."

joana

Gripped with pain and terror, Emilia spoke in fragmented German and Polish.

"No August. Frau Kleist. Prettier."

She kept repeating "Frau Kleist, Frau Kleist." It made no sense.

Things were moving fast. I wanted to run for Dr. Richter but couldn't leave Emilia. She was completely overcome with fear, consumed by pain.

The sailor from the port peered around the door.

"Alfred!"

"Oh, pardon me, Fräulein. I thought you might—" He stopped when he saw Emilia.

"Alfred! Run to the soldiers' ward. Get Dr. Richter. Quickly!"

Emilia gripped the edges of the cot. She screamed, her body vibrating, eyes bulging.

The sailor paled and looked rubbery.

"Alfred! Shore up! Go get Dr. Richter."

He turned, as if in a trance, holding the door frame and talking to himself. And then he was gone.

"Come, Emilia, breathe with me," I told her. We locked eyes, breathing rhythmically.

Emilia stopped, her mouth pulled with pain. She screamed,

words and blood pouring from her lips. *"Liar. Liar. Help me, Mama!"*

I had never seen such terror. Where was Dr. Richter?

I couldn't step away for the chloroform. Blood dripped from Emilia's lip. Her face was slick with sweat. She cried out again, louder, excruciating.

"MAMA!"

The baby's head suddenly appeared.

"Push!" I told her. What was the word for *push* in Polish? I tried to use expressions and gestures. She understood.

She pushed and screamed.

"Don't stop! Push!"

She bore down, her clenched fists shaking, the pain so intense it strangled her screams.

The tiny child met my hands.

"Yes, yes!" I told her.

I looked down. A perfect little bird had fluttered into my arms.

Emilia gasped for breath, then sobbed and covered her face. "Liar. Help. Mama."

"It's over," I told her. "It's all over. You have a baby girl, Emilia. A beautiful baby girl."

florian

I brought the shoemaker and the wandering boy up to the projection room to sleep. I cocooned the small boy in my long wool coat, folding the collar over as a headrest. He slept soundly with his rabbit and remained asleep after I woke.

The shoe poet was already awake, staring at my boots.

"You altered the heel yourself. You did a fine job. You are a craftsman?" he asked.

"Of sorts," I said. If he knew, would he turn me in?

"Six years," said the shoemaker. "This war has stolen six years from the world. I was born in Germany and have lived here my entire life. I have dear friends who are Russian. They tell me the Russian people are suffering terribly. Stalin, Hitler"—he lowered his voice to a whisper—"there is no happy ending here."

I nodded, reflecting upon his words. What would it mean to be German after the war? What would it mean to be Prussian? I checked my watch. "We should wake the little one."

"I suppose, but I look at the boy and I envy his quiet sleep, his innocence," said the old man.

"Where did he come from?" I asked.

"He wandered out of the woods. An address in Berlin was pinned to the front of his coat. But I wonder, who's waiting

236   *Ruta Sepetys*

for the little lad? What if the address is an orphanage? He told Joana that he was with his granny, but one day she didn't wake up."

I could feel my face moving, betraying my desire to remain unaffected.

The old man nodded. "There's a saying, 'Death hath a thousand doors to let out life; I shall find one.' We all have a door that waits. I know that. I accept it. But the children. That's what I struggle with." He shook his head. "Why the children?"

"But the boy is the reason you were given a pass for a ship. He was too young to go alone."

"Yes, yes, I've thought about that. Perhaps the children are little cherubs, looking after withered men like me."

"Which ship will you be on?" I asked.

"The *Gustloff*. And you?" he asked.

"The *Gustloff*," I said.

We shared a quiet smile.

emilia

I stared at a jar of cotton balls on the metal table. Small white clouds trapped in glass. I wanted to lift the lid and let them fly away with my secrets.

I was still alive. Why?

The doctor cleaned and examined the baby while Joana tended to me.

"You did very well, Emilia," she said, softly wiping the hair from my eyes.

I stared into the bright ceiling lights until my eyes hurt. Everything hurt. My strength dissolved into exhaustion.

Wasn't a person supposed to feel better after telling the truth? Perhaps there was no peace because Joana hadn't understood or hadn't heard me. Was it enough to admit the lie to yourself and the heavens, or did you have to tell someone who listened?

For months I had done so well. Most days I actually believed my own story. Yes, August Kleist existed. He visited the farm for a while during my stay. He carried wood for me, climbed the ladder so I didn't have to, shared his plums, and defended me in front of his mother. He did it all because he was a kind person. But I didn't exist for him the way he existed for me. He left before it happened.

238   *Ruta Sepetys*

It was a windless day in May when the Russians arrived at the farm. The air hung still and their boots echoed on the stones as they approached. Mr. Kleist had broken his own arm to avoid recruitment into the people's army. He claimed it was an accident, but I had peeked at his preparations in the barn. He was home in a sling the day the Russians arrived.

Mrs. Kleist and her daughter, Else, came outside as the soldiers approached. Mrs. Kleist quickly told Else to go inside. But Else didn't move. Her feet seemed attached to the ground. I had been picking mushrooms in the forest and was hauling my baskets to the cold cellar. I hid behind a large tree.

Mrs. Kleist carried the ax in the family, but I could see from my hiding place that her nerves were unsteady. Mr. Kleist talked too much when the Russians arrived. It annoyed them. They wanted food, vodka, wristwatches. And Else.

"*Urri, urri*, yes," said Mrs. Kleist. "Martin, give them your watch. Immediately."

A soldier took a step toward Else. Mr. Kleist began to whimper but his wife stepped in quickly to negotiate.

"No! This one *krank, krank*." She was telling the soldiers that Else was diseased. "We have one who is much prettier."

My blood thickened. My skin stung. No. She wouldn't.

"*Emilia!*" she yelled for me. She spotted my basket peeking out from behind the tree and commanded me forward.

"You see? So pretty. Very, very pretty. Take her instead."

The soldiers looked at me with their dead faces.

A trail of mushrooms spilled behind me as they dragged me to the cold cellar.

• • •

Joana carried the tiny swaddled baby over to my cot, cooing and kissing her head.

The doctor approached as well. "She's quite small, but seems healthy. Have you chosen a name yet?"

A name? I shook my head.

"Ah, you understood! You do understand a bit of German. Wonderful. Well, you can think about a name. Good work, Joana." The doctor left the room.

I was so tired. I closed my eyes and waited for the sound of Death's key in the lock.

florian

I would try to board early. A cute little boy and a hobbled old shoemaker might mask my arrival nicely. We left the theater and walked out into the road. The streets were alive, moving and swaying with hordes of people pushing toward the pier. Hungry dogs roamed and barked, abandoned by their masters because they weren't allowed on ships. Children, separated from their parents, wailed on the sidewalks, frantic and freezing. Some crouched in dark doorways of abandoned buildings, gnawing on moldy bread and the peels of sugar beets.

The small boy clung to the shoe poet, who was having difficulties navigating the shoving mob. He swatted people's ankles with his walking stick to clear a path.

"Up we go," I told the small boy. A pain in my wound surged as I lifted the boy onto my shoulders.

"Yes, wonderful idea," said the shoemaker. "Thank you." The old man fell in step with another white-haired German. "What do you hear?" asked Poet.

"On Christmas Eve, a German sub sank a troopship in the English Channel. They say there were thousands of American soldiers on board who drowned."

Were Americans dying by the thousands as well? Nazi

propaganda portrayed America as racially impure, a nation of mongrels, *The Land Without a Heart.*

The deep booming of an artillery shell rumbled in the distance. People in the crowd screamed and pushed forward. Women's faces were flaked with mud and ash, camouflage from the Russians they'd applied while trekking through the woods. Refugees rummaged through deserted sleds and luggage.

"Take those boots," called the shoe poet to an old man picking through a pile. "They're better than your own." The man nodded in acknowledgment.

Stories spread through the packs of people as we walked. A woman ran to a girl near us.

"Hurry! Russian planes dropped phosphorus on a mass of refugees. It blinded them and they had to roll in the snow."

Whispers filtered that the Allies had cut off access roads and train routes. We were surrounded. The crowds became denser, more suffocating as we approached the port. Panicked refugees trembled as they lined up at registration stations. Babies were used as pawns, passed from one person to the next as they approached for registration.

A woman grabbed my arm. "How much for the kid? They won't let me on if I don't have a kid."

The wandering boy's legs tightened on my shoulders.

"He's not for sale," I told her.

"Everyone has a price," she said.

"But clearly not everyone has a soul," said Poet, raising his walking stick to the woman. "Step away from the child."

There appeared to be several checkpoints. No one was allowed through without a boarding pass. I unbuttoned my coat, enduring the freezing temperature in order to allow the bloodstains on my shirt to be visible. I had another stain, of course. One that wasn't visible.

Sippenhaft. Blood guilt. It was a law of the Nazi regime. If a family member had committed a crime or treason, his blood was considered bad. It was an old practice, holding family members responsible for the crime of a relative.

My father made maps for the men who attempted to assassinate Hitler. He was taken to Berlin and hanged in the gallows of Plötzensee prison. And now I was smuggling Hitler's most prized treasure, along with a map and key to the Amber Room in my boot heel. There was no question. Beck blood was bad.

We approached the entrance to the harbor, cordoned off by a line of armed guards.

A shiny black Mercedes slowly carved through the crowd. Soldiers moved a barrier and allowed the vehicle of well-dressed women and officers in uniform to pass.

No. It wasn't. It couldn't be. That wasn't Gauleiter Koch, was it? Anxiety played tricks with my mind.

A soldier marched up and down the line of waiting passengers. "Have your papers and passes ready for inspection, please."

A vein began to pulse at the base of my throat.

joana

Her words replayed in my head.

No August. Russians. Frau Kleist. Take her. She prettier.

My stomach rolled. How I hoped I was wrong. I looked over at Emilia, fast asleep on the cot. She had talked of August and the farm. Her face lit up when she spoke of him. But in the throes of labor she had also screamed *liar* and pleaded for her mother to help her.

I looked at the little bundle. She was perfect, asleep like her mama.

Three more pregnant women had arrived and were resting comfortably in the makeshift maternity ward.

Dr. Richter entered with another man in tow.

"Joana, this is Dr. Wendt. He just arrived from the Naval Medical Academy in Gdańsk. He'll be joining us for the voyage." Dr. Richter gestured to the baby. "Joana handled our first delivery this morning."

I shook the new doctor's hand. "I'm so glad you're here. I'm more comfortable assisting."

"Looks like you did a fine job," said Dr. Wendt.

"Boarding has begun and passengers are filing in as we speak," said Dr. Richter.

"When are we expected to sail?" I asked.

"Quite soon," he replied. "We'll have seven expectant mothers and a hundred and sixty-two wounded men. That could change, of course. If you see anything suspicious, we'll need to report it."

Suspicious. A perfect description of handsome Florian Beck. Where was he now, I wondered.

emilia

I woke, disoriented. Joana wanted me to move, to walk a bit. I didn't want to. I was finally warm. No one would bother me for a while. And I was so tired. I pulled the sheet up to my nose.

She brought me pea soup and sat at my bedside. Whenever she left, she returned quickly. Joana looked at me differently now.

She understood.

She knew.

"The Prussian?" I asked, wondering about the knight.

"I don't know," she said.

"You hope," I told her.

She laughed.

Her smile suddenly faded and she looked straight at me. She leaned over my cot and took both of my hands in hers. Her eyes, filled with compassion, began to well up. Joana then whispered the words I had waited so long to hear. I knew Mama would say them if she could. But Joana spoke them, slowly and deliberately, clutching my hands between hers.

"Emilia, I am so very sorry."

My chin began to tremble. My throat tightened. I nodded and warm tears spilled down my cheeks.

"I'm sorry," she repeated, squeezing my hands.

"Me too," I whispered.

florian

We approached the embarkation officer, the wandering boy between us.

"Well, hello, there."

The officer spoke directly to the boy. Smart. Children spill the truth.

"Hallo, I'm Klaus."

"Give me your papers, please, Klaus."

The shoemaker handed over the boy's papers along with his own. I thrust mine out as well.

The officer opened the old man's papers and looked at his pass. He leaned over and specifically addressed the boy. "And, Klaus, who is this?" he asked, pointing to the shoemaker.

"Opi," replied the little boy.

Grandpa. Yes, he was like a grandpa. That was a good reply.

"And this gentleman?" He pointed to me.

My name. No one knew my name, except Joana. What if he called me what the others did—the Prussian? Or the spy?

"Onkel." The boy smiled.

"And what is Uncle's name?" the officer asked.

The little boy turned to me and saluted, as he had on the road. "Herr Beck."

The officer laughed.

The wandering boy thrust out his rabbit. "*Mein Freund*."

"Looks like your friend lost an ear in battle. Might have to send him to the infirmary." The officer turned to me and gestured to my shirt. "Looks like you lost some blood in the war yourself."

I nodded. "Shrapnel." I buttoned up my coat to escape the cold.

"Do you have a medical exemption?" he asked.

"Yes."

He handed back our papers. "Proceed to the next embarkation point."

He had looked at my papers, but only glanced at my boarding pass. We walked into the harbor.

Every inch of the dock was covered with soldiers, supply trucks, passengers, and luggage. There were entry lines for each ship and additional lines for each gangway.

The boy bounced on his toes.

"Yes, it's quite exciting," said the shoe poet. "And I believe that ship, in basin number nine, the very big one, is ours."

The *Gustloff* was the most imposing ship in the harbor. Her build was clearly that of a leisure cruise ship. Several decks, lots of places to hide. I spied anti-aircraft guns positioned on the deck. The ship was armed.

"Hey! Hey, you," the giant woman yelled, and gestured to us through the crowd.

"Well, hello there, Eva!" The shoe poet waved.

"Boy, you're lucky ducks. I was just about to throw your bags off."

The little boy ran and grabbed the shoemaker's carpetbag.

"Well done, Eva. Thank you," said the old man.

"You have no idea how I suffered for this stuff, waiting in the cold. And why? None of you cared enough to wait for our wagon."

"Enough about the luggage. Did you get registered for a ship, dear?" asked Poet.

"Yes, yes. I'm on that one. *Hansa*," she said. "Which one are you on?"

The little boy pointed to the *Gustloff*.

Eva looked at me and laughed. "You too, huh? I wonder how you managed that. I'm going to board. I'm freezing and it stinks like rotten death. Here, take Joana her suitcase. I know she'll want it. Tell her I said good-bye. She was the only one of you that I liked. Sorry." She set the case at my feet. "Well, nice knowing you."

"Wait." I grabbed her by the coat. "What are the next lines for?" I asked.

"Inspection," she said. "They're examining everyone's luggage."

SALT TO THE SEA   249

joana

Emilia pretended to sleep. I had to raise her spirits. The baby would need to nurse. She had to hold and feed her baby. If she didn't, the doctors might become suspicious. If they figured out she wasn't Latvian, Dr. Richter would report her. I would be held responsible for smuggling her on. My stomach turned.

A woman approached. "Excuse me, miss. There's someone in the hallway who would like to speak with you."

The sailor Alfred paced through the corridor.

"Hello, Alfred." I decided to ask: "Have you seen my patient today, the one from the movie house?"

"No, I haven't. But I'll keep an eye out for him," he said.

"Please let me know if you see him."

He shifted from one foot to another, rubbing the tangle of raw meat that was his hands.

"Oh, Alfred, your hands," I said.

"Actually, I didn't come about my hands. I came—well, what I wanted to say . . . I have been informed that you have a suitor, but I'm well acquainted with the long-distance love affair. You would do well to take a stroll with me on the promenade deck later this evening. We can discuss our sweethearts back at home." He grinned. "Tell me, do you like butterflies, Fräulein?"

Ruta Sepetys

What was he talking about? Was he asking me on a date? Oh, no. Kissing Alfred would be like chewing a mouthful of crackers. I shook off the thought.

"Well, Alfred, I think we'll all be extremely busy before we sail. I don't think I'll have time to take a walk. Honestly, I'd be surprised if you had time either."

Dr. Richter approached. "Joana, could you assist me, please? The girls have just arrived from the sanatorium. We need to determine where to put them. Perhaps you could help them get settled?" The doctor looked at Alfred. "What are you doing here?"

"Documenting the medical procedures of the evacuation, sir," said Alfred. "Someone must verify that work is actually being done." He turned on his heel and strode off.

SALT TO THE SEA   251

florian

The temperature hovered near zero, but I was sweating.

Luggage inspection.

I watched the flow of passengers approach the front of the line. Most of the discussions were about items too large to take on board: antiques, furniture, expensive carpets. And then I saw them. Wooden crates, similar to so many I had carefully belted and fastened, stood in stacked rows, surrounded by armed guards. Of course. The Nazis were not only boarding passengers, they were loading their looted art and treasure onto the ships. My curiosity burned. What was in the crates?

People cried when their large items were refused. I carried only Joana's small suitcase and my pack. The little boy had no luggage, the shoe poet only a carpetbag and his shoe-repair kit. I was about to give Joana's suitcase to Poet when an armed sentry corralled us into line.

"Step ahead. Make room, please."

German efficiency worked against me. They were fast. Before I could finalize a plan we were at the front of the line with our papers. The guard behind the table was older, seasoned. He flipped through the identity papers, examining our photos against our faces. Another soldier walked around us, examining our belongings. The older guard behind the desk then

252   *Ruta Sepetys*

looked at our boarding passes. He pointed to the shoemaker and the boy.

"You two. Proceed to the gangway." He then pointed at me. "You, proceed to the table behind me. Additional inspection."

Additional inspection. My heart punched in my chest. I had forgotten to open my coat, to display my wound. I acted like I was reaching for papers and released the buttons. Brittle cold rushed in around my torso. I hoped it would mask my perspiration, my desperation. I prayed the inspection officer would be a booby like the sailor I had duped.

He wasn't.

He was in his late twenties, blond, with fair, almost waxen, skin. He looked like one of Hitler's prized Aryans from the propaganda posters. He leaned back, teetering on his chair in a long oilskin coat, basking within his power and authority. Two other soldiers stood nearby, hanging on his every word, laughing when they were supposed to. I approached the table and set down the suitcase. My pack hung on my back behind me. In it were pistols, ammunition, forgery materials, my notebook, and the Führer's most beloved treasure, the amber swan.

The blond officer leaned forward. His chair fell to the dock with a thud.

"Papers."

I handed him my identity card and the boarding pass.

"What's in your suitcase?" he asked.

"It's not mine. I'm delivering it to my nurse on board. It belongs to her."

"Your nurse? My, my, you have your own private nurse?"

SALT TO THE SEA   253

He looked to the soldier on his right. "This one has his own nurse."

"I bet he does." The soldier laughed.

"Looks like you need a nurse." He pointed a pencil at my bloodstained shirt. "Show me."

"Excuse me?"

"Let's see this bad wound that requires a personal nurse. I think I may want one myself. I need to see what's required."

I quickly lifted my shirt and revealed the massive gash.

The officer twisted his face. "Nasty. The skin's nearly grown over the stitch. Might be too late to take them out. What's the name of the nurse you say is on board?"

I hesitated. It wasn't fair. I didn't want to implicate her. "Joana Vilkas," I said quietly.

The other soldiers whistled. "Litwinka."

"What?" I didn't understand.

The inspection officer laughed. "It's the nickname for your pretty Lithuanian nurse. There aren't many female personnel on board, so we've named them all."

He leaned back on his chair again. "I think there's something missing here."

Sweat beaded beneath my hairline.

"You have civilian papers and you're trying to get on a ship. Yet you're an able-bodied young man who could be serving the Reich."

I leaned forward and stared him down. "I am serving." I pulled the additional paperwork from my coat pocket and threw it on the table.

He laughed and began narrating for his buddies. "Let's see, fellas. Here we have . . . an official medical testimony signed by Litwinka. Such a pretty signature she has. Shrapnel. Oh, and deaf in one ear, too. That's convenient. Let's see what other love notes he's got." He opened the thick cream paper, saw the seal at the top, and stopped talking. He scanned through the letter and looked up at me, angry.

"When you are asked for papers, you are to provide all of your papers."

I allowed all of the ferocity of the past years to rise up inside me. Like a boiler about to blow, I leaned over the table.

"I will be happy to tell Gauleiter Koch that you unnecessarily held his injured courier in the freezing cold, delaying his mission and wasting the services of a nurse he himself arranged. Koch's mood of late hasn't been very forgiving."

He stared back at me, wanting desperately to jump the table for a fight. Part of me hoped it would come to fists. I wanted to batter this blond idiot senseless.

He pushed the stack of papers back at me and gave a nod toward the gangway.

Adrenaline charged through me. I wanted to knock his teeth out more than I wanted to board the ship. I stuffed my papers away and buttoned my coat.

"Say hi to Litwinka for us." He whistled to the guard at the gangway and pointed to me. "That one's going to the infirmary."

I felt his eyes on me, following my steps up the gangway and into the ship.

SALT TO THE SEA   255

alfred

Fulfilling a woman's request swayed emotions, giving a man the upper hand. Hannelore's heart always seemed to soften when I brought her sweets or swept the sidewalk. Yes, if I wanted to bait the pretty nurse, I must fulfill her request. I would find the young recruit.

I walked through the halls, looking for the tall rogue. If he were on board, he would be easy to find. There weren't many men his age in civilian clothes.

"Frick," someone called to me from a group. "We need you to issue life vests."

I put my hand up in protest. "My apologies, gentlemen. I'm on an important assignment."

"*Bettnässer*," the sailor replied. They all laughed.

Bed wetter.

I scraped at my hands. They would be sorry they had laughed. Very sorry.

The ship's speaker system buzzed with announcements, calls for lost and found children, and misplaced belongings. No smoking belowdecks. Life jackets must be worn at all times.

After several rounds of the ship, I felt energized both in body and in mind. Perhaps there was something to this physical fitness curriculum the military recommended. As I rounded the corner on the upper promenade deck, I saw the old man and the little boy. The boy was hard at work, shining shoes for coins.

"Greetings. I'm looking for the young fellow from the movie house. Have you seen him?"

The old man's eyes narrowed to unbecoming slits. He looked down at my boots. "I saw you do it, you know."

"Do what?" I responded. Had he seen me snatch the crystal butterfly?

"You took your boot to that poor dog."

"Oh that." I sighed. "Our Führer would remind you that it makes no sense to support the weak or crippled. In nature, the weaker species simply die." I leaned in toward him, examining his face. "I believe some might classify you as weak? Now, have you seen the fellow from the movie house?"

"What do you need with him? He had to wait for additional inspection."

"Inspection, right. Very careful we must be. Can't allow any riffraff or deserters," I said. I left their footwear enterprise and went down a few decks to the gangway entry.

"I've been sent to find a young civilian man who just boarded. Tall, brown hair."

"We just sent someone to the infirmary who matches that description. Maybe that was your man?"

I ran to the closest stairwell. I spotted the recruit and called out. He stopped and I made my way up. He looked genuinely happy to see me.

"Well, you're exactly who I was looking for." He clapped me on the shoulder and we continued up the stairs.

SALT TO THE SEA   257

joana

I held the small bundle next to Emilia, hoping she would make eye contact with the child. The new physician, Dr. Wendt, appeared.

"Joana, a sailor is around the corner asking for you. He seems . . . eager."

I walked out. Alfred again. He grinned and waved me forward. "Follow me."

Didn't he have work to do? "Alfred, I can't. I'm very busy."

"Come along. Come along."

I felt sorry for Alfred. I had known boys like him in school—desperate to be a man, yet trapped in his own mind. Girls joked that boys like Alfred made a cow's milk dry up.

Alfred stopped at the infirmary and made a grand gesture with his arm. "Ask and you shall receive."

My stomach gave a little hop. Sitting on a cot in the corner was Florian. Near his feet sat my suitcase. I tried to mask my excitement at seeing him. "My suitcase. Thank you, Florian."

Alfred looked at me and raised his eyebrows. "And?"

"And thank you, Alfred," I said.

Alfred paused, eyebrows arched, staring at me.

Florian nodded to him in quiet dismissal. "Thanks again."

"Right, yes," said Alfred. "Must get back to work. I'm very busy." He walked off.

I made my way over to the corner, through the rows of wounded soldiers. "You made it," I said. I could feel myself smiling.

"Almost didn't. There's a Nazi on the dock who doesn't like me much."

"And you brought my suitcase. So you found Eva? What about Poet and the boy?"

"They're on board. Eva's on the *Hansa*. She said to tell you good-bye." He shifted to look at my face, then reached out and touched my arm. "You okay?"

I nodded.

"Can you take these stitches out?"

I walked over to a table to retrieve the necessary instruments. I was sad to hear about Eva. We weren't given a chance to say good-bye properly.

I returned and Florian began unbuttoning his shirt. The dried blood on his skin now resembled powdered dirt. "Do you have any other clothes?" I asked.

"Are you saying my wardrobe is lacking?"

I smiled. "Very funny. Lie down." I sighed.

"That was a big sigh. What's wrong?" he asked.

"Emilia had the baby."

"The baby didn't make it?" He seemed genuinely upset.

"The baby's fine." I shook my head. "But Emilia isn't."

"What happened?" he asked.

I began removing the stitches. What could I tell him? How much would he even understand? He stared at me. Was he waiting for the story or just looking at me? I took a breath.

"There is no boyfriend," I whispered. "The family she was staying with gave her to the Russians to save their daughter. The boyfriend was a story she made up to continue on. She won't really look at the baby yet."

His face changed. Sincerity and sadness erased the bravado. "That kid. She's a warrior."

"Yes, but fighting who?"

He looked at me, surprised. "Everyone. Everything. Fighting fate."

"Now I understand. She clings to you because you saved her from the Russian in the forest. You're proof that there are still good men in the world."

"Stop. Don't say those things." He stared at the wall.

I pulled the last of the stitches from his muscular torso.

"How long until we sail?" he asked.

"They say we'll leave soon."

"I need to find somewhere out of sight," he whispered. "Do you know of a place?"

He had boarded, but now he wanted to hide?

I shook my head. "I don't know the ship well yet. I'm constantly getting lost." I watched him button his shirt. "Florian, will you do something for me? Will you come say hello to Emilia? Please? It would really lift her spirits."

260   *Ruta Sepetys*

emilia

Was I dreaming? Was the knight really walking toward me? I sat up quickly. His eyes immediately shifted to the baby.

"Yes, that's the beautiful girl," Joana told him.

The knight stopped and raised his arms. "No pink hat? Where's your pink hat?" he asked.

I pointed to a heap of coats. The knight dug through and retrieved the knit cap. He then gently lifted the baby and tucked the hat over her like a blanket. She sat like a little crescent moon in the curve of his arm. He walked over to me.

He looked from the baby to me and then back to the baby.

"Hmm. Your eyes. Your nose. Pretty," he said. He put his lips against the top of the baby's head and closed his eyes. He looked beautiful. Joana stared at the knight. She thought he was beautiful too.

He opened his eyes and whispered to me. "Kind of incredible. She is you, she is your mother, your father, your country." He kissed her head and leaned down to whisper in my ear.

"She is Poland."

My arms lifted and reached for the child.

florian

We left the Polish girl holding her baby. Joana followed me out of the maternity area, her face a mixture of shock and confusion. She grabbed my arm and pulled me behind a door.

"What just happened in there?" she whispered. "Who are you?"

I shrugged. "I like kids." I lifted my pack onto my back. "But now I need that sailor to help me find a place to hide."

"Why is he helping you?"

I tried to suppress a smile. "I told him he would get a medal."

"No, you didn't," said Joana.

"I did."

"You're awful." She laughed.

"I'm awful? Then why are you laughing?" I asked.

She laughed even harder. "I don't know. I shouldn't laugh."

"So stop laughing."

She laughed more, leaning against my shoulder. Her face smelled of soap.

"You look nice clean," I said.

Her laughter eased and she smiled. "Thank you. And thank you for bringing my suitcase." She stood on her toes, took my face in her hands, and kissed me.

My arms were around her. I kissed her back. And kissed her again.

"And thank you," she whispered, looking into my eyes. "For Emilia."

She slid from my arms and walked off.

joana

The hallway narrowed and tightened with oncoming passengers. I turned the corner to the glass enclosure of the promenade deck. Frozen constellations of ice laced the edges of the window. I put my fingers on the chilled glass, staring out but not looking. I was supposed to be the smart girl. What was I doing? He was younger. I knew nothing about him. He was clearly involved in something deceitful. But if he could be so gentle with the baby, so kind to Emilia, could he really be a bad person?

I kissed him because of Emilia.

My conscience tapped at me from behind the glass.

Or maybe I kissed him because I wanted to.

And oh, my, it was nothing like chewing crackers.

I turned around and leaned against the window. January permeated the glass and my blouse. For the first time in a long time, my body felt warmer than the outside air.

Some passengers were visibly relieved and excited to be on board. Others appeared nervous, flittering around like caged birds. I was part of the relieved group. How lucky I was to be on such a large ship. I loved the hulking *Gustloff* with its thick steel walls and multiple levels. Dr. Richter had told me that the cruiser was only eight years old, but hadn't sailed in four years. The lack of use had left everything in fine order. Once we left Gotenhafen, the voyage to Kiel would take only forty-eight hours. I would then board a train and finally reunite with Mother.

So much had changed since I left Lithuania. Mother said my father and brother were probably fighting in the woods. Could they really survive living in underground bunkers?

The *Gustloff* was my bunker. I felt a deep breath take hold. All the struggle and worry. Could it nearly be over?

alfred

Hello, my butterfly,

I know the separation is difficult and it must be lonely to fly by yourself. But soon our great country shall prevail and the dutiful will stand on pedestals of honor. The day is coming.

I am relieved to report that the boarding procedure is well under way and that I am warm. Some of the other sailors had to haul life rafts in the freezing cold. I can't imagine where they found such a quantity of rafts.

We are told that we will board even more passengers but I don't know where we shall fit them. The upper cabins are occupied by the privileged and the refugees have gladly taken to the mattress pads. The ship is not even moving, yet some passengers are wearing life vests. They look quite silly.

The Wilhelm Gustloff is now a living, breathing city. Enterprise is afoot. People barter their belongings and a shoemaker and his apprentice repair shoes on the upper promenade deck. They have amassed quite a sack of coins for their efforts.

I'm sure you are wondering about the activities I wrote of earlier. My friendship with the young recruit has developed quite nicely. We share important conversations on all matter of topics.

Alas, I'm no longer the dreamy boy you'd wave to at the edge of the school yard. I am a man in uniform now.

Each day I find myself in deeper allegiance to our country and our Führer, Hannelore. As such, I have helped the recruit find secret accommodation on board to assist in fulfilling his mission. He was so much obliged that he once again mentioned that upon arrival in Kiel he will promptly recommend me for a medal of valor. Just another one to add to the pile, but appreciated nonetheless. After all, everything I achieve, everything I have done, it is all for you. For you and for Germany. Surely you know that, don't you, Lore?

emilia

The tiny baby nuzzled against me. The knight said she was part of Mother, part of Father, part of me. If she was part of us, I wanted her to know our city of Lwów. She should know Poland. Looking at the child, I suddenly became hungry for my country, for its fat bees carrying nectar from apple flowers and for the birds singing in clusters of hazel.

How would she know the truths from the untruths? Would she believe that Poles, Jews, Ukrainians, Armenians, and Hungarians had all coexisted peacefully in Lwów before the war? That I often made tea and doughnuts with Rachel and Helen in our kitchen?

Food. I wanted her to know our food. How my hands missed the feel of dough dusted with flour. My ears missed the snap of apple pancakes in the pan and my eyes missed the rainbow of fruits and vegetables sealed in jars on the shelves. War had bled color from everything, leaving nothing but a storm of gray.

I wanted her to know not only Poland, but *my* Poland.

I pulled her close and whispered in Polish: "There were no ghettos, no armbands. I often fell asleep to a breeze floating through my open window. It's true. It was like that once."

florian

The interior of the chimney measured about five meters wide. There was a ladder and a ledge of ample width to lie down on. It was cold and I couldn't sleep. The chimney was secluded, but it could also be my downfall. If someone looked in and saw me, they would immediately know I was hiding. Should I have stayed in the infirmary? I might have been better camouflaged there, warmer. Closer to Joana. But if the Nazi from the harbor came on board, he'd look for me in the infirmary.

I was weighing my options when the hinges on the door rotated.

The sailor climbed up the ladder and took a seat next to me.

"I've come with news," he announced.

"Oh yeah, what's that?"

He rubbed his blistered palms together. "I have just observed from the top deck the arrival of hundreds of female naval auxiliaries. They are well dressed and quite clean."

"They're bringing the women's auxiliary on board?" Maybe that meant we'd leave soon.

"Yes, there are hundreds of them and they seem quite plucky."

"Where are they going to put them?" I asked. "Are there enough cabins available?"

"Oh no. All of the cabins are quite full already. But I

imagine there are those on board who might offer a warm cot." He snorted with laughter.

I leaned back against the cold chimney wall. Had this guy been broadsided with a brick at some point?

"How long have you been in the service, sailor?" I asked.

He stared at his feet, hesitating. "As we share confidences, I will be truthful. I was a late recruit. I had wanted to be part of the youth organizations, but the physical drills were quite rigorous and placed heavy emphasis on athletic competition. I can see you have gifts of strength and coordination. I do not. I cannot run very fast or jump very far. My gifts lie in other areas. My father was terribly disappointed but Mutter was relieved. Although Mutter of course loves the Führer, she wasn't quite inclined to serve me up. I'm an only child."

"Your mother loves the Führer, eh?"

He looked at me, his eyes sober and sharp. "Of course. We all love the Führer, sir. As the papers say, 'The good German fights for the Führer.' I certainly do. I will admit that I'm too tenderhearted and at times felt sorry for someone or other who could not be part of the master race, but now I banish such impure thoughts. Such is the nature of sacrifice, is it not?"

His impure thoughts were radically different from my own.

He stared at me. "You agree, of course? We are good Germans."

His eyes lingered. His speech pattern carried an unsettling cadence. I suddenly had an overwhelming urge to knock him off the ledge. But instead I just nodded.

"We are good Germans. So do you think you could find me some food?" I asked.

joana

The maternity ward was now full. Three of the women were quite close to their time. Emilia whispered to her baby, inspecting her tiny hands. When I was a little girl I had two baby dolls and carried them everywhere. Then I became competitive in school and had no time for dolls. I turned away from Emilia and her daughter, trying to swallow past the strange knotting in my throat.

A soldier in a green uniform and black jackboots walked in. "Joana Vilkas."

The soldier had yellow hair and fair, almost translucent skin. He looked like the men referred to as "purebloods," portrayed on the German signs. "Can I help you?"

"I'm here about someone that *you* helped." He stood completely still. "One of your patients—the one with a shrapnel wound and a damaged ear."

Emilia's posture tightened. She pulled the infant close and kept her eyes on the soldier.

"Can you confirm the name of the patient with the shrapnel wound and the bad ear, Miss Vilkas?"

I walked over to him and lowered my voice. "I'm not at liberty to give out the patients' names. I'm sure you understand."

He became annoyed. This man wasn't used to being refused.

SALT TO THE SEA   *271*

"If I am not mistaken, miss, you are *Volksdeutsche*, a Lithuanian who was allowed to repatriate into Germany. Your liberty belongs to Adolf Hitler. We can certainly hand you back over to Stalin." He grinned, pleased by the bully within him. "But we wouldn't want to do that. You're too pretty. So can you confirm, then, the name of your patient with the shrapnel wound and damaged ear?"

"I'm not sure I remember," I whispered. "Maybe Friedrich? Or Fritz?"

The soldier seemed to consider this. What did he already know?

His eyes narrowed. "Florian, perhaps? Surname Beck?"

He knew more than he was letting on.

"Yes, that might be it."

"Where did you encounter him?"

"In transit. He was bleeding and suffering a fever. Is there a problem, sir?"

The soldier ran his finger along the edge of the metal table, as if checking for dust. "If you are telling the truth, then no, there is no problem. But if you are assisting or harboring a deserter, Miss Vilkas, then yes, there's a big problem."

"He has papers. Did Herr Beck show them to you?" I folded a piece of linen to busy my trembling hands.

"He showed me his papers. He also showed me his attitude. It was only after I pressed that he showed me *all* of his paperwork."

I tried to deflect but dig. "Then you understand the nature of his situation?"

Ruta Sepetys

"Yes, he's a courier for Gauleiter Koch. He was wounded and says Koch appointed you as his personal nurse."

My breath stopped but my hands kept moving. Gauleiter Erich Koch appointed me? What was he talking about?

He shook his head. "But there was something," he said, looking at Emilia and then at me. "I didn't believe him. I'd like to take another look at his papers. I sent him to the infirmary but I can't seem to find him there. Would you happen to have a duplicate of the medical testimony you signed for him?"

Medical testimony. That I had signed. What had he done? "I'm sorry, there have been so many," I said.

"Yes, there are a lot of wounded. So I've sent a wire to Koch's office for confirmation, but thought you might be able to solve the matter more quickly. Did you see him?"

"Yes. I removed his stitches."

Emilia squirmed in protest, wanting to defend Florian.

"What did he say?" asked the soldier.

"Just that he was tired." Emilia shot me a ferocious look. "And . . . that he had wanted to board the *Hansa* instead."

"*Hansa?*"

The wandering boy ran in, chest heaving beneath his life vest, tears streaming down his face. He held up the stuffed rabbit. The remaining ear dangled from a strand.

"Oh no!" I exclaimed. He nodded, pouting.

"Don't you worry, we'll fix him right up." I turned to the soldier. "Are we through, sir? As you can see, I'm about to go into surgery."

emilia

Florian Beck. The knight was Florian, like Saint Florian, the patron saint of Poland. The Nazi soldier had tried to cause problems. He was clearly full of hate. If he discovered I was Polish, he would throw me off the boat into the Baltic.

Joana paced the floor, sewing the ear of the rabbit back onto its body. She was mad or thinking. Maybe both. The wandering boy walked over to my cot and peeked at the baby.

"Hallo," he said to her. "I'm Klaus."

I looked at the boy. His cheeks were red, burned from the cold and wind. The large blue life vest dwarfed his body and hung down to his knees. He was alone, like me, but he was only six years old. Where were his parents? Mama said that a transplanted bud doesn't prosper. The shoemaker loved him, though. I could tell. He would take care of him, protect him, unlike Frau Kleist.

"Four years. We've kept you for over four years," Frau Kleist used to complain. "Do you know what that's cost me?"

"My father will come for me," I told her. "He will pay you."

She whipped around, furious. "Your father's dead. Why do you think I'm so annoyed?"

Dead.

Her words had squeezed at my throat, run down through my windpipe and strangled the air from my lungs.

"It's not true," I whispered.

Please. It couldn't be true.

August appeared at my side. "Of course it's not true." He pulled me by the arm. "Come on, Emilia, let's snip the roses for the jam." He shot his mother a fierce look.

The old feelings of fear began to churn within me. The baby stirred in my arms. I looked down. Her little head bobbed, almost nodding at me. And then our eyes fastened. Her sweet yet steady stare calmed me. My shoulders released and the fear dissipated.

The shoemaker arrived in the maternity ward, panting and out of breath. "You must wait for me, Klaus. These old sticks can't move as fast anymore." He saw the baby and his hands flew to his face.

"Look, look. A miracle, indeed."

"Isn't she beautiful?" said Joana.

"What's beautiful," said the old man, "is that she has beaten this war. You saw it on the road. Ingrid through the ice, death and destruction all around. Look what's transpiring down on that pier. Frantic desperation. The Russians are just around the corner."

He moved forward and gestured to the baby. "Yet amidst all that, life has spit in the eye of death. We must find her some shoes."

SALT TO THE SEA   275

alfred

Dear Hannelore,

Night falls in the harbor. I sit, reflecting on all that has happened. Do not be misguided by my poetic inclinations. I am not only a watchman. I am a thinker, Lore, and I have been thinking. I have been working in service to a man of great charge. We have a confident understanding of one another and share many attributes. This evening we discussed loyalty. I assured him of my allegiance to Germany's fight. I also confessed of once feeling sympathy for those who are inferior. Be assured that I pull at the roots of these sympathies. I know they are a weakness. They must be torn from the garden. We are good Germans. It is our birthright. As such, it is our duty to sift the sands, preserve the gold, and with it build a stronger national vertebrae.

I believe you're also familiar with moments of weakness? I recall your deep sighs of admiration as I swept your sidewalk. Oh yes, dear one, I noticed. I am much more observant than those pests of Hitler Youth.

I will admit, Lore, that I was surprised when Mutter held me back from Hitler Youth. My father was ashamed that I was not deemed ready to join the others. He feared consequences. But then I grew tired of those pushy boys and realized I was intended for something much more important. Although it took nearly five years for me to join the war effort, I have finally found my calling here in Gotenhafen. My qualities are finally recognized by one of my own, a recruit of steadfast courage. Yes, it is calming in an indescribable way to find oneself. Few men have that opportunity. I am one of those men.

I now understand what it is to feel superior. And I quite like it.

florian

Breath fogged from my mouth. My stomach rumbled. I thought of our warm kitchen at home in Tilsit, the soft ring of the lids trembling on their pots, and my sister's laughter echoing throughout the house.

When my mother died of tuberculosis, my father's greatest concern was Anni. "How will I raise a proper girl on my own?" he said.

Anni was thirteen when I last saw her. She would be nearly sixteen now. Would I recognize her if I passed her on the street? Where had she been and what had she experienced?

The door squealed. "Anyone hungry up there?" yelled the voice.

Such an idiot. "Shh," I reminded him once again.

"Ah, yes, we must be covert." He climbed the ladder. "I feel my physique responding," he announced. "I have made exercise a priority and am seeing benefits. In fact, I believe the benefit now expands to my hands, which seem to be improving."

I didn't want to think about his clotted hands. "What have you brought to eat?" I asked.

He removed the shoulder strap and handed me my canteen. It hadn't felt that heavy for a long time.

"Thank you." I drank immediately. He then produced a

large chunk of bread from inside his shirt along with a slice of meat wrapped in paper.

"Most are eating pea soup, you see, but that would be quite challenging to transport," he explained.

"When are we leaving?" I asked.

"Word is that we could depart any minute."

An artillery blast sounded in the distance. He twitched and plastered himself against the wall of the chimney.

"Still miles away," I told him. "But they're advancing." I pictured my father's maps. I could see swarms of Russians plowing into East Prussia toward the coast of the Baltic Sea, flattening Germany's Wehrmacht, and all of us, in the process.

He scratched his wrist. "May I ask, are you good with weaponry?"

I nodded. "You?"

"Better with my mind," he said. "I'm what is commonly referred to in philosophical circles as 'a thinker.' I prefer to capture all angles mentally. I observe. I am a watchman."

"But sometimes there's no time to think," I told him. "We just have to act."

"I quite disagree, respectfully, of course. I see many who act on instinct, which I believe is wrong. Through instinct we succumb to weakness and emotion. Careful thought and planning, mental construction, is always best."

The impulse to hit him returned. I swallowed the last of the bread.

"'Obstacles do not exist to be surrendered to, but only to be broken,'" said the sailor. "I think of this wisdom often. Of

SALT TO THE SEA   279

course you're familiar with these words. You've read Adolf Hitler's *Mein Kampf*?" he asked.

I didn't answer the question. "You know, you strike me as an intelligent guy. It might be better for you to think for yourself, rather than memorizing the words of others."

"Why, thank you. Mutter always praises my sharp mind." He turned to me, his top lip curled in a grin. "And I do think for myself. But the wisdom of the Führer, it fills me with an indescribable command." His grin widened and he began to recite, "'Only in the steady and constant application of force lies the very first prerequisite for success.'"

He stared at me, pupils dilated. "Isn't that beautiful?"

I didn't respond. Small hairs on the back of my neck lifted in warning. This guy wasn't a sailor. He was a sociopath in training.

"Have you seen the nurse?" I asked him.

"I'll go get her," he said eagerly.

"No—"

But he had scrambled down the ladder and out the door before I could stop him.

joana

I took a breath, trying to control my anger. How could he do this to me?

Tomorrow morning I could walk down to the pier and find the blond soldier. I could tell him that I realized I was mistaken. I didn't write any sort of medical testimony, that I knew nothing of it. The soldier had said I was *Volksdeutsche*—of German ancestry. It was true. Germany had saved me from Stalin. What now did I owe to Germany?

"Joana."

The voice came soft from over my shoulder. I turned. Emilia stared at me, her eyes full of concern.

"No," she whispered. "Please."

Were my thoughts visible?

"Excuse me, Fräulein." Alfred stood at the edge of the ward. "A certain gentleman has requested an audience with you," he said.

"Where is he?" I asked.

"I will take you," he said. "You might want to bring your coat."

I tried to hurry Alfred, but it was no use. The ship was so overcrowded it was impossible to move quickly. How many thousands of people had they boarded?

SALT TO THE SEA

"But when will I see them?" sobbed a young girl in the corridor.

"Don't cry, sweetheart," said an old woman. "You were lucky to be the one chosen in your family. Your mother will come for you in a couple years. You'll see, the time will go quickly."

The crying girl looked to be ten or eleven. How would she make it on her own? "Alfred, there are so many. They'll have to remove some passengers, won't they?" I asked.

"No. I've heard that we have over eight thousand already and we are still boarding."

Eight thousand? The ship's capacity was not even fifteen hundred. We passed cabins intended for four people. A dozen were squeezed in, trying to sleep, suitcases and luggage stacked to the ceiling.

"This is quite civilized," said Alfred. "This afternoon over three hundred girls from the naval auxiliary arrived. They are at the very bottom of the ship. In the drained swimming pool."

I realized how fortunate I was to be in the maternity ward. There was space and relative calm. We waded through the sea of people toward the stairwell. Some were wearing life vests, which took up even more space.

We climbed the stairs. The air became cooler. I put on my coat. Alfred stopped me and put his finger to his lips. We let some people in the stairway pass. He then opened a small door in the stairway and pulled me by the sleeve of my coat.

We were inside a hollow chamber. "Where are we?" I asked.

"In the chimney," he announced.

282 *Ruta Sepetys*

"Shh," echoed from above. I looked up and saw Florian climbing down an interior ladder.

"Alfred," I said. "Would you mind leaving us for a moment?"

florian

She slapped me.

When I didn't react, she raised her hand again. This time I caught her arm.

"How dare you," she breathed.

"What are you talking about?" I said. Her face was an inch from mine.

"You know what I'm talking about," she whispered. "You forged a letter. You said I was appointed by Erich Koch. Do you know what they could do to me?"

I let her go. "What happened?"

She threw her arms in the air. "The blond Nazi, the one you mentioned, he came to the maternity ward looking for you."

"What did you tell him?"

"I told him nothing. That I knew nothing." The speed of her words increased. "But he told me he had seen your papers, that you're a courier for Koch, and that Koch appointed *me* as your nurse!"

"Shh," I repeated. "That sailor is probably listening to every word."

"He should," she whispered. "He thinks he's a hero, helping you with some spy mission for the Reich."

"That guy is no hero. You need to stay away from him."

"You're putting us in terrible danger. It's not fair. Eva said you were a spy. Ingrid said you were a thief. I should have believed them."

What were my options? She could turn me in.

Would she?

joana

We stood staring at each other.

"Tell me what you want to know," said Florian.

"Are you really carrying something for Gauleiter Koch?"

"No. I'm carrying things for myself," he said. "A piece of art."

"You stole art?"

"No. The Nazis stole art."

Was he telling me that he had taken art from the Nazis? "Stop being so cryptic."

He sighed, then spoke in a whisper. "I'm a restoration artist, Joana. I repair and restore works of art. Initially, that's why I wasn't drafted. I worked at a museum in Königsberg. I preserved and packaged art for the museum director and his contacts. But then I learned that they were using me."

"So you stole some art to get back at them?"

"Not just 'some art.' A priceless piece." He paused. "Let's just say that I've taken a piece that will leave a puzzle incomplete."

None of it made sense. And either way, I didn't want to be implicated.

"Do you love your country? Do you love your family?" he asked.

"Of course," I told him.

"So do I. I have a younger sister out there somewhere. I'm all she has left. I think of her every day. My father made maps. He worked for the men who tried to assassinate Hitler. So the Nazis killed my father and sent a bill to our house. Three hundred reichsmarks for his execution. Do you understand? The Nazis wanted me to pay them for murdering my father. How would you feel if Stalin demanded payment for killing someone you love?"

"Stop."

"Well, you're acting so virtuous. You're harboring a Polish girl and her baby in the maternity ward."

"Lower your voice. That's different and you know it. She's a victim. I need to help her," I said.

"It doesn't matter. If they find out that you falsified the identity of a Pole and brought her on board, taking a space for a German, you're done. We're both up to our necks. But I won't turn you in. Poet's not going to turn us in. I'm not a spy, Joana. I'm not working for anyone. I'm working for myself, for my family, and others like mine. If anyone discovers the truth, I'll tell them that I forged the letter and that you knew nothing about it."

"What if they don't believe you?" I asked.

"I'll show them. I'll take out your letter and my notebook. I'll show them how I practiced forging your signature."

"What letter?"

He paused, then pulled in a breath. "The note you left in the kitchen at the manor house. I took it."

"You took my note?"

I had worried so intensely about that piece of paper, that they would find my name in that house. Florian had it the whole time.

"I took the note because I was trying to protect you," he whispered.

"Well, protect yourself. That soldier told me that he's wired Koch about you."

The door opened and Alfred's pale face appeared. "Pardon the interruption. Would you mind if I left my post to use the facilities?"

"Not at all," I said. "I'm leaving."

emilia

The ship was full of unnatural sounds. Steel doors clanging, hollow footsteps, desperate echoes. Nature, the outdoors, even the farm, it all felt so far away.

I had worked so hard for the Kleists. Frau Kleist claimed everything I did was wrong but she was all too happy to let me clean, cook, and preserve for her. The cold store cellar on the edge of the property became my favorite place. On hot days I'd sit on an apple box outside with the cool stones against my back. August repaired the shelves for me when he was home. Else would linger nearby, begging for a spoonful of rose petal jam.

It wasn't Else's fault.

But I wondered.

Did she ever think of it? Did she remember the trail my heels carved in the dirt as they dragged me across the yard? Did my screams echo in her head as they did in mine?

Or perhaps, like me, she tried to forget it all and think instead about a spoonful of rose petal jam.

florian

Was she telling the truth? Had the soldier really contacted Koch's office or did she say that because she was mad and wanted to scare me?

I waited until the middle of the night when I hoped everyone would be asleep. I had noted toilet facilities in the corridor as the sailor walked me to the chimney. I quietly slipped out of the small door with my pack, keeping my head down.

People occupied every possible space, yet my lavatory visit went undetected. I then went to the maternity ward to see Joana. If what she said was true, the ship would be swarming with soldiers hunting for me at first light.

I peeked in but didn't see her. The Polish girl slept, the baby cradled in her arms. I walked to the infirmary. It was a solemn sight, wounded men on wooden pallets lined within a foot of each other. Joana tended to a soldier nearby. Their words were easily heard in the quiet dark.

"Well, you're not wearing a wedding ring," said the soldier.

"No, but I told you. I have a boyfriend. Now, you rest quietly and let me finish with this bandage."

"Let me be your boyfriend, just for tonight," pleaded the soldier.

My fingers curled into a fist.

"Please, just let me finish," said Joana, her voice taut.

The soldier continued to pester. He grabbed her with his good arm. "C'mon, give me a little kiss."

"Hey." The word came out before I could stop it.

"There you are," said Joana. "I was just telling Sergeant Mueller about you. I'm almost done here."

I stepped back into the corridor to remain out of sight from the men.

Joana walked out of the infirmary. "What do you want?"

"Does that happen often?" I asked.

"They're delirious." She sighed, fatigued, and tucked a curl behind her ear. "I'm busy. What do you want?"

What did I want? I wanted the war to be over so I could ask her out.

"I need to know. Did the soldier really say that he had wired Koch?" I asked.

She looked up at me. I couldn't read her expression. I told myself that her eyes weren't pretty and that I didn't want to kiss her. She just stared.

"Did he really say he had contacted Koch?" I repeated.

"Yes," she finally whispered.

SALT TO THE SEA   291

alfred

Arguments began before the sun rose. Flotation rafts, life vests, weather. The commotion was unsettling to my mind. I decided it would be best to descend to E deck to check on the hundreds of ladies in the drained pool. It was quite warm at the bottom of the ship. I wondered if the women might shed their uniforms for comfort. They played cards, slept, combed their hair, huddled in groups, and preoccupied themselves in general feminine behavior. I found them fascinating to observe and decided to remain concealed for one, maybe two hours, to further my studies.

At ten o'clock my surveillance was disrupted by a group of soldiers who marched onto E deck, sending the girls into a flurry. They announced they were looking for a specific passenger. It was the perfect time to present my services. I stepped out of the shadows and approached the men. The leader was a fine specimen, hair as yellow as the sun and clear, unblemished skin.

"Good morning, sir. Might I be of service?"

The soldier seemed surprised by my presence.

"He's been spying on us all morning," said one of the women. "He's harmless."

The other girls laughed.

I did not appreciate their laughter at my expense, nor did I like the feeling it created inside of me. I suddenly detested these insipid women. They were disgusting and stupid.

"Who are you looking for? We've seen a few fellas wander down here," said one of the girls from inside the drained pool. "Can you describe him for us?"

The soldier knelt down at the edge of the pool. "Tall guy, long brown hair, civilian clothes. Bloodstained shirt. Name is Florian Beck. He's probably trying to stay out of sight. Gauleiter Koch has a message for him."

They would quickly realize their error in their laughter toward me. I was, after all, soon to receive a medal. I cleared my throat. "Excuse me, sir, but I may be able to deliver that message to your desired party."

The soldier threw a glance at me over his shoulder. "I wasn't talking to you. Get lost." The girls giggled.

They were dismissing me. Laughing at me. The familiar anger began to rise.

I did not serve this soldier.

I did not serve my father.

I served only one.

The one.

"Heil Hitler!" I yelled, slicing my right arm through the air in salute. I turned on my heel and walked out.

joana

I placed the baby in Emilia's arms and leaned down to whisper, "I told Dr. Richter I found a Latvian to translate. I think he believed me." Emilia didn't look convinced. I righted my posture and my voice. "Have you thought of a name yet?"

She nodded, smiling. "Halinka."

"Halinka. That's a beautiful name," I said.

"My mother's name was Halina. My father always called her Halinka."

I thought of my own father. How long would the Soviets occupy our country? Eva had said the occupation could last as long as ten years. That couldn't be true.

I heard the stiff step of boots. The blond Nazi entered the room.

"Good morning, Litwinka. Ready to sail?"

"Can't be soon enough," I replied. "What do you need?"

"Are you always so serious?" he asked, sauntering toward me. "I was just down on E deck. The girls in the pool are much friendlier."

"Perhaps they're not as busy as I am."

"I'm busy too," he said. He removed his brimmed hat and placed it under his arm. "I'm still looking for your patient,

294   *Ruta Sepetys*

Florian Beck. The office received a return wire from Gauleiter Koch." He stared at me.

He was alone. Relaxed. If Florian was to be arrested, there would be rushing, searching, more soldiers. "What's the message?" I asked.

"Ah, you're interested?" he said.

My curiosity burned. I reluctantly gave him my best smile, trying to coax details from him. "A nurse is always interested in her patients."

"Can I be a patient?" he asked. His smugness was annoying. This was the type of man who looked at a picture on the wall and instead of admiring the photo, looked at his own reflection in the glass.

I forced myself to flirt with him and stepped in close. "Let's see how well you communicate with the nursing staff. Read me the message."

He removed a piece of paper from his pocket and read:

"*Have Beck contact me directly. Tell DRL dead. Keys needed. Urgent.*"

I repeated the message in my mind, memorizing it. I stepped away from him and back toward Emilia. Gauleiter Koch had sent a direct message. Florian wasn't lying.

"Well?" said the soldier.

"Sounds like you'd better deliver that message to Herr Beck."

"Yes, but he seems to have disappeared," he said.

"I told you, he wanted to board the *Hansa*."

"*Hansa* is pulling out now."

"Well, then I guess you've missed your chance, haven't you?"

florian

The Prussian. That's what Joana called me.

I thought of the Prussian flag, a black eagle on a white background. What would happen to the kingdom of Prussia and its forty million inhabitants? Its legacy reached back to the thirteenth century, but now lay crushed underfoot. Can history disappear if it's written in blood?

A noise roared. I nearly fell off the ledge in the chimney. My heart hammered.

Was it an alarm? An air raid?

And then I realized. It was the air horn.

The ship was finally departing.

I peeked through the seam in the steel and immediately wished I hadn't. The scene below was horrifying. I had never seen such desperation. Those left behind on the dock were frantic to come on board. Faces contorted as they screamed and begged.

Mothers tried hurling their infants to passengers up on deck, but they couldn't throw high enough. Their babies smashed against the side of the ship and plunged into the sea. Women screamed and dove into the water after the children. A man dressed as a woman was beaten by a sentry when he tried to rush the gangway. I watched it all from above, sick with sympathy as they cried and screamed that they would die if they were not allowed to board. The *Gustloff* was their only hope.

I clutched my pack, shaking my head in disbelief.

The *Gustloff* was my only hope, as well.

And I had made it.

alfred

Good afternoon, my little Lore!

I am elated to report that we have finally departed this infernal port. The gangways were lifted around 12:20 p.m. amidst the wails of the unworthy on the dock. We have exited the mouth of the harbor and are on our way to Kiel, cutting through the sea like Neptune with his trident. The weather, however, is proving a challenge. The winds blow fierce. We are battling quite a vicious snowstorm.

Unfortunately, our departure was not without incident. We are nearly ten times over capacity. My superior estimated that fifty thousand refugees still remained in the port when we pulled up anchor. The refugees screamed and cried, begging for passage. I tried to comfort them with the wisdom of Don Quixote and called out, "Until death, it is all life!" but that did not seem to bring them peace.

I feel quite exceptional to be taking part in Operation Hannibal's evacuation. Although I refuse to think of him, I daresay that man who is called my father would be proud if he should see me now. People speak of the Allies and their famous evacuations. But now Hannibal will soon reign in the history books. Speaking of history books, just think, Lore, your beloved will soon be receiving a medal. I will be officially recognized in the annals of German history . . . oh my . . . quite a lot of movement. The swaying. I'm sure this is temporary. They will steady the vessel. Yes, they must. Although I am of steely constitution, the other passengers cannot endure over forty hours of this. Certainly not.

I leaned over and threw up on my shoes.

emilia

As the hours passed, I felt increasingly nauseated. Joana said it was too cold and windy to take air on the top deck. Instead, she wrapped cold towels around my feet. It helped. Others were more seasick than I was. The baby slept, unbothered. After bouncing for months on the run, the sway of the sea soothed like a lullaby.

I hadn't planned for this. I was certain the birthing would kill both of us, just as it had Mama. Yet somehow, after five cruel winters of war, I was still alive. I adjusted the baby in my arms. What was happening? Could I have been wrong about the sign?

I had received the sign six years ago. It was Saint John's Night, the longest day of the year. Mama loved Saint John's celebration—a night of bonfires, singing, and dancing. The tradition called for girls to make wreaths of flowers and candles. At dark, they would light the candles and send their wreaths floating down the river. Legend said that the boy who retrieved your wreath downstream was the boy you would marry. The year Mama died, the older girls let me make a wreath of flowers and candles with them. I chose all of Mama's favorites—hibiscus, roses, poppies, and dried herbs.

After setting the wreaths to water, the girls danced around

the bonfire. I decided to follow my pretty wreath. I padded barefoot in the grass along the river, watching the flowers and candles turning slowly in the water. I walked quite far. My wreath suddenly bounced, catching on something beneath the surface. It stopped in the center of the river. One of the candles tipped onto the flowers. The herbs caught on fire.

I sat in the grass and watched my wreath burn and sink, quietly sealing my fate.

I had expected everything to end. But now, I began to think that maybe the sign had been wrong. I had fought so hard and overcome so much. Something changed when the knight arrived. Maybe he truly saved me, had pulled my burning wreath from the water. After all, in Poland, Saint Florian was fighter of fire.

For the first time in years, people cared for me. Protected me. I looked down at Halinka. I could actually feel her. She was mine. I was hers. Her perfect cheeks and fingers were pink, just like my hat. What the knight said was true. She was part of me, my family, and Poland.

I had to consider the possibility.

Maybe the storm was finally behind me.

florian

I waited in the chimney, shivering, still tormented by the departure scene on the dock. The ship swayed as it cut through the stormy swells. My stomach lifted up and then dangled back down. I had to think of what lay ahead.

When I left, the Amber Room was packed in crates in a secret underground room in Königsberg Castle. The map to the underground vault, along with the key, was still in my boot heel. Only three people knew of the location:

Me. Dr. Lange. Gauleiter Koch.

I thought of my father's maps and pictured Kiel, tucked within a crease of northern Germany. Kiel was approximately a hundred kilometers from Denmark and only eighty kilometers from where my sister was sent to live with our old greataunt. If I could get there, I would stash the swan in her barn until the war was over.

If.

That meant I would have to disembark in Kiel without incident. Without suspicion. If the blond soldier had told Koch that I was on the *Gustloff*, would someone be waiting for me in Kiel? The boat's motion was too severe to forge new papers. And then I remembered.

I dug through my pack and found it. The identity card of

302   *Ruta Sepetys*

the German soldier that the Polish girl had killed in the forest. When we reached Kiel, maybe I could leave the ship as a
wounded soldier.

But once again, I would need Joana's help.

alfred

Every lavatory was occupied or soiled. I stumbled to the infirmary, stepping over bundles of life jackets and coats that passengers had peeled off. The ship was so very hot, so foul-smelling of sickness. The last I overheard, we were carrying more than ten thousand passengers. Sailors were discussing whether the ship should follow a zigzag course to evade lurking submarines and whether the navigation lights would be illuminated. I was too sick to care.

The nurse was tending to soldiers when I arrived.

"I am here for self-admittance," I announced. My legs began to tremble. "Please show me to a cot immediately."

"Oh, Alfred, I'm sorry you're seasick. But this ward is for the wounded."

My stomach rolled in protest. "I am, in fact, wounded. My constitution has been destroyed by the enemy. The enemy is the sea."

"Is this your first voyage?" asked the nurse.

"Indeed, and at this moment I have pledged it shall be my last."

"Shake it off, sailor," said an officer from his cot. "Go up top and get some air. Look at the horizon."

"That really does help," agreed the nurse.

304   *Ruta Sepetys*

"Please," said a wounded soldier. "Don't baby this guy. He loses his lunch and he's crying? I've lost an arm."

I tried to turn in his direction. "Seeing that your safe delivery to Kiel relies upon me, sir, perhaps you should have a bit more compassion for a fellow comrade. I will remember this." I walked out of the infirmary and slumped against a wall in the corridor.

Dear Hannelore,

It is at crossroads such as these that my mind often questions the very integrity of man. Forgive me if I speak beyond your comprehension, but if we share unity of purpose, stand upon the same team, shouldn't we try our best to assist one another? I fondly remember when we were once on the same team. It was for a game in the street. Do you recall it? You were wearing a short pleated skirt and a green ribbon in your hair. The game was brief because your mother quickly called you away, but for those fleeting moments, Lore, we were joined in common purpose. Purpose and principles are so very important.

It confounds me when people don't assist or even welcome those on their own team. But it troubles me more when people welcome those from an opposing team. Have you ever considered these thoughts, Hannelore? Have you ever reflected on this idea with regard to your own mother and father, how your mother's perfection was chipped by her judgment? I once asked your mother why she chose to marry your father. Do you know how she replied? She said the oddest thing.

"Because I love him."

joana

"I promise."

Was it the way he said it? Was there something that lingered behind it? Or was it just my own pathetic loneliness that made me grab the scissors?

Florian appeared as I was walking between the maternity ward and the infirmary. I hadn't been sure he was still on board. Secretly, I was happy to see him. Why was it so hard to stay angry with some people?

"Please. It will only take a few minutes." He smiled. "I promise."

I quickly followed him to the stairs. He leapt up, taking them in twos, agile even with his pack. We crept through the small doorway in the stairwell up to the chimney.

"Are you sure you want me to do this?" I said.

"It's the best option I have right now." He leaned his back against the door. "In case someone tries to open it."

"Move your foot," I told him. I stepped between his legs. "Okay, now come down a bit." He shimmied his back down the door, sliding his legs alongside mine until our faces were level.

"How much?" I asked.

"As much as you can."

306 *Ruta Sepetys*

I ran my fingers through his hair, trying to stand it up at the roots. That would make it easier to cut. It was thick and soft near the scalp. "You have nice hair," I told him.

He reached out and gently slid one of my curls between his fingers. He closed his eyes. "Maybe you'd better start."

I grasped a piece of his hair with my left hand and snipped with my right. He opened his eyes and looked at the chunk suspended in my fingers. We both laughed.

I cut most of the hair and then trimmed as tight to the scalp as I could. It was difficult near his ears. I moved in close, trying to be as gentle as possible. He put his hands on my waist. Was he keeping a safe distance between us?

"Don't worry, I'm not going to kiss you. I'm hard at work here," I teased. He didn't reply.

"So," he said awkwardly, trying to make conversation. "I've been to Lithuania."

He was being honest. I decided I should be too. "I know," I told him. "The first night in the barn, when I took out the shrapnel. You said some things."

His face clouded. "Oh?"

"You said you had once visited Lithuania. You also said you had to recover to find Anni."

"Oh, well, that's not too bad. I already told you that Anni is my sister."

I nodded and clipped closer to his scalp. "And you told me I was pretty. You said you were a good dancer and asked if I had a boyfriend."

"Well, that's . . . embarrassing," he said.

SALT TO THE SEA   *307*

"You were delirious. You didn't know what you were saying." I continued cutting, aware of both the silence and the sensation of his hands around my waist. He finally spoke.

"The night that I said those things—did you tell me anything?"

I stopped clipping and looked at him. I nodded. His fingers pressed gently against my back. He pulled me in closer. Then closer still. I put my mouth to his ear. It was barely a whisper.

"I told you that I'm a murderer."

florian

Her hips were in my hands. Her lips were on my ear. And then the word came out of her mouth.

Murderer.

I moved my head back and laughed. "That's supposed to be my good ear, but it sounded like you said 'murderer.'"

She said nothing, just stared at me, her eyes pooling with tears. What? She wasn't joking?

"I," she began slowly, taking a breath, "killed my cousin."

I felt my eyes widen. She nodded. Tears dropped onto her cheeks.

"My—my cousin Lina," she stammered. "She was my best friend. When we fled from Lithuania, my father repeatedly told me not to leave anything or speak to anyone. But I couldn't leave without saying good-bye to Lina."

Tears streamed down Joana's cheeks. Her breathing fluttered. It pained me to see her crying.

"I wrote her a letter, explaining that we were on Stalin's list because my father had joined an anti-Soviet group. I gave the letter to our cook and asked her to mail it. I never should have put those things in writing. After we fled, the NKVD ransacked our house. My father's secret contact wrote to us and said the NKVD had my letter."

SALT TO THE SEA   309

"The cook gave your letter to the NKVD?"

"Yes," she whispered. "My mother said she was probably trying to protect herself. When the Soviets came looking for us we were gone. But based on my letter they located Lina's family and took them instead. My father's contact corresponded with Lina's neighbor. She said they were arrested and deported to Siberia."

She tried to wipe her tears. "Two years ago our neighbor sent a letter with a coded message saying that my uncle was tortured and died in a gulag."

I pulled her in to me. The pieces slid into place. Joana felt responsible for her cousin being sent to Siberia.

"When was that?" I whispered.

"Four years ago. June of '41," she cried.

From what I'd heard, Stalin's torture in Siberian gulags was brutal. Her cousin was probably dead. I wanted to say something to comfort her, but I wasn't good at this kind of thing. "Maybe she got away somehow. Maybe she's still alive."

Joana brightened. "Do you think so?" she asked. She dabbed her eyes. "I feel so guilty. My freedom cost her family their lives. The drawing you found in my suitcase. It was from Lina. She was so talented and was just about to start art school."

"Stop talking about her in past tense. She could be back in Lithuania soon." The positivity seemed to comfort her.

We stood in silence. Her honesty and guilt, they made me like her even more. I tried to wipe her tears. She resumed my haircut.

"So what are you going to do when we arrive in Kiel?" she asked.

Kiss you, I wanted to say.

"Let's see. First, try not to get arrested. Second, try to find my sister and protect her until the war ends. What about you?"

"Try to communicate with my mother to find out about my family." She finished cutting and brushed the hair off my shoulders.

"There you are, Prussian. I think it looks nice. You could use a shave though."

My hands were still on her hips. I stared at the amber pendant around her neck. "Call me Florian, not Prussian, okay?" I pulled her close. "And I wasn't delirious," I whispered. "I do think you're pretty. Take a break and meet me later," I told her. "Let's meet here at nine thirty."

She seemed to think about it, then smiled and nodded. She moved toward the door. "I wasn't going to tell you because I was mad, but that blond soldier came by before we sailed. He received a message from Koch," she said.

My head snapped up.

"Yes. It said, 'Have Beck contact me directly. Tell DRL dead. Keys needed. Urgent.'" She reached out and touched my cheek. "See you at nine thirty." Joana slipped out the small door.

A root twisted in my stomach. Dr. Lange was dead. Who had gotten to him?

I would be next.

SALT TO THE SEA   311

emilia

Joana returned, smiling. Had she left to see the knight? When birds pair, their plumage becomes more vibrant. I noticed that with the knight and Joana. Their feathers had changed since we arrived in the port. Something was happening between them.

The deep swaying of the ship increased. "The weather must be getting worse out there," Joana commented, looking toward the ceiling. "We're lucky to be inside."

Cheerful melodies piped through the ship's speakers. The music was suddenly interrupted by an anniversary radio broadcast from Adolf Hitler. Exactly twelve years ago to this day, January 30, he was appointed chancellor of Germany. It was hard for me to understand Hitler's German as he yelled through the speakers. I caught one sentence and it gave me shivers.

"When was the helpless goose ever not eaten by the fox?"

alfred

I collapsed among the refugees on the floor of the music room. My throat burned from the nonstop retching of phantoms in my stomach.

A little girl played with a floppy stuffed bear near my feet. She stopped and stared at me for a long while.

"Stupid girl, it isn't polite to stare. Especially at someone in my condition," I informed her.

She giggled, bent her bear over at the waist, and pretended it was vomiting.

"Oh, isn't that funny?" I reached out and clawed a button eye from the bear's face.

florian

I made my way down to A deck to check on the wandering boy. He slept, his head in the shoe poet's lap.

"You've cut your hair. You look almost respectable." The old man laughed. "Sit a while. Rest. The ship is doing the traveling for us."

"Yes, at least we don't have to walk," I said.

"Ah, but remember, the poet Emerson said that when we have worn out our shoes, the strength of the journey has passed into our body." He nodded and winked. "Wisdom pays the largest debt to his shoemaker."

We sat in silence. I admired this kind man. Why couldn't I have apprenticed with someone like him, instead of Dr. Lange? If I had listened to my father, how different would things be? I gestured to the boy. "He's lucky to have you."

"No, I am the lucky one," said the shoe poet. "The boy keeps me kicking." He looked at me and his face softened. He extended his hand. "I'm Heinz," he said.

I shook his hand. "Florian."

He held my hand for an extra beat, staring at me. "The children and young people, you are the unlucky ones. This war has murdered many futures. Are your parents still alive?" he asked.

314 *Ruta Sepetys*

I shook my head.

"Ah, I thought so," he said, patting my knee. "You are a wandering boy too."

"Will you give the little one to the Red Cross in Kiel?" I asked.

"I don't think I could bear it," said the shoemaker. "I quite like being *Opi*. I've got the address in Berlin that was pinned to his coat. I'll take him there myself and see what comes of it." He sighed. "But who knows how long Berlin will hold. Do you have other family?" he asked.

"A sister, Anni. I haven't seen her in three years. I don't know if I'd recognize her."

"You'll recognize her. Your feet will steer you in her direction." The old man leaned back and hummed the melody of "Lili Marleen." It made me think of Joana.

"Are you married, Heinz?" I asked.

"I spent fifty-five years with the love of my life. I lost her last July." He gestured to the boy. "Just when you think this war has taken everything you loved, you meet someone and realize that somehow you still have more to give."

"I know what you mean," I said, looking at my watch.

"I know you do." He smiled. "And she's worth it too."

SALT TO THE SEA   315

joana

9:15 p.m.

Fifteen minutes. Then I would see Florian. I smiled, remembering Eva's comment that he wasn't too young for me. I hoped Eva was comfortable on the *Hansa*.

BANG!

A massive jolt. My head hit the wall. Lights flickered.

Emilia was on the floor.

What was happening?

BANG!

Total blackness. Women screamed.

BANG!

Alarm bells shrilled. The entire maternity ward suddenly tilted toward the front of the ship. Dim emergency lights began to glow.

emilia

BANG!

My body was thrown from the cot.

I hit the floor.

BANG!

Pitch-black. I crawled. I couldn't see the baby.

I yelled for Joana.

BANG!

Screaming.

Glass breaking.

Alarms ringing.

alfred

We were twenty-five nautical miles offshore.

BANG!

Something slammed into the port side of the ship.

What was that?

BANG!

Another explosion. Darkness. I could not breathe.

BANG!

Panicked screams filled my head. My body shifted.

The ship was listing.

The nose was going under.

florian

BANG!

Our bodies slammed into each other.

The old man grabbed my arm. "Did we hit a mine?" he whispered.

BANG!

The little boy stirred. "Opi?"

"Yes, yes. I'm right here." The old man quickly tightened the straps on the boy's life vest.

BANG!

And then I knew.

Torpedoes.

joana

I stood, not knowing what to do. Where were Dr. Wendt and Dr. Richter? I helped a screaming pregnant woman off the floor. She gripped my arm in terror.

"Please. Help me!" she pleaded.

Emilia grabbed Halinka. She wrapped her in a pillowcase and then quickly spiraled a sheet around her. She looked at me and shouted, pointing up with her finger.

The ship's tilt increased. Everything in the room slid. The pregnant woman's nails pierced my skin.

Emilia sprang into action. She put on her coat and pink hat, grabbed a life vest from the corner and tied it on. She held the swaddled baby in one arm and threw life vests from the corner to everyone. I grabbed a vest with my free arm and put it around the pregnant woman.

"Let's all stay calm," I said. "We'll wait for Dr. Wendt or one of the captains to advise us. I'm sure they'll make an announcement."

"No!" Emilia yelled, gesturing frantically. "Coat. It's cold. Up. Now!"

Emilia was saying we had to go up top into the cold.

Emilia was saying the ship was sinking.

320   *Ruta Sepetys*

emilia

The image of the burning, sinking wreath flashed before my eyes. Noise increased from the corridor.

I called out to the women. "Hurry! Take your coats. Wrap up. The cold will kill you." Was anyone listening? Did they understand me? Didn't they realize that we had to get out of the metal container?

The boat carried more people than the population of some cities. I thought of the ship's many levels. Thousands of passengers would surge toward the top. The stairways would be jammed. No one was moving fast enough. I ran around the area, swatting at them like pigeons.

Joana wanted to wait for instructions. No.

We had to move. Now.

I looked down at the tiny baby. Her eyes were open wide, staring into mine.

She began to cry.

alfred

Emergency lights blinked on. A sailor ran through the heaps of refugees, instructing everyone to put on life vests.

"What happened?" I yelled to him.

"Torpedoes. A Russian sub."

We had been torpedoed by a Russian submarine? The ship's list increased dramatically. Things began sliding down the angled floor.

Suddenly, the grand piano in the music room rolled fast, crushing the little girl with the bear in its path before crashing into the wall and releasing a discordant cry. Passengers shrieked and wailed, trying to help the girl who now resembled smashed fruit.

Burning bile rose in my throat.

A woman sitting nearby held her infant out to me and screamed. "Help us! What do we do?" She reached for me.

I picked up the life vest near the feet of the mangled girl. I slipped it over my head.

"You should probably leave," I told the woman.

I pushed my way to the stairs.

florian

The corridor was jammed with passengers.

"Torpedoes! The submarine is under the ship," someone yelled. Panic flared into a desperate rush of yelling and pushing.

I slung my pack onto my back. I grabbed the little boy and picked him up.

"Do we have to leave the boat?" asked the boy.

"Yes. Hang on to my middle. Tight. Do not let go."

"Opi!" yelled the boy.

"Yes, yes, Opi's here," said the shoe poet. "I'm here."

"Do you have our coins?" called the boy.

"Yes, I have the coins," he replied.

My mind raced through the layout of the ship. We were on A deck, front dining hall. We had to climb up, two decks to Joana. Then up to the sundeck. I thought of the four levels below us. The boat tilted farther. Frantic screams splintered through the dark passageway. We would soon be trapped.

"Hurry," shouted the old man. "Wait, Florian, where's your life vest?" he asked me.

Alarm bells continued to shriek.

"Walk in front of me," I yelled to the shoemaker. "I can lift you if I need to."

The boy on my front, my pack on my back, we pushed our

SALT TO THE SEA   323

way through the sea of people toward the stairs. The boy clung to my neck, his legs around my stomach, feet locked at the ankles under my pack.

The width of the crowd knocked the fire extinguisher from the wall in the stairwell. It fell and exploded, sending foam everywhere. People began to slip and fall. Others simply scrambled over them. I felt the crunch of bodies underfoot in the dark and the little boy's panting breaths in my hair. I pushed Poet up in front of me. People grabbed and clawed at my back. I leaned forward, trying to stay upright. And then I felt a pull on my shoulder. It was the strap on my pack.

It snapped.

joana

Announcements crackled through the speaker system.

"Remain calm. Proceed in an orderly manner to the top deck."

Dr. Wendt burst into the maternity ward.

"Don't listen to the announcements. Get the women on deck and into lifeboats. Quickly!"

"What should we take?" I asked, moving toward my suitcase.

"Nothing!" he said. "Just take your life vest, hurry!"

I corralled the women out of the ward and directed them to the stairwell. The hallway was already flooded. Where was Emilia? Icy water seeped through my boots.

"Erika!" a desperate man shrieked. "Erika, where are you?"

The boat was nose-first and tilting left, to port side. The stairs slanted at an awkward angle, making them even more difficult to climb. The lifeless body of a child lay trampled near the stairs. I tried to stop and pick him up but the surge of the crowd knocked me forward.

Thousands of piercing screams filled the stairwell. "We're going to drown!" a woman cried. A gunshot echoed somewhere below. Further panic swelled through the mass of people on the stairs. I was moving but not sure I was even walking. People clambered over one another as they climbed. The weaker ones fell backward and were sucked underfoot, unable to pull themselves up.

The stairway became choked. The ship tilted deeper into the water. The woman was right.

We were all going to drown.

alfred

I ran downhill along the tilting corridor, freezing water up to my knees. A small boy swam by me. All of the passengers seemed to be going the other way. But I knew something they didn't. There were interior ladders inside the ventilation ducts. I pushed past people, continuing on my way.

"Sailor, please," someone called out behind me.

I reached the end of the corridor. Another sailor appeared. He grabbed me by the shirt.

"Hurry, we have to get everyone out of the cabins and up on deck!" he said.

"How severe is it?" I asked.

"Three torpedoes. E deck, the engine room, and the forward compartments are destroyed."

E deck. The swimming pool. The naval auxiliary girls were on E deck. The sailors' bunks were in the forward compartments.

The sound of joists snapping and rivets popping echoed through the stairwell.

"She's going down," said the sailor. "Grab a coat if you can find one." I followed him onto the upper promenade deck, taking a coat from a woman who was struggling with her life vest.

The sailor began smashing and breaking open cabin doors

SALT TO THE SEA   327

that had jammed. He shuttled people toward the stairs. "Come on!" he shouted to me. "Get these people out!"

"Yes, everyone, hurry," I said to myself. I opened a door.

A woman and child lay bloody on the floor. In the center of the cabin, a naval officer stood with a gun to his head.

I watched, somehow fascinated. Would he do it?

He turned and pointed the gun at me.

I ran back to the ventilation ducts.

I am a thinker. I am thinking.

Torpedo strike: Approximately 9:15 p.m.

Ship's capacity: 1,463.

Passengers on board: 10,573.

Lifeboats: 22.

But then I remembered.

Ten of the lifeboats were missing.

emilia

I made it to the top deck. Snow whipped, stinging my face. I clutched the baby. The wind lashed, trying to pull us over. The nose of the *Gustloff* was already beneath the water and the ship was rolling onto its left side. The icy deck glimmered, slick. I crouched down and crawled with Halinka, speaking to her in Polish. *Nie płacz.* Don't cry.

The night was dark. The sea churned, boiling and angry. Huge waves crashed against the ship. A sailor fired a flare. It soared high, a red shooting star illuminating an endless snow-filled sky. Frantic passengers tried to run as soon as they emerged from the stairs. I watched as they slipped and skidded across the icy deck, screaming and plunging into the water like human raindrops.

People cried. They fought. Sailors yelled. A grown woman kicked a teenager out of the way, ignoring her pleas for help. I stopped and crouched farther down with Halinka, holding her soft, warm body close to mine. I sang *All the little duckies* and hooked one arm around a metal railing on the deck. The ship submerged deeper into the sea.

Sailors struggled with the frozen winches that held the lifeboats on the left side.

The lifeboats on the right side were unusable, suspended high out of the water.

But I wasn't looking for a lifeboat.

I was looking for the knight.

florian

We made it to the top deck.

"Hang on to me," I yelled to the old man.

"Wait. It's slippery. Our shoes will slide," shouted the shoe-maker. "We must crawl."

Hordes of people emerged onto the icy deck. A man began to run. His feet slipped out beneath him. His body sailed through the air, his back snapping in two against the ship's rail before bouncing into the sea.

I saw a lifeboat, only half full, lowered into the water. It had two sailors in it. The winds and sea spray whipped against our faces, making it hard to see or even move. People scrambled to the next boat, fighting and jumping to get in. Someone cut the back rope but the front rope didn't release. The boat overturned and dangled, spilling all of the people into the deep black to drown.

Screams of death filled my good ear. The other half of my head felt detached, muted.

"Where is your life vest?" yelled the shoemaker to me as he clutched the wandering boy.

I had been hiding. I hadn't been issued a vest.

Some passengers dove off the ship rather than wait for a boat. Countless bodies bobbed in life vests in the water.

"Look for our girls," said the shoemaker. "Where are the girls?"

SALT TO THE SEA   *331*

joana

I emerged up top into the freezing wind and snow.

I had lost sight of Emilia on the stairs. I yelled for her and looked for her pink hat. Dr. Wendt and Dr. Richter were already on deck loading the wounded into a boat. I directed the remaining pregnant women to them. They gave me a life vest. I put my arms through it and tied the strings in the front.

"Please," a girl cried to me. "My cousin is down on the lower deck. Please, help me go find her."

Her cousin. Thousands were on the lower decks. Thousands were trapped.

The ship suddenly groaned and shifted into a deeper tilt.

"Get in a boat. Now!" I yelled to the girl. I directed her toward a lifeboat.

I grabbed a railing near the staircase. A loud *crash* thundered from behind. The enormous anti-aircraft weaponry slid across the deck, broke through the rail, and smashed onto a lifeboat that had just been lowered. The weapons, the boat, and all of the passengers sank quickly beneath the surface.

A scream erupted from within me.

Ruta Sepetys

alfred

I had made it up top. Everyone was screaming. Screaming was not thinking. Passengers struggled toward the rail and the lifeboats. I watched them cry, yell, and beg for help. Beg for life.

The scene played as if to music. People looked to me, eyes panting and desperate. Their hands reached for me in choreographed synchronization.

Save me. Save me. Save me.

We crawled on the slippery deck. An injured woman grabbed my ankle.

"Please, help me!" she shrieked. The salt of her tears had smudged her eye makeup.

I nodded. Yes, she would need help to fix her ruined face.

Panic required me to take action. I could not. The chaos disrupted my ability to focus, pulling me instead from reaction to observation. My arm began moving, turning the invisible crank of Death's music box. Somewhere inside, I didn't want the melody to end. I saw Captain Petersen lowered with passengers in a boat. My intelligence then called to me. If our captain was leaving, surely I should depart as well.

A lifeboat. Yes, I would get in a lifeboat.

The blisters on my hands popped and bled. I wiped them off on the wool coat I had taken from the passenger. I shoved through the thick crowd to the rail. And then I saw the recruit, the old man, and the little boy.

The recruit was screaming. Veins bulged in his neck. His mouth contorted as he summoned all of his strength to roar one, single word.

Joana.

florian

The few remaining boats were filling fast. My pack swung from my shoulder on the single strap, causing me to slip and lose balance.

I saw the pink hat through the crowd. And then I saw Joana. The Polish girl was crawling behind with the baby. I moved through the throngs of people toward them. The sailor, Alfred, crept slowly in my direction.

"Joana, Emilia, hurry! Women and children first," I yelled.

Joana turned, saw the Polish girl, and grabbed her.

"Hurry!" I repeated to Joana. "Get in the boat. I'll help her in with the baby."

"Take the little one," shouted Poet, frantically pushing the wandering boy through the crowd. "Please, take him," he pleaded.

"*Opi!*" the boy screamed, fighting to get back to the shoemaker.

A sailor helped Joana down a rope ladder into the lifeboat. She reached up for the baby.

The Polish girl refused. She motioned for me to get into the swaying boat.

People pushed past. The boat began to fill.

"*Go!* Get into the boat!" I yelled.

"She only trusts you," shouted Joana. "She wants you to bring the baby down."

"Damn it." I handed Alfred my pack. "Hold this."

The shoe poet tossed a life vest over my head. I took the baby from the Polish girl and climbed down into the boat.

"There's too many people," someone screamed. "We're going to capsize."

"Only one more," a sailor said.

"Wait! *No!*" I yelled. "We have more people."

"One more," the sailor repeated.

"Emilia, hurry!" screamed Joana.

Emilia stared at us from above, then quickly pushed the wandering boy into the boat on top of us. The ropes snapped and our boat dropped down into the water.

Emilia was still on deck.

I was holding her baby.

Alfred was still on deck.

He was holding my pack.

joana

Our boat dropped down into the black water.

I screamed for Emilia.

Florian screamed for his pack.

Huge waves battered and tossed us. A woman vomited in her lap. A deep rumbling sounded from the ship as it slid farther beneath the water. The wandering boy stood up in our lifeboat, his tiny arms stretched up toward the ship. "*Opi*," he wailed. "*Opi!*"

A tuft of white hair appeared. "I'm coming, Klaus!" echoed from above. The shoe poet leapt feetfirst off the ship, plummeting toward the sea.

"Poet!" I screamed.

He plunged into the water nearby. Florian handed me the baby and jumped up to dive in after him. A wave threw our boat and Florian stumbled, slamming onto the pin holding the oar. The wandering boy grabbed his coat. The boat pitched and hurled.

"Row away," someone yelled. "When the ship goes under it will suck us down with it."

"Wait," said the wandering boy, frantically searching the water. "Wait for my Opi."

SALT TO THE SEA   *337*

"Heinz!" Florian called into the darkness, his voice breaking with emotion. "Heinz, are you there?"

But the shoe poet did not reappear.

Florian grabbed my arm. "The sack of coins. The old man tied the bag to his belt. He gave me his life vest."

"*Opi!*" sobbed the wandering boy. "No, please, *Opi.*"

Poet.

Our blessed shoe poet. Our Opi.

Our one light in the darkness.

He was gone.

alfred

The lifeboat was in the water. I was not in it.

No operable boats remained.

Some people had jumped down after the lifeboats. I was not a good jumper.

I was afraid to jump.

Shouting. Crying. Gunshots.

The ship slid deeper into the sea.

And then someone was pulling, yanking at me.

The young Latvian woman who gave birth was screaming in my face and dragging me. The ship's list increased and so did my terror. I stumbled behind the girl, my back feeling so heavy. And then we passed two rafts, stuck together with ice. She began kicking at them frantically, to dislodge them from the deck. One of the rafts came loose. The girl pulled me down onto it.

And then we began to slide.

emilia

The raft was sheet steel with large buoyancy floats on each end. Planks of wood stretched across the tanks with netting in between. The ship tilted and our raft began to skid. Like a winter sled racing down an icy hill, we skated across the deck.

Metal scraping. People screaming.

I grasped tightly to the netting. Our raft launched out into the sea.

Items tumbled into the water behind us with a splash. Luggage. Empty rafts. Empty bodies.

A crowded lifeboat floated nearby. Drowning people in the water clung to the edges of the boat, desperately trying to pull themselves in.

"Please," begged a teenage boy. "I'm so cold. Please let me in." He gripped the side of the lifeboat, struggling to pull himself up.

"It's too crowded. It will capsize," argued the people in the boat.

"Could you please warm my hands then? *Please, help me?*"

They did not warm his hands. They beat at the teenager's fingers until he released his grip and slipped beneath the surface with a few small bubbles.

"Come!" I yelled to the people in the water. "We have room

on the raft." And then an enormous wave lifted the raft and pulled us away from the sinking ship.

How foolish to believe we are more powerful than the sea or the sky. I watched from the raft as the beautiful deep began to swallow the massive boat of steel.

In one large gulp.

joana

The baby. The wandering boy. What was I to do?

florian

The Polish girl. My pack. Where were they?

emilia

The knight. He had the baby. I knew he'd be a savior.

alfred

Bodies were strewn like human confetti. Would I still get my medal?

florian

The tail of the ship was all that remained sticking out of the water. People dangled from the railings, their legs swinging wildly. The glass-enclosed sundeck at the back of the ship was packed with hundreds of trapped passengers. They banged their desperate fists against the glass. The water inside rose higher and higher. A brave sailor, balancing on the stern, hacked at the glass with an ax, trying to free the trapped people. The glass would not break. He swung harder, then lost his balance and fell into the sea. We watched in horror as the people behind the glass began to drown.

A lifeboat floated near the back of the *Gustloff*. In it sat a captain and several sailors.

Thousands of lifeless bodies floated around us. I searched for Heinz and the sailor with my pack. A young girl kicked and shrieked in the water next to our lifeboat.

I removed my life vest and threw it to her. "Grab my hand," I told her.

"No!" yelled a woman in our boat. "She'll turn us over!"

I stood and leaned over the side. Our lifeboat tipped toward the water. Everyone screamed. I reached down and grabbed the girl by her hair. She gripped my arm and I pulled her into the boat. She fell, soaked and exhausted at our feet.

A woman in a fur coat yelled at me. "You had no right! You're endangering everyone!"

"Shut up!" I roared. My body shook with anger. "Do you hear me? Shut up!" Everyone fell quiet. The wandering boy hid his crying face in the crook of his arm. Joana reached up to me.

I slumped down beside her and dropped my head into my hands.

Fate is a hunter.

Its barrel pressed against my forehead.

joana

The dark air was full of screams. Snow and sleet blew horizontally, battering our faces. A lifeboat near ours was sandwiched full of crying women and children. Florian saw them and stood up.

"They need someone to row their boat."

My free hand grabbed at his back. "Stay," I begged him. "Please, Florian. Stay with me."

"I'll go." The husband of the woman in the fur coat stood up. The woman yelled and berated her husband as he bravely jumped from our boat into the other.

Floating in the sea of black, we were forced to witness the massive and grotesque deaths of thousands of people. I clutched the baby tight and closed my eyes. But the scenes continued to play in my mind: The severely angled deck. A woman throwing her baby down to a sailor. He reached. He missed. The child hit the steel raft and then rolled off into the sea. Thousands of desperate people jumping, kicking, gulping. Seawater filling mouths and nostrils, collapsing lungs. High waves, angry sea, snow, and wind.

The injured soldier who had begged for a kiss now floated dead near our lifeboat, his head strangled in the netting of a raft. So many people needed my help. And now I could do nothing. The frigid temperature of the water would induce immediate and lethal stress on their hearts. They would die of hypothermia. Instead of helping, I was forced to watch the panorama of catastrophe unroll before my eyes.

Guilt is a hunter.

I was its hostage.

emilia

A whitecap tossed us beyond a cluster of rafts, most of them empty. Less than an hour had passed since the ship was torpedoed. Thousands of dead bodies, eyes wide, floated frozen in life vests. In the darkness, closer to the sinking ship, I thought I could make out the silhouette of lifeboats. We were much farther from the ship than the others. The sailor was sick into the water. I pulled the pack from his arm. He thanked me and leaned farther over the edge of the raft.

I had the knight's pack.

The knight had the baby.

The knight would want his pack.

I wanted my baby.

Pain ripped through my chest. I wanted her. I wanted my baby.

A deep popping came from the ship. Its bones were snapping, breaking from the contortion pressure. The rounded stern sloped vertically toward the sky. People dangled from the railings, screaming. Others plummeted backward to their death. An explosion detonated from within the boat under the water. Suddenly, the entire ship lit up. A blaze of glittering lights brightly illuminated the water and the grotesque scene. I stared at the massive twinkling ship. A groan, like a deep

Ruta Sepetys

yawn, sent echoes across the waves into my face. And then the lights vanished. The boat disappeared into the black. The huge steel city—and thousands trapped inside—was sinking to the bottom of the sea.

A momentary quiet followed, leaving nothing but the sound of the wind and waves. We bobbed up and back, up and back, waves lapping and curling, the sound of crying filtering through the dark.

Next to me in the water, a young woman floated silently in a life vest. Her skirt rose up in a perfect circle around her. She turned in slow pirouette, dead arms outstretched, snow dusting her dark hair like powdered sugar. A set of false teeth drifted by on a piece of wood and faded into the darkness.

The lifeboats were too far away to yell. I didn't have an oar. I scanned the water for something to row with. Bobbing all around us were tiny children. The weight of their heads, the heaviest part of their bodies, had flipped them over in their life vests. With each wave, small corpses knocked against my raft. I was surrounded by hundreds of drowned children, heads in the water, their little feet in the air.

> *All the little duckies, with their heads in the water*
> *Heads in the water.*

It was my punishment. Honor lost. Everything lost.
Shame is a hunter.
My shame was all around me now.

alfred

My angel, Hannelore,

The night is dark. I scarcely know where to begin. I am floating on a buoyed raft in the Baltic Sea. My ship, the Wilhelm Gustloff, she is gone. We left Gotenhafen at lunchtime on January 30. I thought it such a perfect departure date. After all, January 30 was the birthday of Wilhelm Gustloff, for whom the ship was named, and also the anniversary of Hitler's rise to power.

The voyage began this afternoon, with more than ten thousand passengers on board. Yes, ten thousand. I was gripped with seasickness from the start. It was crippling in a way that forced interruption of my duties.

Several hours into our journey to Kiel, at precisely 9:15 p.m. per my watch, the ship was struck by three torpedoes. It began to sink. Alarm bells hammered and we were mustered to boat stations. Passengers were seized with savage panic. It would be inappropriate for me to document the scene for you. You see, the dark corridors I ran through felt like a lumpy mattress, the kind I detest. But I soon realized that it was, in fact, a carpet of bodies that I was walking over. The three explosions tore not only through the ship, but also the passengers. I asked a young girl in the corridor to move. When she didn't respond, I nudged her. Her round

352   *Ruta Sepetys*

head, the shape of a summer peach, rolled and she was missing half of her face. I can't stop thinking of it. I'm grateful you weren't here to witness such haunting devastation.

The sinking took just under sixty minutes. The Gustloff's final dive will pull her deep, to the bottom of the Baltic Sea. I estimate the water temperature to be approximately four degrees Centigrade at this time of year. It is quite impossible for a body to survive in that cold for any length of time. As a result, the many thousands of people I now see in the water will surely perish, despite their life vests. I am fortunate to have station on a raft, joined by a young Latvian woman whose newborn baby was snatched into a lifeboat without her. The waves are enormous and I am plagued with illness, constantly spilling my stomach over the side of the raft. My uniform is soiled. I seem to be missing a shoe.

Floating amidst this darkness and death, I have time not only for reflection but for honesty. I am now faced with the unbearable truth. How, Lore, could I truly love you? I could not, I should not—not after what you said, what you so rudely announced to everyone in the street. Yet the infatuation preserves and satiates me in an indescribable way. Perhaps it fences the fear.

So I cling to it.

You see, fear is a hunter. It encircles us when we are unarmed and least expect it. And then we are forced to make decisions.

I made the right decision. I tried to help.

You tried to pull your shade, to keep me out. Your decision, Hannelore, was the wrong one.

florian

"The ship, it's under," said Joana, her teeth chattering. Her voice was barely a whisper.

I counted nearly fifty people in our large lifeboat. We could have fit more.

The shoemaker.

The Polish girl.

Gone.

The cold on the open water would kill us. I called out to the little boy and pulled him onto my lap. I turned my body and straddled the bench in the boat. "Do the same," I told Joana. "We'll put the kids between us. Put the baby under your blouse and coat, against your skin."

She turned toward me, holding the baby. I moved as close as I could. I wrapped my arms around her, sheltering the children from the elements. Our heads touched.

"Can you hear me?" Joana whispered. Her voice sounded thin, frightened.

I nodded and turned my good ear toward her.

"It's so cold. Will anyone come for us?" she asked.

The air was black. The moon hid behind the clouds, unable to stomach the wretched scene. I looked out across the water, thousands of corpses floating silently. So many children. The girl I had pulled into the boat was already dead. She lay blue and lifeless at our feet. How would the Nazis report the news of the sinking? But then I realized.

They wouldn't report it at all.

"Will anyone come for us?" repeated Joana.

"Yes," I lied. "Someone will come for us."

With the threat of Russian submarines in the area, most ships would probably detour to avoid us.

Everything I ran with was in my pack—my papers, the forged documents, my notebook, and the swan. All the running, the hiding, the lies, the killing, for what? The endless circle of revenge: answering pain by inflicting pain. Why did I do it?

The strange sailor had not made it to a lifeboat. There were none left. I looked down at my boots. My heel was still intact. Had the map and key survived? Did it matter? Water slowly crept through a crack in the bottom of our boat. The precious treasure would end up at the bottom of the Baltic.

So would I.

Maybe the Amber Room truly did carry a curse.

During my weeks on the run I had imagined every scenario. I had counted all of the ways I could die. They were gruesome, frightening. I had carefully planned how I would defend myself, what weapon I would use. But this, I had never imagined. How do you defend yourself against the prolonged, insufferable agony of knowing you will surrender to the sea?

SALT TO THE SEA   355

joana

The black water lapped against the side of the boat. Snow drifted down around us. In the quiet dark, Florian began telling me things. He told me of his mother, how he missed her, how he mourned the mistakes with his father. He spoke of many people and places.

He was telling me things now because he knew we were going to die.

I thought of my mother, waiting patiently for me to arrive, worrying about her only daughter, perhaps her only surviving family member. How would she hear the news? Everyone knew the story of the big ships, *Titanic* and *Lusitania*. I looked toward the thousands of corpses floating in the water. This was so much larger. More than ten thousand people had been on board the *Gustloff*. The gruesome details of the sinking would be reported in every world newspaper. The tragedy would be studied for years, become legendary.

I sat, wrapped up with a handsome thief, an orphan boy and a newborn baby between us. I thought of Emilia standing on the deck of the *Gustloff* in the freezing wind, handing her baby to Florian. She had looked down at us in the lifeboat, her blond hair blowing beneath her pink hat.

"One more."

That's what the sailor had said.

Most would have fought to be "the one." They would have insisted they ought to be "the one." But Emilia had pushed the wandering boy into the boat, sacrificing herself for another. Where was she now? Had she gotten into a boat? I thought of frightened yet brave Emilia, and I started to cry.

I wanted my mother. My mother loved Lithuania. She loved her family. The war had torn every last love from her life. Would she have to learn the grotesque details of our suffering? Would news make it to my hometown of Biržai, to the dark bunker in the woods where my brother and father were thought to be hiding?

Joana Vilkas, your daughter, your sister. She is salt to the sea.

We floated in the blackness, bobbing along the waves. A woman in the boat announced the time every thirty minutes. There was no more splashing in the water, only the quiet echoes of crying. We sat, snow falling from an infinite sky.

We waited.

We drifted.

And then I felt Florian's face in my hair. He was kissing me. He kissed my head, he kissed my ear, he kissed my nose. I looked up at him. He took my face in his hands.

"There's a light. A boat is coming," he whispered.

alfred

Dear Hannelore,

The news is grim, the night so very cold. To warm myself I think of summer in Heidelberg. I see you there. I can see you here now, your dark hair against your snug red sweater. I saw a lot of things back home, but most did not credit me for my observant nature. Instead people, like my naïve Mutter, insisted I was suited for bakery work. "How doth we judge a man . . ." I can't recall the rest at this time. People knew I had thoughts, but never wanted to hear them from me. I had more than thoughts. I had theories, plans. Do you remember on the sidewalk when I began to tell you of them? You were so enlightened you ran away, probably to share them with others.

Hitler, he understands my theories. And I, his. Protection of the sick, weak, and inferior is not sensible. That is why I told the Hitler Youth boys about your Jewish father. Do you understand that I was trying to help, Lore? Your mother is not Jewish. I thought surely you would have had sense enough to tell the officers that your mother was a gentile, that you would have aligned yourself to the greater being inside you.

But you decided otherwise.

And now, years later I am still confused by our final conver-

sation. Do you remember it? I remember it so clearly. I ran out onto the sidewalk as they were taking you away. I told them that half of you was part of the master race. You stopped in your tracks and whirled to face me.

"No," you yelled. And then you screamed so very loud.

"I am Jewish!"

Your words echoed between the buildings and bounced down the street.

"I am Jewish!"

I am certain everyone heard your proclamation. It almost sounded like pride. And for some reason those words are now caught, like a hair, in the drain of my mind.

"I am Jewish!"

emilia

We tossed for such a long while. At times I thought I saw tiny faint lights in the distance, but the waves had carried us too far to tell. Where was the Russian submarine that had torpedoed the ship? Was it underneath us? I clutched the knight's pack in front of my body to shield me from the wind. Having his pack made me feel close to him. He was a good man. Thoughts of him made me warmer. I just needed to wait until sunrise. How long would that be? Perhaps seven or eight hours?

I could make it. *I'm coming, Halinka.*

The sailor alternated between talking and heaving over the side of the raft. He was pointing his finger at me, speaking of Hitler. He kept calling me Hannelore. It frightened me. He frightened me. There was a look behind his eyes. I had seen it in the port. Frau Kleist had the same disapproving look.

His speech became slow and slurred from the cold. He was delirious. He threw his hands in the air, repeating the word *Jewish*. It made me think of my sweet friends Rachel and Helen from Lwów. How we used to sing as we collected mushrooms in the forest when they visited me. How we'd be covered in flour and sugar after rolling plum dumplings. How I missed them.

The sailor began talking about a medal. His medal. He then insisted that the medal was in the knight's pack.

"Did you take my medal? Are you a thief?" he asked, deranged from the cold. He crawled over to me and started grabbing at the pack. I swatted his hands away. He became more insistent.

I shouted at him. His face pinched at my words.

I hadn't realized: I was speaking Polish. I was so tired of the game. What did it matter now? "*Nicht Deutsche,*" I yelled. "*Polin.*"

He stopped and wobbled in front of me, confused. "What? You are Polish?"

"I am Polish!" I yelled.

He wagged a delirious finger at me. "Filthy Pole. You liar! Finally, I will serve my country. I am a hero, Hannelore. *Einer weniger!*" he bellowed.

Einer weniger. One less.

He leaned over and tried to shove me into the water. I kicked him with all of my remaining strength. He fell backward on the raft, chanting and repeating, "Hero, hero." He pulled himself to a crouch, then leaned in, eyes narrowed. He began reciting. Or was he singing?

"*Poles, Prostitutes, Russians, Serbs, Socialists.*"

He took a breath, tightened his lips, and spit on me, then resumed singing.

"Stop, please," I begged.

He did not stop. He grabbed at me. I fought and clawed as he sang.

"Spanish Republicans, Trade Unionists, Ukrainians . . ."

He paused and then jumped to his feet.

"YU-GO-SLAV!"

His shoeless foot slipped on the icy surface and he dropped, his forehead smashing against the steel corner of the raft. He lay still, motionless. Then slowly he began to move. He pulled himself up, his face covered in blood, eyes wide with momentary inquisition. He parted his lips to speak. His mouth formed a small smile as he whispered.

"But-ter-fly."

His torso swayed. He was gravely injured. I reached to steady him but he jerked away, violently recoiling from my touch.

He lost his balance and fell backward into the water.

There was brief splashing. The freezing water quickly strangled his screams.

And then it fell quiet. I waited, listening for a long while. The sailor, the self-professed hero, he was dead.

I was alone.

Again.

I hugged the pack and sang songs to Halinka in the darkness. Once in a while I saw something float by. After a time, the waves calmed slightly and cradled me up and back in their arms. I dozed a bit and wondered how many hours were left until sunrise. I imagined the sun warming me and showing me where I was.

Just a little longer now.

It was very dark. My body felt relaxed but heavy.

I was so tired.

My breathing slowed, quiet. Never had I felt so drowsy.

Then I saw something. I blinked softly. It was still there. Yes. It was coming closer, cutting through the water toward me, gradually becoming brighter.

Light.

joana

Florian was right. The light was a ship. The passengers in the boat with remaining strength waved their arms to be seen by the searchlight scanning the water. Florian moved to row us toward the rescue ship.

The baby stirred. The wandering boy looked up at me. "A boat has come to pick us up," I told him.

"Is Opi on the boat?" he asked.

Sailors unfurled a large knotted net down the side of the ship. I didn't know if I had the strength to climb up. My hands were numb with cold.

"Are you a good climber, Klaus?" Florian asked the wandering boy.

The boy nodded.

The lifeboat swung up next to the ship, bobbing frantically. Florian kept his feet in the boat and held on to the nets. Two sailors scrambled down to help people up.

"We've got a newborn baby," Florian told them. The sailors took the baby from me and carried her up. The children were brought up next, and then all of the adults. I tried to check the pulse of those who remained in the boat. Five, wet and without coats, were dead of hypothermia.

Soon Florian and I were the only two left.

364   *Ruta Sepetys*

"You first," he said. "I'll be behind you."

My fingers were too frozen. I couldn't move them. I had to climb by putting my elbows in the ropes of the net and pushing up with my legs. I was nearing the top. My foot suddenly slipped on the slick rope and kicked back, hitting something.

I heard Florian yell. I screamed and felt a heavy jerk on the net.

The sailor on deck reached over and grabbed me. "Keep climbing," he commanded. "Don't look down."

"Florian!" I screamed. There was no reply. "Florian!"

The sailor leaned over the edge, grabbed me by the shoulders, and pulled me onto the swaying deck of the ship. I turned to look down.

Florian was gone.

florian

I was falling, the black, frothy water coming at me. I grabbed for the net. My body wrenched. My shoulder popped and separated from the socket.

I felt my grip slipping.

Slipping.

My fingers released and I plunged into the sea. The freezing water carved into me like knives puncturing my skin. Pain surged in my chest and traveled across my arm. My body pulled down and down.

I was disoriented.

Everything was dark.

Which way was up? Where was the surface?

I was losing breath, my head spinning.

And then I heard her voice, calling to me from above the water.

"Kick! Kick your feet!"

She was yelling to me. The voice was suddenly close, warm and present, in both of my ears. "Kick your feet!"

Propel myself upward. Yes, okay.

Up.

My head rose above the water. I gasped, choking as I pulled air into my lungs.

"There!" yelled a sailor. My shoulder screamed with pain as they pulled me onto a raft.

joana

The sailors had him on a raft.

"Florian!" I screamed. I tried to climb over the side.

"Stay where you are," insisted the sailor. "They've got him."

Florian looked up. He motioned for me to remain on deck. The two brave sailors who had jumped into the water after him were boosting him up the net. They pushed him over the side and he collapsed in a heap.

The wandering boy threw himself onto Florian, sobbing and crying.

"I'm okay, Klaus. Just a little cold and wet."

"We have to get him warm immediately," I said.

We followed the sailors as they moved him belowdecks. I quickly stripped off his icy clothes and wrapped him in a big blanket.

"Not exactly how I envisioned that part," he said quietly, with a grin.

"Hush." I pulled the blanket tight and kissed him. The sailors gave him some dry clothes.

People ran in front of us, shrieking and crying for those they had lost. One man went mad, tearing at his hair, talking nonstop of chickens and the chicken car.

A sailor walked among the passengers.

"What vessel is this?" Florian asked him.

"You've been picked up by *T-36*, a German torpedo boat."

An explosion detonated beneath the boat. People screamed.

"Stay calm," said the sailor. "We're releasing depth charges. There are still Russian subs prowling the area."

Submarines. We were still in danger.

They gave us hot drinks and soup. The warmth brought tingling and pain. The wandering boy cried of aches in his legs and feet. And he cried for Opi. The baby whimpered for Emilia. We settled onto the floor with piles of blankets, huddling together for warmth.

Florian reached down and took my hand. "I heard you," he whispered.

"What?"

"When I was underwater. I heard you telling me to kick my feet. Thank you."

I looked up at him.

What was he talking about?

florian

Joana lay with her head on my shoulder, cradling the baby. The little boy slept in a bundle under my good arm. The brave rescue crew worked with precision, moving the boat and plucking people from the water.

I had been certain I was going to die.

The baby slept. Where was the Polish girl? Had she been picked up? I looked at the wandering boy, asleep. Heinz had his papers, the address in Berlin.

Heinz.

Our shoe poet, our friend. Opi. I fought the emotion that stirred.

The sailors walked among the people who had been rescued. They spoke to each passenger, asking questions and giving instructions. Joana opened her eyes and looked up at me.

"They're asking everyone for their name and information. They say we're going to Sassnitz, on the German island of Rügen." She squeezed my hand.

I bent over and kissed the top of her head. I then leaned back against the wall and closed my eyes.

My name and information.

Who was I?

I looked down at Joana and the children.

Who did I want to be?

emilia

The lace curtain flapped in the kitchen window. The breeze today was the kind you opened the shutters for, the kind that carried away old sin and flakes of sadness. The sun streamed through the window, blooming light through a jar of amber honey on the sill. I dipped my fingers into the cool sack of flour, sprinkled a handful across the board, and began to roll out the dough. Rachel and Helen were coming for tea after synagogue. They would be thrilled to have their favorite doughnuts with rose petal jam. Father would eat the leftovers for breakfast.

Something stirred by the sideboard.

"I see you, Halinka." I laughed. My daughter peeked out from behind the cabinet.

"What are you sneaking around for?" I asked.

"Fairy bread." She giggled. She was a beautiful whisper. If only I imagined her, my little bird could always be with me.

"Get a plate," I told her.

She ran to the cupboard and returned with a plate, already licking her lips.

I cut a thick slice off the loaf while she sprinkled sugar onto the plate. I spread a layer of butter on the piece of bread and handed it to her. She gently pressed it facedown in the sugar.

She then peeled it back up, slowly, careful not to lose a single crystal.

Halinka carried her fairy bread to the back door of the kitchen, which stood open to the unfenced yard and wildflowers. I had just returned to my dough when my daughter began jumping up and down.

"Mama, they're back!" She dashed out into the yard, her silhouette fading, disappearing into the glistening sunlight.

I ran to the door just in time to see the storks soaring overhead.

"Did you see them, Emilia?"

I nodded, turning toward the voice.

My beautiful mother walked toward me through the grass with my baby brother.

"Did you see them, sweetheart?" she whispered. "They've come home."

Mama smiled wide. She kissed me, handed me a jar of jam, and then walked into the kitchen. I leaned against the warm door frame, allowing the golden heat to envelop me.

I turned the lid and lifted the rose petal jam to my nose, savoring the scent. I raised my face to the sun. My war had been so long, my winters so cold. But I had finally made it home. And for the first time in a long time, I was not afraid.

SALT TO THE SEA   373

florian

I sat on the porch, my hands trembling and cold. The fear never disappeared, but with each year it retreated slightly, a tide of memory sliding back out to sea. The terror returned mainly at night, but Joana was always there to chase it away.

And then, after more than twenty years, a letter arrived.

I thought it was behind me, that what remained was only suffering's ghost. I had run and tried to hide, but it was no use.

Fate is a hunter.

So fate had found its way to me across the ocean, tucked in an envelope. I thought long and hard about whether I should write back. Finally, I did.

And now another envelope had arrived. It had the same return address.

A reply.

Answers.

I took a breath and tore it open.

25th day of April, 1969

Bornholm, Denmark

My Dear Florian,

I was so full of joy to receive your response to my letter. Although it must certainly sound strange, for all these years—twenty-four to be exact—it has felt that I have known you. Yes, of course I understand it took time and careful thought for you to reply. My apologies for the delay as well, I required assistance with my German. Part of me feared, dear child, that you would never reply at all. I spent quite a long time debating whether I should actually post the first letter, wondering if it would even find you. I wrote it the very same day I read the article in the newspaper. Initially, it simply seemed like an interesting story—a young swimmer from America who longed to compete in the summer games, but her nationality was in question because she had been born on a ship. Can you imagine my shock when I read these words in print from the swimmer, Halinka, herself:

"My birth mother was on a German ship that sank during the war, the Wilhelm Gustloff. My mother saved me and also my older brother, Klaus, during the sinking. I am told she was very brave. We know nothing of her except that she was Polish and her name was Emilia."

Her name was Emilia.

Of course it could have been coincidence, but when

SALT TO THE SEA   *375*

you and Joana were named in the article, I knew. Emilia, Florian, Joana. This was not a coincidence. I contacted an acquaintance in America who helped me retrieve your address through a telephone directory in the library. I'm so grateful she did.

In your letter, you gently asked if I had revealed anything. Let your heart be still, I have not. You also asked how it happened. I am so grateful that you want to know and I hope it will bring you comfort.

She arrived in February.

Niels had left to check the evening nets. He was gone quite long, so I followed to see if he needed assistance. It is difficult to describe the feeling, seeing the raft tapping against the shore of our land. It seemed she was softly knocking, asking would we please allow her in.

Countless things have floated up onshore over the years. There is a museum on the island of Bornholm, full of items. But this, of course, was different. She arrived not on a public beach, like most of the bottles and floats. She came directly to us, in our sandy backyard, defying tides and the elements.

Although I'm sure it sounds ghostly and terrifying, it was not. And to this day, I really cannot describe why. We sat, staring silently into the fire that night. So many questions. Where had this lovely young girl in a pink woolen cap come from? How long had her trip taken? How had she suffered? And then of course we thought *of her family. Who was missing their beautiful daughter?*

We couldn't sleep. We left our bed in the dark. The large rucksack had defrosted near the fire and Niels brought it into the kitchen. We removed all of the items and placed them on the table. Certainly nothing made sense. But then Niels found your little notebook. The writing was so small we could not read it without a strong magnifier. The details were cryptic. We loved your tiny sketches, signatures, and the brief entries about your family and Joana.

But this, scratched into the margin, was what we needed—

Emilia. Pink hat. Poland.

We only realized that your abbreviation Willi G implied Wilhelm Gustloff when Niels heard a report from Sweden years later about the sinking. We were shocked to learn the ship had been carrying ten thousand people. More than nine thousand perished.

Your Emilia was one of them.

We contacted the occupying German authorities, but they were uninterested because she was not a soldier. We contacted the Red Cross. We knew if we mentioned the small box, many would come. So we did not. We wanted someone to search for Emilia, not for the spoils of war. Twenty-four years have passed and even now my heart goes still when I hear a knock on the cottage door. But so far, no one has come. I will leave it to you and Joana to decide whether to share this information with Halinka. In the meantime, I have buried the items from your pack as you requested.

So, dear one, I have grown old now and my Niels is gone. Receiving your kind letter brought such peace to my heart, knowing that you, Joana, Klaus, and Halinka are together in America along with a child of your own. I do understand how you have struggled for this new life. The sinking of the Gustloff is the largest maritime disaster, yet the world still knows nothing of it. I often wonder, will that ever change or will it remain just another secret swallowed by war?

You wrote that Emilia was your savior and that she is ever on your mind. Please do know, Florian, she is ever in my heart as well. War is catastrophe. It breaks families in irretrievable pieces. But those who are gone are not necessarily lost. Near our cottage, where the small creek winds under the old wooden bridge, is the most beautiful bed of roses.

And there Emilia rests. She is safe. She is loved.

Affectionately,
Clara Christensen

AUTHOR'S NOTE

This book is a work of historical fiction.

The *Wilhelm Gustloff*, the Amber Room, and Operation Hannibal, however, are very real.

The sinking of the *Wilhelm Gustloff* is the deadliest disaster in maritime history, with losses dwarfing the death tolls of the famous ships *Titanic* and *Lusitania*. Yet remarkably, most people have never heard of it.

On January 30, 1945, four torpedoes waited in the belly of Soviet submarine *S-13*.

Each torpedo was painted with a scrawled dedication:

For the Motherland.

For the Soviet People.

For Leningrad.

For Stalin.

Three of the four torpedoes were launched, destroying the *Wilhelm Gustloff* and killing estimates of nine thousand people. The torpedo "For Stalin" failed in its tube and did not launch. The majority of the passengers on the *Gustloff* were civilians, with an estimated five thousand being children. The ghost ship, as it is sometimes called, now lies off the coast of Poland, the large gothic letters of her name still visible underwater.

Over two million people were successfully evacuated during Operation Hannibal, the largest sea evacuation in modern history. Hannibal quickly transported not only soldiers but also civilians to safety from the advancing Russian troops. Lithuanians, Latvians, Estonians, ethnic Germans, and residents of the East Prussian and Polish corridors all fled toward the sea. My father's cousins were among them.

My father, like Joana's mother, waited in refugee camps hoping to return to Lithuania. But that did not happen. Baltic refugees waited half a century before they could return to their nation of origin. Most who were forced to flee established new lives in different cities and countries. The evacuees walked, rode cratered trains, and fled over water.

The *Wilhelm Gustloff* was not the only ship destroyed during the evacuation. The SS *General von Steuben* was also sunk by the submarine *S-13*, claiming the lives of 4,000. The sinking of the MV *Goya* claimed the lives of 6,500 passengers. The ships *Thielbek* and *Cap Arcona* were carrying Jewish prisoners from concentration camps. The ships were bombed and sunk by British RAF planes, killing over 7,000. It is estimated that in the year 1945 alone, over 25,000 people lost their lives in the Baltic Sea. For months, bodies drifted ashore in various locations, haunting the coastline and its residents. Even today, some divers report a strong presence in the water near the enormous sea graves.

The Amber Room, once called the Eighth Wonder of the World, disappeared during the war and remains one of the most

SALT TO THE SEA   *381*

enduring mysteries of World War II. The Amber Room was last seen in 1944. Many treasure hunters have gone in search of it and some have suffered terrible fates during their quest. Over the years, pieces of the room have allegedly been found. But where exactly is the Amber Room? Reports have claimed that murderous Nazi leader Erich Koch was kept alive through the 1980s because he possessed information on the room's whereabouts. But who knows the real story? Some say it was hidden in a salt mine or beneath a castle, others claim it rests in an underground bunker in the forest, and some believe it was loaded onto the *Wilhelm Gustloff*.

There are many important stories of World War II. Much has been documented about combat, politics, guilt, and responsibility. Suffering emerged the victor, touching all sides, sparing no nation involved. As I wrote this novel, I was haunted by thoughts of the helpless children and teenagers—innocent victims of border shifts, ethnic cleansings, and vengeful regimes. Hundreds of thousands of children were orphaned during World War II. Abandoned or separated from their families, they were forced to battle the beast of war on their own, left with an inheritance of heartache and responsibility for events they had no role in causing. Many experienced unspeakable atrocities, some miraculous acts of kindness by complete strangers. The child and young adult narrative is what I chose to represent in the novel, seeing the war through the eyes of youths from different nations, forced to leave everything they loved behind.

For many, war redefined the meaning of home. Emilia's

birthplace of Lwów, Poland, is now part of Ukraine. Florian's East Prussian Tilsit and Königsberg are now Sovetsk and Kaliningrad, Russia. Much of East Prussia is now part of Poland. Joana's country of Lithuania was occupied by the Soviet Union for over fifty years until regaining its independence in 1990.

Every nation has hidden history, countless stories preserved only by those who experienced them. Stories of war are often read and discussed worldwide by readers whose nations stood on opposite sides during battle. History divided us, but through reading we can be united in story, study, and remembrance. Books join us together as a global reading community, but more important, a global human community striving to learn from the past.

What determines how we remember history and which elements are preserved and penetrate the collective consciousness? If historical novels stir your interest, pursue the facts, history, memoirs, and personal testimonies available. These are the shoulders that historical fiction sits upon. When the survivors are gone we must not let the truth disappear with them.

Please, give them a voice.

RESEARCH AND SOURCES

The research and investigation process for this novel was a global, collaborative effort that carried me to half a dozen countries. That said, any errors found herein are my own.

Claus Pedersen in Denmark worked with me for over three years on this project. He read, he researched, he translated, and he traveled to Copenhagen and Brussels to meet with me. I am indescribably grateful for his help, hard work, and most of all, his friendship.

Agata Napiórska in Poland was the first person to champion this book. Dedicated and beautifully passionate, she met me on four separate trips to Warsaw, Gdynia, Gdańsk, and Kraków and connected me to many people and places.

Over forty years ago, Polish divers Michal Rybicki and Jerzy Janczukowicz were among the first to explore the sunken *Gustloff*. Their first dive required Soviet approval. Michal and Jerzy agreed to assist with my research and spent countless hours with me in Gdańsk, sharing unforgettable details of the tragedy and gravesite beneath the sea.

Michal Rybicki and Dorota Mierosławska helped me retrace the steps of the millions of evacuees who ran for their lives. Together we walked the path of the refugees through former East Prussia (now Poland) to the lagoon in Tolkmicko, Frombork (Frauenberg), and Nowa Pasłęka. They took me to the port in Gdynia (Gotenhafen) to study the departure of the

384   *Ruta Sepetys*

Wilhelm Gustloff and the geographic execution of Operation Hannibal. Michal photographed our research and Dorota filled me with the magic and love that is Poland. This book would not be possible without them.

My father's cousin, Erika Demski, fled from Lithuania through East Prussia and obtained a pass to sail aboard the doomed *Wilhelm Gustloff.* By a twist of fate, she missed the voyage and sailed on another ship. Erika and her husband, Theo Mayer, who now reside in Belgium, shared the incredible story and encouraged me to write about the disaster.

Bernhard Schlegelmilch, a historian born in former East Germany, spent long days touring me through Berlin, digging up details of World War II, and bringing the time period to life.

A world-renowned deep-sea diver from England, Leigh Bishop has explored over four hundred shipwrecks, including the *Titanic* and *Lusitania.* Mr. Bishop shared with me the haunting details of his unforgettable experience diving the *Wilhelm Gustloff* in 2003.

Rasa Aleksiunas and her son, Linas, generously shared the amazing story (with all of the original documents and even the strap from the life vest) of her father, Eduardas Markulis, a twenty-two-year-old Lithuanian from Šiauliai who survived the sinking.

Ann Mara Lipacis and her brother, J. Ventenbergs, from Riga, Latvia, both survived the sinking. They were six and ten years old. Mrs. Lipacis and Mr. Ventenbergs shared first-hand accounts and memoirs not only of the sinking, but of losing their beloved mother, Antonija Liepins Ventenbergs, who remained on deck to allow children into the lifeboats.

Lorna MacEwen in the UK shared personal details and photos with me. Her mother, Marta Kopaite, was a young Lithuanian nurse who walked over minefields to Gotenhafen and boarded the *Wilhelm Gustloff*. She survived.

Lance Robinson in South Africa shared the story of his mother, Helmer Laidroo, a fifteen-year-old Estonian girl who survived the sinking of the *Gustloff*.

Mati Kaarma in Australia shared the story and background of his family who fled from Estonia. His parents took a train to Germany and his grandparents, who opted for passage on the *Gustloff*, did not survive.

Gertrud Baekby Madsen in Denmark shared a detailed account of her evacuation from Tilsit and the treacherous trek across the ice.

Edward Petruskevich, curator of the Wilhelm Gustloff Museum, patiently answered many of my questions. His incredible website provided invaluable source material: www.wilhelmgustloffmuseum.com.

Author and journalist Cathryn J. Prince answered countless e-mails and generously shared her research findings, contacts, and knowledge.

Charlotte and William Peale organized research material and read early drafts.

This novel was built with bricks from the following books, films, and resources. I am enormously indebted to them:

Abandoned and Forgotten: An Orphan Girl's Tale of Survival During World War II, by Evelyne Tannehill.

The Amber Room: The Fate of the World's Greatest Lost Treasure, by Adrian Levy.

Battleground Prussia: The Assault on Germany's Eastern Front 1944–45, by Prit Buttar.

Before the Storm: Memories of My Youth in Old Prussia, by Marion Countess Dönhoff.

Bloodlands: Europe Between Hitler and Stalin, by Timothy Snyder.

The Captive Mind, by Czeslaw Milosz.

Caveat Emptor: The Secret Life of an American Art Forger, by Ken Perenyi.

Crabwalk, by Günter Grass.

The Cruelest Night: The Untold Story of One of the Greatest Maritime Tragedies of World War II, by Christopher Dobson, John Miller, and Ronald Payne.

The Damned Don't Drown: The Sinking of the Wilhelm Gustloff, by Arthur V. Sellwood.

Death in the Baltic: The World War II Sinking of the Wilhelm Gustloff, by Cathryn J. Prince.

Die große Flucht: Das Schicksal der Vertriebenen, by Guido Knopp.

Die Gustloff-Katastrophe: Bericht eines Überlebenden, by Heinz Schön.

Forgotten Land: Journeys Among the Ghosts of East Prussia, by Max Egremont.

God, Give Us Wings, by Felicia Prekeris Brown.

Handmade Shoes for Men, by László Vass and Magda Molnar.

Lwów, A City Lost: Memories of a Cherished Childhood, by Eva Szybalski.

Oral History Sources of Latvia: History, Culture and Society Through Life Stories, edited by Māra Zirnīte and Maija Hinkle.

The Painted Bird, by Jerzy Kosinski.

The Rape of Europa: The Fate of Europe's Treasures in the Third Reich and the Second World War, by Lynn H. Nicholas.

Rose Petal Jam: Recipes and Stories from a Summer in Poland, by Beata Zatorska and Simon Target.

Shoes: Their History in Words and Pictures, by Charlotte Yue and David Yue.

Sinking the Gustloff: A Tragedy Exiled From Memory, by Marcus Kolga.

Token of a Covenant: Diary of an East Prussian Surgeon 1945–47, by Hans Graf Von Lehndorff.

The Vanished Kingdom: Travels Through the History of Prussia, by James Charles Roy.

The following people and organizations contributed to my research and writing efforts:

Henning Ahrens; the Bihrs; Dr. Richard Butterwick-Pawlikowski; Ulrike Dick; Angela Kaden; Helen Logvinov; Jeroen Noordhuis; Jonas Ohman; Xymena Pietraszek; Julius Sakalauskas; Carol Stoltz.

Ancestry.com; the Balzekas Museum of Lithuanian Culture;

Bornholms Museum; Der Spiegel; the Federal Foundation of Flight, Expulsion, Reconciliation in Berlin, Germany; Historical Museum of the City of Kraków; Inkwood Books; Kresy Siberia Virtual Museum; Letters of Note; the Museum of Genocide Victims in Vilnius, Lithuania; the Museum of Occupation in Riga, Latvia; the Regional Historical Center of Eindhoven, Holland; the Rockefeller Foundation Bellagio Center; Steuben Tours; the Wilhelm Gustloff Museum: www.wilhelmgustloffmuseum.com.

The greatest *Wilhelm Gustloff* archivist was undoubtedly Mr. Heinz Schön. Mr. Schön served as assistant purser on the *Gustloff,* witnessed and survived the sinking, and devoted much of his life to documenting the disaster. Heinz Schön passed away in 2013. At his request, his remains were taken to the bottom of the Baltic Sea to rest upon the sunken *Gustloff.* He is gone but his legacy and research remain a gift to us all.

I am grateful to the following *Wilhelm Gustloff* survivors who throughout the years have bravely given several very detailed interviews about their experience:

Ulrich von Domarus; Irene Tshinkur East; Heidrun Gloza; Waltraud Lilischkis; Ellen Tschinkur Maybee; Eva Merten; Rose Rezas Petrus; Helga Reuter; Inge Bendrich Roedecker; Eva Dorn Rothchild; Willi Schäfer; Edith Spindl; Peter Weise; Horst Woit.

Several people agreed to be interviewed for this project but requested to remain anonymous. Revisiting tragedy chisels the heart. They subjected themselves to the discomfort of painful memory for the sake of this novel and I am eternally grateful.

SALT TO THE SEA   *389*

ACKNOWLEDGMENTS

Many writers create and succeed on their own. I am not one of them.

My incredible agent, Steven Malk, guides and inspires my every step. I could not dream of a better mentor and friend.

Liza Kaplan, my tireless editor, and Michael Green, my brilliant publisher, devoted years to this novel and the associated journey. They are my heroes. Thank you to Shanta Newlin, Theresa Evangelista, Semadar Megged, Talia Benamy, Katrina Damkoehler, and my Philomel family for giving history a voice and my stories a home.

None of this would be possible without the beautiful people at Philomel, SPEAK, Penguin Young Readers Group, all of the Penguin field reps, Writers House, and SCBWI.

My sincere gratitude to my wonderful foreign publishers, sub-agents, and translators for sharing my words with the world.

The hands and heart of Courtney C. Stevens have touched every page of this novel.

My writing group sees everything first: Sharon Cameron, Amy Eytchison, Rachel Griffith, Howard Shirley, and Angelika Stegmann. Thank you for ten years of dedication and friendship. I couldn't do it without you and would never want to.

Fred Wilhelm and Lindsay Kee helped me spark the title and Ben Horslen contributed across the ocean.

Yvonne Seivertson, Niels Bye Nielsen, Claus Pedersen,

Mike Cortese, Gavin Mikhail, Beth Kephart, Genetta Adair, Ken Wright, Tamra Tuller, the Rockets, JW Scott, Steve Vai, the Lithuanian and Baltic communities, the Polish community, the Myerses, the Reids, the Smiths, the Tuckers, the Peales, and the Sepetyses all contributed to my writing efforts.

Heartfelt thanks to my biggest supporters—the teachers, librarians, and booksellers. And most of all, my sincere thanks to the readers. I appreciate each and every one of you.

Mom and Dad taught me to dream big and love even bigger.

John and Kristina are my champions and the best friends a little sister could ask for.

And Michael: his love gives me the courage and the wings. He is my everything.

PRESENT-DAY OVERVIEW
DENMARK
SWEDEN
Steuben
BORNHOLM (DENMARK)
Kiel
Sassnitz
Berlin
GERMANY
CZECH REPUBLIC
Heidelberg

discussion questions

1. *Salt to the Sea* is told in multiple first-person narratives. How do you think this literary method strengthens the story? If only one character had been chosen to narrate, which would you choose and why?

2. As the novel opens and readers are introduced to each of the four protagonists, they are told by Joana, "Guilt is a hunter." Florian states, "Fate is a hunter." Emilia shares, "Shame is a hunter." And Alfred declares, "Fear is a hunter." What makes this common refrain such a powerful one? How does it immediately capture the internal conflict of each of these characters? What roles do guilt, fate, shame, and fear play in their respective lives?

3. Considering each of the main characters' perspectives, in what ways is *Salt to the Sea* a story about things that have been lost? What does each character find along the way?

4. Repeated attention is called to Emilia's pink hat. What do you think the hat symbolizes? How else does color play a role in the book as it pertains to the story and its characters?

5. Describe Florian, Emilia, Joana, and Alfred. What makes them dynamic characters? What are their strengths and weaknesses? While they each have their own unique story and come from different backgrounds, how are they similar to one another?

6. Why is Alfred unable to understand why Hannelore proudly proclaims, "I am Jewish!" as he tries to argue that half of her is "part of the master race"? What was your reaction to learning of Alfred's role in the removal of Hannelore and her father?

7. Describe the "Alfred" in the imaginary letters written to Hannelore. How is he different from the "Frick" observed by those with whom he works and interacts on the *Wilhelm Gustloff*? What does this dual perspective say about his character?

8. Why does Emilia attempt to conceal her pregnancy? In what ways do her memories and fantasies of August Kleist help her persevere through her trauma?

9. Florian's father tells him, "You are Prussian. Make your own decisions, son." What does he mean by this? In what ways do his words affect Florian's decisions? In your opinion, does Florian succeed in heeding his father's advice?

10. What is the significance of the title, *Salt to the Sea*? Given the magnitude of the tragedy of the *Wilhelm Gustloff*, does it accurately describe the events and relationships portrayed in the novel?

in conversation

As mentioned in my author's note, I received assistance from many while writing *Salt to the Sea*. For this edition, I'd like to introduce you to a few individuals who shared their knowledge or direct experience of the history, the time period, and the ship. I hope you find their insights as generous and fascinating as I do.

—*Ruta Sepetys*

LEIGH BISHOP
Diver

Leigh Bishop is a world-renowned deep sea diver, acclaimed for his shipwreck explorations and underwater photography. He has explored hundreds of sunken ships, including the legendary *Titanic* and *Lusitania*. Leigh's detailed account of diving the *Wilhelm Gustloff* in 2003 brought chilling insight to the disaster.

1. Before diving and exploring the *Gustloff*, in what ways did you prepare?

With any shipwreck expedition there is inevitably a degree of preparation involved, and the *Gustloff* dives were no different. The wreck lies below a depth limit endorsed by recreational divers and therefore falls into a technical dive category. By using special closed-circuit rebreather technology rather than traditional scuba equipment, we could recycle the onboard gases breathed and extend our time spent actually physically exploring the wreck. The Baltic Sea, however, is very cold, which means the divers had to prepare for low temperatures and in-water survival with drysuit heaters to see them through the extended decompression times. Perhaps the main thing that hung across all the divers' minds was the possibility of confronting the vast amount of human remains that were likely to be found inside the wreck. The psychology of dealing with such a likelihood on an unprecedented scale was something the team could never prepare for.

2. You have explored and photographed dozens of sunken ships, including the *Titanic* and the *Lusitania*. In what way was your exploration of the *Wilhelm Gustloff* different from other explorations?

Upon surfacing from my first dive to the *Wilhelm Gustloff*, I waited patiently for the dive boat to pick me up. As it attended to other divers who had surfaced prior, I had time to reflect on my dive. I had swum completely around the stern and witnessed the large Gothic lettering spelling out the name *Wilhelm Gustloff* spanning almost the entire counter stern of the wreck. Whilst reflecting, I was utterly haunted by a presence that something had happened at this very spot where I now waited, as if a cold chill had crossed the hairs of my back, as if something evil was here with me, perhaps people from the past watching me. A presence I had never felt before—not even when we arrived at the site of the *Titanic* only months before in the same year.

3. What was most surprising about the sunken *Gustloff*?

What was most surprising about the *Gustloff* was just how well the wreck was preserved, something that struck me immediately as the wreck came into view. The environmental impact on the wreck is unlike others that lie in more temperate waters, such as the famous RMS *Lusitania*. The reason for this is the naval worm, *Teredo navalis*, responsible for eating wood of shipwrecks, which is less active in the Baltic Sea because of the low salinity levels. The teak decking of the wreck was all still very much in place, and the stern poop deck was really quite remarkable. As I set my tripod up to shoot long-time exposure photos, I spared a moment to think of the people who maybe gathered on that very deck as the ship was sinking. Shadowing above me as I swam the decks were the haunting davits and, again, I thought about how cold it had to have been for them to freeze in place, unable to launch the lifeboats to save at least some of the many victims the ship took with her.

4. How is the wreck of the *Wilhelm Gustloff* regarded within the dive community?

Wilhelm Gustloff has taken legendary status amongst the diving community. Few have dived into the cold depths to witness the history that is the *Gustloff*, but many would give their right hand to simply set eyes on the famous wreck. Today a no-diving policy hangs over the wreckage, and visitors, if any, are on a strict permit-only basis. With today's modern technology any vessel nearing the navigational sinking position are quickly intercepted by Polish authorities.

CATHRYN J. PRINCE
Author and Journalist

Cathryn J. Prince is the author of *Death in the Baltic*, a compelling and comprehensive nonfiction book about the *Wilhelm Gustloff* disaster. Cathryn provided tremendous help during my research process. She shared her contacts, notes, and interview findings from her meetings with survivors. Visit her website at **cathrynjprince.com**.

1. How did you approach your research of the *Wilhelm Gustloff*—including survivor testimonies, documents, artifacts, etc.—to create a nonfiction narrative for your book *Death in the Baltic*?

I approach every book I write as a journalist; that's how I got my start in writing and I continue that work now. Of course in this case I am reporting on the past. To me the story of the *Wilhelm Gustloff* is not only the story of a ship's sinking. It is the story of how the people came to be aboard this ship. It is about what it was like to come of age in a part of Nazi Germany that until the early 1940s had remained in some ways isolated from what was happening in Berlin.

I knew from the outset that the survivors would be the heart of the book. Without their accounts, the book would simply be a litany of events. My research took me to the US National Archives, the US Holocaust Memorial Museum, and the German Federal Archives. The rich trove of original source documents and oral histories I found gave me the glue that held the story together.

At every turn I needed to ask—what were the ramifications and implications for each action in the book? I also needed to anchor each person to the time and place, and to do that it was important to fill in the gaps of their lives before and after the sinking. Lastly, my goal was to get readers to care about each person. But before we care about what happens to, say, Helga Reuter Knickerbocker, we've got to know a bit about her childhood. We need to know little things about Helga, like she loved her older sister, she enjoyed summers on the Baltic Sea, and she loved the window seat in her bedroom.

2. During your research and interviews with survivors, what made the greatest impression on you?

War shapes so much of who we are as a nation, and a world. I've always been interested in not just the strategy, tactics, and politics of war—but what civilians and soldiers endured on the most basic level. I'm interested in war as a time of transformation—for individuals and society. The story of the *Wilhelm Gustloff*, with all its human drama, not only resurrects history but raises provocative questions about loss, survival, and how those impacted continue on year after year, decade after decade.

For me the greatest impression I was left with is how the sinking haunts each survivor in very different ways. One can't stand under a shower head anymore because it reminds her of near-drowning, another has turned a study into a shrine of sorts, another only spoke about it because she wanted people to know about her cousin who died on that day.

Spending time with these men and women, now in their late seventies and eighties, was to see someone instantly transported back to that time period; to see them as they were when they were ten, fifteen, or seventeen.

3. Why do you feel it's important for people to know the history of the *Wilhelm Gustloff*?

Because history is defined as much by what becomes part of the official record as by what is left unrecorded, few know this story. In this case, German censorship, Soviet suppression, and Western indifference buried the *Gustloff*'s story. Refusing to let the flailing Third Reich hear of defeat, Hitler prohibited officials from reporting the sinking. The Soviet Union suppressed the story partly because it doubted the integrity of the submarine commander and partly because to talk about the *Gustloff* might have cast light on their own atrocities. In the West, the event remained buried, first because of war fatigue and then because it was overshadowed by the Cold War.

In time German war guilt accomplished what government censorship could not. In the same way that survivors of the Dresden firebombing had difficulty finding an audience receptive to listening to and learning about their ordeal, so too did survivors of the *Wilhelm Gustloff*. Mourning was seen as tantamount to clinging to an immoral and evil past.

For more than seventy years this story has been relatively hidden, as the victims inspired little sympathy after their role and their countries' role in World War II. After all, WWII, perhaps more than any other war in recent history, is still portrayed in stark lines of black and white. Knowing the story of the *Wilhelm Gustloff* allows to us to understand that nothing is black and white.

EDWARD PETRUSKEVICH
Curator, *Wilhelm Gustloff* Online Museum

Edward Petruskevich has assembled the world's largest public online collection of artifacts relating to the MV *Wilhelm Gustloff.* His knowledge of the ship, together with the museum pieces, helped me visualize and build the narrative around the ship. Visit the museum at **wilhelmgustloffmuseum.com**.

1. Approximately how many items, and what types of items, are currently in the collection of the *Wilhelm Gustloff* online museum?

The collection currently consists of almost 3,350 original photographs and is continuously expanding. The majority of these photographs are of the *Wilhelm Gustloff* from her first rivets of construction to her final days in Gotenhafen. Others include memorials, drawings, and wreck photographs taken from 1945 to the present. The online museum also showcases 280 daily agendas and menus from the *Wilhelm Gustloff* that were used onboard, and 230 artifacts from the ship. Many artifacts are souvenirs that were created to be sold in her gift shop during her 1938–1939 passenger voyages and primarily include small china pieces, pins, and cap tallies. Some of the more unusual souvenirs are a pillowcase embroidered with the *Gustloff,* a Norah Wellings sailor doll, and nautical flag bracelet that spells out the ship's name. Other items include a handwritten journal from her official maiden voyage, a 1:100 scale model of the *Wilhelm Gustloff* built in 2009, and many original books and magazines chronicling the ship throughout her career.

SALT TO THE SEA 405

2. Which items do you consider the most unique and how did you come upon them?

The most unique artifacts from the *Wilhelm Gustloff* come from her final voyage and wreck since so few have been made public. The collection has two boarding passes that belonged to Käthe Kraus for her evacuation voyage, which I found through a military collector in an online auction. There are currently only five of these passes known to exist that were printed on the ship's own printing presses just before departure. I also have a piece of wreck wood that washed up in Leba, Poland, on February 11, 1945, and was carved into a figure of the Madonna. It was then presented to survivor Waltrud Grüter, who kept it with a pin she wore the night of the sinking, which is also part of the collection. The centerpiece of the online museum is a section of the *Wilhelm Gustloff*'s Neptune tile mosaic from her swimming pool. This was by far the most beautiful room on the ship, and it is where the second torpedo hit, killing nearly all of the 373 Women's Naval Auxiliary who were housed there for the voyage. After the ship sank, she was imploded to prevent her from being a navigational hazard and the explosions ripped through the pool housed on the forward E deck. A friend of mine who made several dives on the *Wilhelm Gustloff* found the tile lying in the mud after it fell out of the ship, and it remained in his basement for several years after he raised it to the surface. He decided it needed a better home where people could view it, and I purchased it from him in 2016.

3. What do you hope visitors will come away with after visiting your *Wilhelm Gustloff* online museum? What can artifacts teach us about the *Wilhelm Gustloff*?

One of the important things to me is that people understand the *Wilhelm Gustloff* wasn't just a means to an end during the closing days of World War II. She was once the flagship of the Kraft durch Freude* fleet and laid the groundwork for future generations of ships with her open spaces, single class, and cruising capabilities. She became highly successful as a passenger ship. The artifacts that come from her cruising days give a glimpse into the structured voyages of the Third Reich and the propaganda that was constantly drilled into the minds of Germany's citizens. A journal written during a voyage to Italy gives a lot of praise to their leader for allowing them to have such enjoyable adventures. Many of the items recovered from the *Wilhelm Gustloff* expressed praise for Hitler and all he has given his people, including the *Wilhelm Gustloff*, which was a very effective propaganda tool herself.

I believe the best way we can remember the disaster and the *Wilhelm Gustloff* herself is to tell her story through artifacts and what they represent. The love letters written by sailors to their sweethearts impart a dire need for the war to come to an end, and express the same hopes and fears those on the Allied side had. The boarding passes that were to be the salvation of those fleeing the advancing Red Army ended up being the holders' demise. A

---

*The Kraft durch Freude was a leisure organization established by Nazi Germany to encourage tourism and the ideology and practice associated with the twentieth-century German Nazi Party.

Kriegsmarine blanket that a weary survivor had wrapped around himself as he climbed a rope ladder up the side of the T-36 after the *Gustloff* had been sunk. A simple piece that shows the longing to stay warm while its holes show the struggle of staying alive in the middle of the sea. Each of these artifacts shows us that she wasn't just a ship that was sunk with a heavy loss of life, but the *Wilhelm Gustloff* emphasized what was going to mirror the very best of Germany in the 1930s and the very worst in the 1940s. Over 100,000 people sailed and stayed on the *Gustloff* during her life, and each person and artifact has a story to tell. Calling the ship "it" soon turns into "she" as a mass of steel and wood seemingly turns into a humanized character. Eventually, those on board give her a more affectionate name, the Willi G, and for some, her loss equates to losing a family member. Looking beyond politics and race, gender and affluence, it is a story about people. People so unimaginably exhausted and hysterically seeking a way to escape death in one of the darkest chapters of our history. It is also a story about the *Wilhelm Gustloff*: the ship that so many looked to as a vessel of hope, but that delivered them to the perilous fate they were trying so desperately to avoid.

MARA LIPACIS
Wilhelm Gustloff Survivor

Born in Latvia, Mara Lipacis was six years old when she boarded the doomed *Wilhelm Gustloff* with her mother and older brother. As the ship was sinking, Mara's brother was separated from the family. Although young Mara was handed down into a lifeboat, her mother remained on deck. Mara generously shared her experience with me, some of which she recounts here.

1. Please give us a brief account of your experience onboard the *Wilhelm Gustloff*, who accompanied you, and a bit about your experience when the ship sank.

I remember a gray sky, cold wind, and crowds of people as my mother, brother, and I boarded the ship, lying on a mattress with suitcases by our heads in a large hall with lots of people around, rushing up a crowded hall, standing on a sloping, cold, crowded deck, then very few people on the deck, then my mother lifting me into a sailor's arms, then holding on to the seat of the lifeboat as it was riding through large waves.

2. What is your most vivid memory of the sinking?

There are a couple of scenes that have stayed in my mind:

1) Holding on to my mother's hand in a crowded corridor in order to get to the deck with people pushing and shoving each other.

2) While in the lifeboat, seeing the *Wilhelm Gustloff* with

lights ablaze turn onto one side and go underwater. In my mind I remember seeing my mother standing on one deck but I do not know if this can be true even though our lifeboat was not far from the ship.

3) Hanging on to a rope with all my strength while being pulled up from our lifeboat to the torpedo boat that rescued us.

3. What role did others, including your mother and brother, play in your survival?

My mother unselfishly handed me to a sailor who put me on the lifeboat and remained standing on the sinking ship in hope that I would have a small chance to survive. My ten-year-old brother saved me from being sent to an orphanage and an unknown future when he saw me standing in line with other small rescued children on the boat in Sassnitz.

4. In what ways do you feel that the sinking of the *Wilhelm Gustloff* differs from the *Titanic*?

The sinking of the *Titanic* was an accident caused perhaps by carelessness and overconfidence. The sinking of the *Willhelm Gustloff* was intentional and represents the horror and cruelty men are capable of inflicting on each other.

MICHAL RYBICKI
Diver and Architect

Nearly half a century ago, Michal was among the first to explore and sketch the entire sunken *Gustloff*. Together with his dive team, Rekin, he was one of the few to enter the interior of the ship, swimming between decks and exploring inside the main rooms and cabins. Originally from Lwów, Michal introduced me to Poland and the region of former East Prussia. Together we walked the path of the refugees, envisioning their hope and hardship.

1. What year did you first dive the *Wilhelm Gustloff* and what sort of permission did you need to explore the wreck?

The very first free-swimming scuba divers' descent to the *Wilhelm Gustloff*'s wreck took place in the summer of 1973. I was very involved in organizing the project and, with two other divers, I explored the wreck a number of times. In total, I explored the wreck for over seven hours.

I'm sure there were some explorations done before us, by the Russians and by Poles, commissioned by state institutions. But as they were poorly equipped, wore iron shoes and large metal helmets, they were unable to see properly (let alone search) the inside of the wreck. Nevertheless, their reports were beyond imagination.

Under the guise of the "Search for the Amber Room," our dive team finally received the blessing from appropriate authorities and received assistance from several state companies. We were

SALT TO THE SEA   *411*

granted formal permission from the Main Maritime Office and were assigned to thoroughly investigate "Underwater Obstacle #73." This meant we had to precisely examine the position of the wreck, describe its condition, and locate any and all high elements protruding above the water level. Situated close to a busy fairway used by tankers, these elements were considered dangerous and had to be detonated to clear the way.

As an architect, I was asked to draw a sketch of the sunken *Wilhelm Gustloff* wreck. (See page 419.)

2. Describe what you saw and experienced during your dive.

Sitting on the side of our base ship and looking down at the water, I found myself pensive and painfully aware that forty-five meters below rested the remains of thousands of people who, in deadly panic, had to leave their homes and, in freezing temperatures, ran from the approaching Soviet Red Army. People from thousands of little towns and villages. People of all ages and statuses, some in horse-drawn carts and carriages, some afoot, other on bicycles. Children, mothers, some of them pregnant, the old, the young, some sick, my God, so many—millions of them—with desperation and hope in their hearts, running for their lives, heading toward the last evacuation points on the coast of the Baltic Sea. Some tried for passage in Piława (then Pillau), others hoped to cross the frozen lagoon afoot to get to the coast on the other side, and then along the shore to reach Gdansk and Gdynia (then Gotenhafen). Several thousands of them, probably with great relief, finally boarded the *Wilhelm Gustloff*. And there I was, reflecting on those cruel times and all the suffering and tragedy of so many whose roads had ended here below. I knew in a short while I'd dive and find myself among their bodies, in their underwater cemetery. My first descent was to check the anchor. Slowly, with my head down, eyes half-closed and holding the rope, I reached the bottom and found the visibility quite good.

At that point I had to confront the cruel history. I saw blackened human remains, bones, skulls. I saw elements of leather belts, shoes, buckles, bundles of textiles here and there. The sight affected me intensely and remains in my memory. It accompanied me throughout the entire exploration and many years after. I still remember it well.

The wreck was covered with a thin layer of silt and as visibility was very good, I could see the individual layers of paint (the ship had been repainted a number of times). The name *Wilhelm Gustloff* on the side of the ship looked very impressive. We repeatedly swam through the shaft of the cargo hatch in the bow to where the shattered hull rested. I tried to spot traces that divers before us may have left. Rumor had it that over fifty million dollars was deposited in the captain's safe. There was no way for us to confirm it, and we found no evidence whatsoever of any traces of burned-out holes in the sides of the wreck.

There were three of us divers. On one occasion we swam into what used to be a spacious salon (or maybe it was a restaurant?). We found it in total ruin, with piles of debris and rubble. Broken devices, pipes, pieces of furniture, heaters. It was difficult to distinguish because everything was covered in silt. I moved my fin slightly and the silt raised, forming a thick brown muddy suspension which then made visibility poor. We continued to swim through the thick foggy ooze. The length of light coming from my torch was only twenty centimeters. Where do we go now?! We couldn't see one another. Suddenly, as if on command, the three of us decided to switch off our torches. After a while we noticed a dim sunlight, delicately penetrating the depth of the water. This enabled us to see the vague, barely visible, outlines of window openings. A bit farther toward the stern, in a gap of a ruptured hull, we saw a strange object; its shape was unexpectedly well-preserved. It turned out to be a chandelier, which, as we later saw in photos of the *Wilhelm Gustloff,* hung in the ship's lounge.

Through the closed portholes we could see into the passenger cabins—mountains of rubble and unidentified remains. Certainly the clearest water and best visibility was at the stern. I could easily identify the reels, construction of the deck, curved bow hold, and stairs on both sides. Because the time we were able to spend at this depth was nearly up, we decided not to push our limits and withdrew from deeper penetration of the inside of the huge wreck. It was incredible to think that if the ship stood on its bow, two-thirds of its height would stick out above the water level. Later, when I was drawing the sketch of the wreck, I had to verify my observations with other divers. The exchange of these observations was, at times, quite emotional.

The *Wilhelm Gustloff* is, without doubt, the largest wreck in the Baltic Sea. It carried thousands of exiles who became tragic victims the minute the deadly torpedoes struck their ship. We were the first civil team of free-swimming divers who were privileged to examine the wreck. It was such a rare opportunity, it's no wonder that each one of us was completely overwhelmed.

3. After so many years, was there still evidence of human tragedy and a human story when you explored the *Wilhelm Gustloff*?

Every descent we made to the wreck brought new discoveries and great emotions. Each one of us, even when exploring the same spots, would notice and focus on different things, have different impressions. Each would question different objects, or pieces of objects, like a cracked porcelain saucer. (Who was its owner? Did it belong with a lost cup in the cabinet of the *Wilhelm Gustloff*'s kitchen?) There were shreds of clothing. There were many shoes. (Were their owners running to safety in them?) There were military belts (maybe they belonged to young soldiers). There was a lovely plated little jug, stuffed with silk scarves, all tightly tucked inside. (Why would such scarves be packed inside a jar? Maybe the owner needed to save every bit of free space? Or was it of great sentimental value to him or her?) With time, the scarves had turned the color of brown silt.

The majority of objects and pieces of belongings that we saw were not on the actual wreck, but were scattered all around it. Most of them were very difficult, if not impossible, to identify. This was due to the disaster, time lapse, and the sea water. To me, every object, even if it was unrecognizable, would trigger my imagination, and, in my mind, I kept returning to the individual tragic experiences of their owners, fleeing from imminent danger of the approaching enemy, only to meet their tragic ends on the ship they hoped would take them to safety.

Because the *Wilhelm Gustloff*'s great mast had to be detonated and removed for safety reasons (it was sticking far too high above the fairway water level and was an obstruction for tankers), we had to remove all the navigation lamps and lighting devices from it. I thought to myself, maybe, just maybe, if they were all switched off during the voyage, perhaps submarine commander Marinesko wouldn't have spotted the ship.

SALT TO THE SEA

4. Several divers have explored the *Wilhelm Gustloff*. In what way do you feel that your dive and experience was unique?

Classic divers, the only ones to have explored the wreck before us, had very limited resources to thoroughly do the job due to defective and imperfect equipment existing and available at the time. They wore heavy metal helmets and iron shoes, and had to be connected to an air hose. Nevertheless, the number of myths, legends, and fantasies about the *Wilhelm Gustloff* wreck was growing and became quite impressive! That was, until 1973, the year we, as free-swimming scuba divers, were permitted to do the exploration. The wreck at the time was officially shrouded in secrecy. Its geographic position was classified and all the information was highly confidential.

Before we went on our dive exploration, we heard many crazy stories about the wreck from so-called eye witnesses, previous classic divers, or foreign journalists. All the nonsense and myths called for verification! There was one constantly repeated "tip," which alleged of a supposedly rectangular opening in the side of the wreck made by some secret "professionals." This suggested that some uninvited guests had been trying to get their hands on some secret and valuable cargo. But neither I nor my fellow divers ever saw such a hole. Not even a trace of it or attempts at cutting it out by a burner.

Whenever conditions allowed, we were able to swim inside the wreck. Between crushed decks and what was left of interior corridors. I was also able to swim alongside the *Gustloff* and make close observations. Unlike those classic divers before us with metal helmets and iron shoes, who were unable to move freely (and thus unable to have a wide view of the lying wreck), I could see it from a ten-meter distance. Just as far as the visibility allowed. As a diver free from weighted and connected equipment, I was able to see the wreck from various angles and I could draw the sketch precisely. Of course, I consulted with my dive friends who took part in the exploration. It took me a sequence of separate dives to complete the sketch.

5. Although other people have investigated this part of history, you live in the region where the refugee evacuation took place. What do you think might have been misunderstood about the legend of the Amber Room or the sinking of the *Wilhelm Gustloff*?

In my opinion, it is hard to definitively state whether or not the Amber Room ever had a chance to be onboard the *Wilhelm Gustloff.* The possibility evokes great interest, even today. Unconfirmed rumors were circulating that the Amber Room was last seen after the *Wilhelm Gustloff* sank. What is certain though is that during the Allied Forces' bombardment of Königsberg, the Amber Room was in Königsberg Castle. In the courtyard of the castle, a lot of melted amber and metal fittings that belonged to the Amber Room were found.

Until 1973, the torpedoing and sinking of the *Wilhelm Gustloff* was considered an outstandingly heroic act. Captain Marinesko, the commander of the Soviet submarine who sank the *Gustloff,* has a monument in his name in Königsberg (now Russian Kaliningrad) and is still very honored and revered.

During our explorations on the wreck of the *Wilhelm Gustloff,* I remember expressions of disbelief and utter surprise on the

SALT TO THE SEA   417

faces of people (even those who knew the history of World War II really well) and their repeated questions: "Is it possible? Isn't the *Titanic* the ship that had the highest number of victims?" And the answer was, "No, the largest maritime disaster is not the *Titanic*. On the *Wilhelm Gustloff* there were five or six times more victims; an entire city of people went down."

It was only then that people learned of this enormous tragedy. And thirty years later, the famous German writer Günter Grass wrote a novel, *Crabwalk*, about it.

This interview was translated from Polish to English by Dorota Mierosławska.

TURN THE PAGE FOR A LOOK INSIDE ANOTHER
NEW YORK TIMES **BESTSELLING NOVEL BY**
RUTA SEPETYS

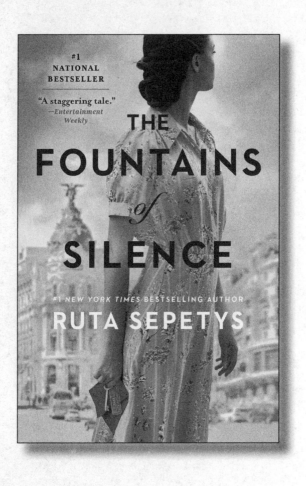

❴ 1 ❵

They stand in line for blood.

June's early sun blooms across a string of women waiting patiently at *el matadero*. Fans snap open and flutter, replying to Madrid's warmth and the scent of open flesh wafting from the slaughterhouse.

The blood will be used for *morcilla*, blood sausage. It must be measured with care. Too much blood and the sausage is not firm. Too little and the sausage crumbles like dry earth.

Rafael wipes the blade on his apron, his mind miles from *morcilla*. He turns slowly from the line of customers and puts his face to the sky.

In his mind it is Sunday. The hands of the clock touch six.

It is time.

The trumpet sounds and the march of the *pasodoble* rolls through the arena.

Rafael steps onto the sand, into the sun.

He is ready to meet Fear.

In the center box of the bullring sits Spain's dictator, Generalísimo Francisco Franco. They call him *El Caudillo*—leader of armies, hero by the grace of God. Franco looks down to the ring. Their eyes meet.

You don't know me, Generalísimo, but I know you.

I am Rafael Torres Moreno, and today, I am not afraid.

"Rafa!"

The supervisor swats the back of Rafael's damp neck. "Are you blind? There's a line. Stop daydreaming. The blood, Rafa. Give them their blood."

Rafa nods, walking toward the patrons. His visions of the bullring quickly disappear.

Give them their blood.

Memories of war tap at his brain. The small, taunting voice returns, choking daydreams into nightmares. *You do remember, don't you, Rafa?*

He does.

The silhouette is unmistakable.

Patent-leather men with patent-leather souls.

The Guardia Civil. He secretly calls them the Crows. They are servants of Generalísimo Franco and they have appeared on the street.

"Please. Not here," whispers Rafael from his hiding spot beneath the trees.

The wail of a toddler echoes above. He looks up and sees Julia at the open window, holding their youngest sister, Ana.

Their father's voice booms from inside. "Julia, close the window! Lock the door and wait for your mother. Where is Rafa?"

"Here, Papá," whispers Rafael, his small legs folded in hiding. "I'm right here."

His father appears at the door. The Crows appear at the curb.

The shot rings out. A flash explodes. Julia screams from above.

Rafa's body freezes. No breath. No air.

No.

> *No.*

>> *No.*

They drag his father's limp corpse by an arm.

"*¡Papá!*"

It's too late. As the cry leaves his throat, Rafa realizes. He's given himself away.

A pair of eyes dart. "His boy's behind the tree. Grab him."

Rafa blinks, blocking the painful memories, hiding his collapsed heart beneath a smile.

"*Buenos días, señora*. How may I help you?" he asks the customer.

"Blood."

"*Sí, señora.*"

Give them their blood.

For more than twenty years, Spain has given blood. And sometimes Rafa wonders—what is left to give?

{ 2 }

I t's a lie.

It has to be.

I know what you've done.

Ana Torres Moreno stands two levels belowground, in the second servants' basement. She rips the small note to pieces, shoves them in her mouth, and swallows.

A voice calls from the hall. "Hurry, Ana. They're waiting."

Dashing through the windowless maze of stone walls, Ana wills herself to move faster. Wills herself to smile.

A weak glow from a bare bulb whispers light onto the supply shelf. Ana spots the tiny sewing kit and throws it into her basket. She runs to the stairs and falls in step with Lorenza, who balances an assortment of cigarettes on a tray.

"You look pale," whispers Lorenza. *"¿Estás bien?"*

"I'm fine," replies Ana.

Always say you're fine, especially when you're not, she reminds herself.

The mouth of the stairway appears. Light from a crystal chandelier twinkles and beckons from the glittering hall.

Their steps slow, synchronize, and in perfect unison they emerge onto the marble floor of the hotel lobby, faces full of smile. Ana scrolls her mental list. The man from New York will want a newspaper and matches. The woman from Pennsylvania will need more ice.

Americans love ice. Some claim to have trays of cubed ice in their own kitchens. Maybe it's possible. Ana sees advertisements for appliances in glossy magazines that hotel guests leave behind.

Frigidaire! Rustproof aluminum shelving, controlled butter-ready.

Whatever that means. Beyond Spain, all is a mystery.

Ana hears every word, but guests would never know it. She scurries, filling requests quickly so visitors have no time to glance out of their world and into hers.

Julia, the matriarch of their fractured family, issues constant reminders. "You trust too easily, Ana. You reveal too much. Stay silent."

Ana is tired of silence, tired of unanswered questions, and tired of secrets. A girl of patched pieces, she dreams of new beginnings. She dreams of leaving Spain. But her sister is right. Her dreams have proven dangerous.

I know what you've done.

"For once, follow the rules instead of your heart," pleads her sister.

Follow the rules. To be invisible in plain view and paid handsomely for it—five *pesetas* per hour—this is the plan. Her older brother, Rafael, works at both the slaughterhouse and the cemetery. Between two jobs he makes only twelve *pesetas*, twenty cents according to the hotel's exchange desk, for an entire day's work.

Ana hands the sewing kit to the concierge and heads quickly for the staff elevator. The morning is gone, but her task list is growing. Summer season has officially arrived at the hotel, pouring thousands of new visitors into Spain. The elevator doors open to the seventh floor. Ana shifts the basket to her hip and hurries down the long corridor.

"Towels for 760," whispers a supervisor who shuttles past.

"Towels for 760," she confirms.

Four years old, but to Ana, the American hotel smells new. Tucked into her basket is a stack of hotel brochures featuring a handsome bull-fighter, a matador, holding a red cape. In fancy script across the cape is written:

Castellana Hilton Madrid. Your Castle in Spain.

Castles. She saw old postcards as a child. The haunting newsreel rolls behind her eyes:

The tree-lined avenue of Paseo de la Castellana—home to Spanish royalty and grand palaces. And then, the bright images fade. 1936. Civil war erupts in Spain. War drains color from the cheeks of Madrid. The grand palaces become gray ghosts. Gardens and fountains disappear. So do Ana's parents. Hunger and isolation cast a filter of darkness over the country. Spain is curtained off from the world.

And now, after twenty years of nationwide atrophy, Generalísimo Franco is finally allowing tourists into Spain. Banks and hotels wrap new exteriors over old palace interiors. The tourists don't know the difference. What lies beneath is now hidden, like the note disintegrating in her stomach.

Ana reads the newspapers and magazines that guests discard. She memorizes the brochure to recite on cue.

> *Formerly a palace, Castellana is the first Hilton property*
> *in Europe. Over three hundred rooms, each with a three-*
> *channel radio, and even a telephone.*

"If you are assigned to a guest in a suite, you will see to their every request," lectures her supervisor. "Remember, Americans are less formal than Spaniards. They're accustomed to conversation. You will be warm, helpful, and conversational."

"*Ay*, I'm always warm and conversational," Lorenza whispers with a wink.

Ana wants to be conversational, but her sister's call for silence contradicts hotel instruction. The constant tug in opposite directions makes her feel like a rag doll, destined to lose an arm.

A man in a crisp white shirt emerges from a door into the hallway. Ana stops and gives a small bob. *"Buenos días, señor."*

"Hiya, doll."

Doll. Dame. Kitten. Baby. American men have many terms for women. Just when Ana thinks she has learned them all, a new one appears. In her English class at the hotel, these words are called terms of endearment.

After what happened last year, Ana knows better.

American diplomats, actors, and musicians arrive amidst the swirling dust of Barajas Airport. They socialize and mingle into the pale hours of morning. Ana secretly notes their preferences. Starlets have favorite suites. Politicians have favorite starlets. Many are unaware of what transpired in Spain decades earlier. They sip cava, romanticizing Hemingway and flamenco. On rare occasion someone asks Ana about Spain's war. She politely changes the subject. It's not only hotel policy, but also the promise she made.

She will look to the future. The past must be forgotten.

Her father executed. Her mother imprisoned. Their crime was not an action, but an ambition—teachers who hoped to develop a Montessori school with methods based on child development rather than religion. But Generalísimo Franco commands that all schools in Spain shall be controlled by the Catholic Church. Republican sympathizers must be eradicated.

Her parents' offense has left Ana rowing dark waters of dead secrets. Born into a long shadow of shame, she must never speak publicly of her parents. She must live in silence. But sometimes, from the hidden corners of her heart, calls the haunting question:

What can be built through silence?

TURN THE PAGE FOR A LOOK AT
OTHER AWARD-WINNING NOVELS BY

RUTA SEPETYS!

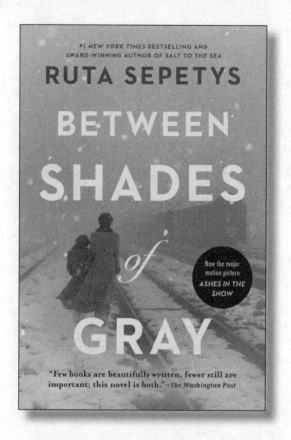

A #1 *NEW YORK TIMES* BESTSELLER
AND WILLIAM C. MORRIS AWARD FINALIST!

"Few books are beautifully written, fewer still are important; this novel is both." —*The Washington Post*

"At once a suspenseful, drama-packed survival story, a romance, and an intricately researched work of historical fiction."
—*The Wall Street Journal*

★ "Beautifully written and deeply felt . . . An important book that deserves the widest possible readership."
—*Booklist*, STARRED REVIEW

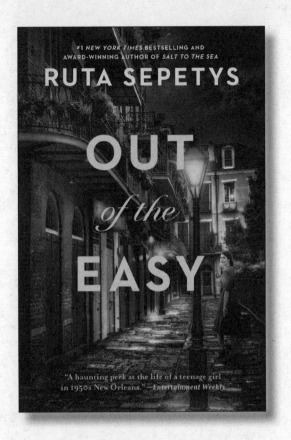

A *NEW YORK TIMES* BESTSELLING NOVEL!

"A satisfying novel, bringing to life the midcentury French Quarter . . . Sepetys writes with rawness and palpable emotional unease." —*The New York Times Book Review* (Editors' Choice)

"A haunting peek at the life of a teenage girl in 1950s New Orleans." —*Entertainment Weekly*

"Sepetys's latest is full of transporting writing, drawing you into a past that is fully reconstructed by her superb imagination."
—*The Boston Globe*

Look for *Ashes in the Snow*, the movie tie-in edition of *Between Shades of Gray*, featuring a behind-the-scenes look at the making of the film!

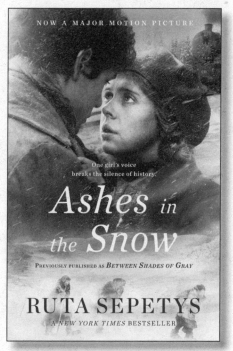

Movie tie-in edition

Now available on DVD!